Reader's Digest

BEST LOVED BOOKS
FOR YOUNG READERS

The Adventures of Huckleberry Finn

A CONDENSATION OF THE BOOK BY

Mark Twain

Illustrated by John Falter

CHOICE PUBLISHING, INC.

New York

Produced in association with Media Projects Incorporated

Executive Editor, Carter Smith
Managing Editor, Jeanette Mall
Project Editor, Jacqueline Ogburn
Associate Editor, Charles Wills
Contributing Editor, Beth Passaro
Art Director, Bernard Schleifer

Library of Congress Catalog Number: 88-63353
ISBN: 0-945260-30-X

This 1989 edition is published and distributed by Choice Publishing, Inc.,
Great Neck, NY 11021, with permission of The Reader's Digest Association, Inc.

Manufactured in the United States of America.

10 9 8 7 6 5 4 3 2

Foreword

TOM SAWYER'S BEST friend was Huckleberry Finn, the envy of all his contemporaries because he smoked a pipe and never had to wash or go to school. But there were too many well-intentioned grown-ups wanting to "sivilize" Huck, so he had no choice but to leave town, quietly. This book is his own ever-memorable account of what followed.

Down the Mississippi he floated on a log raft. And his experiences, recounted in his inimitably racy language, were legion: some hair-raising, some hilarious, some bittersweet and haunting. On the whole he was happy. "You feel mighty free and easy and comfortable on a raft," he decided.

Huck came to value freedom for others as well when he joined forces with Jim, a brave and generous runaway slave. Years ahead of his time (which was the early nineteenth century), Huck learns that the color of a man's skin has nothing to do with his worth as an individual or his right to freedom.

The Adventures of Huckleberry Finn is Mark Twain's masterpiece. Ernest Hemingway said of it that "all modern American literature stems from this one book," and for H. L. Mencken the discovery of *Huckleberry Finn* was "the most stupendous event of my whole life."

Mark Twain (whose real name was Samuel Clemens) grew up beside the "father of waters" and was for a time a steamboat pilot. He knew the river firsthand, and the ways of the river folk—both saints and scoundrels—who throng these pages. He has embodied in the one small raggedy figure of Huck all the toughness and tenderness, all the humor and independence of the American frontier spirit.

Explanatory

In this book a number of dialects are used, to wit: the Missouri Negro dialect; the extremest form of the backwoods Southwestern dialect; the ordinary "Pike County" dialect; and four modified varieties of this last. The shadings have been done in a haphazard fashion, or by guesswork; but painstakingly, and with the trustworthy guidance and support of personal familiarity with these several forms of speech.

I make this explanation for the reason that without it many readers would suppose that all these characters were trying to talk alike and not succeeding.

—The Author

☞ NOTICE ☜

CHAPTER I

YOU DON'T KNOW ABOUT ME without you have read a book by the name of *The Adventures of Tom Sawyer;* but that ain't no matter. That book was made by Mr. Mark Twain, and he told the truth, mainly. There was things which he stretched, but mainly he told the truth.

Now the way that the book winds up is this: Tom and me found the money that the robbers hid in the cave, and it made us rich. We got six thousand dollars apiece—all gold. Well, Judge Thatcher he took it and put it out at interest, and it fetched us a dollar a day apiece—more than a body could tell what to do with. The Widow Douglas she took me for her son, and allowed she would sivilize me; but it was rough living in the house all the time, considering how dismal regular and decent the widow was in all her ways; and so when I couldn't stand it no longer I lit out. I got into my old rags again, and was free and satisfied. But Tom Sawyer he hunted me up and said he was going to start a band of robbers, and I might join if I would go back to the widow and be respectable. So I went back.

The widow she cried over me, and called me a poor lost lamb, a lot of other names, too, but she never meant no harm by it. She put me in them new clothes again, and I couldn't do nothing but sweat and sweat, and felt all cramped up. Well, then, the old thing commenced again. The widow rung a bell for supper, and you had to come to time. When you got to the table you couldn't go right to eating, but you had to wait for the widow to tuck down her head and grumble a little over the victuals. After supper she got out her book and learned me about Moses and the Bulrushers, and I was in a sweat to find out about him; but by and by she let it out that Moses had been dead a considerable time; so then I didn't care no more about him, because I don't take no stock in dead people.

Pretty soon I wanted to smoke, and asked the widow to let me. But she wouldn't. She said it was a mean practice, and I must try to not do it anymore. And then her sister, Miss Watson, a tolerable slim old maid, with goggles on, who had just come to live with her, took a set at me with a spelling book. She worked me middling hard for about an hour, and then the widow made her ease up. I couldn't stood it much longer. Then for an hour it was deadly dull, and I was fidgety.

Miss Watson would say, "Don't put your feet up there, Huckleberry"; and "Set up straight, Huckleberry"; and "Don't gap and stretch like that, Huckleberry—why don't you try to behave?" Then she told me all about the bad place, and I said I wished I was there. She got mad then, but I didn't mean no harm. All I wanted was to go somewheres; all I wanted was a change, I warn't particular. She said it was wicked to say what I said; said she wouldn't say it for the whole world; *she* was going to live so as to go to the good place. Well, I couldn't see no advantage in going where she was going, so I made up my mind I wouldn't try for it. But I never said so, because it would only make trouble, and wouldn't do no good.

Miss Watson she kept pecking at me, and it got tiresome. By and by they fetched the niggers in and had prayers, and then everybody was off to bed. I went up to my room with a piece of candle, and put it on the table. Then I set down in a chair by the window.

I felt so lonesome I most wished I was dead. The stars were shining, and the leaves rustled in the woods ever so mournful;

and I heard an owl, away off, who-whooing about somebody that was dead; and the wind was trying to whisper something to me, and it made the cold shivers run over me. Pretty soon a spider went crawling up my shoulder, and I flipped it off and it lit in the candle; and before I could budge it was all shriveled up. I didn't need anybody to tell me that that was an awful bad sign and would bring me bad luck, so I was scared, and I got up and turned around in my tracks three times and crossed my breast; but I hadn't no confidence. I hadn't ever heard anybody say there was any way to keep off bad luck when you'd killed a spider.

I set down again, a-shaking all over, and got out my pipe for a smoke; for the house was all as still as death now, and so the widow wouldn't know. Well, after a long time I heard the clock in the town go *boom—boom—boom*—twelve licks; and all still again—stiller than ever. Pretty soon I heard a twig snap down in the dark, and I set still and listened. Directly I could just barely hear a *me-yow! me-yow!* That was good! Says I, "*Me-yow! Me-yow!*" soft as I could, and I put out the light and scrambled out the window onto the shed. Then I slipped down to the ground and crawled in among the trees, and, sure enough, there was Tom Sawyer waiting for me.

WE WENT TIPTOEING ALONG a path amongst the trees back toward the end of the widow's garden, stooping down so as the branches wouldn't scrape our heads. When we was passing by the kitchen I fell over a root and made a noise. We scrouched down and laid still. Miss Watson's big nigger, named Jim, was setting in the kitchen door; we could see him because there was a light behind him. He got up and said, "Who dah?" Then he listened some; then he came tiptoeing down and stood right between us. We could 'a' touched him, nearly.

For minutes and minutes there warn't a sound, and we all there so close together. There was a place on my ankle that got to itching, but I dasn't scratch it; and then my ear begun to itch; and next my back, right between my shoulders. Seemed like I'd die if I couldn't scratch. Well, I've noticed that thing plenty times since.

If you are with the quality, or at a funeral, or trying to go to sleep when you ain't sleepy—if you are anywheres where it won't do for you to scratch, why you will itch all over in upwards of a thousand places. Pretty soon Jim says:

"Say, who is you? Dog my cats ef I didn' hear sumf'n. Well, I know what I's gwyne to do: I'se gwyne to set down here and listen tell I hears it ag'in."

So he set down on the ground betwixt me and Tom, and he leaned his back up against a tree and stretched his legs out. Then my nose begun to itch. It itched till the tears come into my eyes and I reckoned I couldn't stand it a minute longer, but I set my teeth and got ready to try. Just then Jim begun to breathe heavy; next he begun to snore—and then I was pretty soon comfortable again.

Tom he made a sign to me—kind of a noise with his mouth—and we went creeping away on our hands and knees. When we was ten foot off Tom whispered to me, and wanted to tie Jim to the tree for fun. But I said no; he might wake and make a disturbance, and then they'd find out I warn't in. Then Tom said he hadn't got candles enough, and he would slip in the kitchen and get some more. I said Jim might wake up and come. But Tom wanted to resk it; so we slid in there and got three candles, and Tom laid five cents on the table for pay. Then we got out, and I was in a sweat to get away; but nothing would do Tom but he must crawl to where Jim was, on his hands and knees, and play something on him. I waited, and it seemed a good while, everything was so still and lonesome.

As soon as Tom was back we cut along the path, around the garden fence, and by and by fetched up on the steep top of the hill the other side of the house. Tom said he slipped Jim's hat off his head and hung it on a limb right over him, and Jim stirred, but he didn't wake. Afterward Jim said the witches bewitched him, and rode him all over the state, and then set him under the trees again, and hung his hat on a limb to show who done it. And next time Jim told it he said they rode him down to New Orleans; and, after that, every time he told it he spread it more and more, till by and by he said they rode him all over the world. Jim was monstrous proud about it. Niggers would come miles to hear him tell about it, and he was more looked up to than any nigger in that country. And he always kept that five-center piece round his neck with a string, and said it was a charm the devil give to him with his own hands. He was most ruined for a servant, because he got stuck up on account of having seen the devil and been rode by witches.

Well, when Tom and me got to the edge of the hilltop we looked away down into the village and could see three or four lights twinkling, where there was sick folks, maybe; and the stars over us was sparkling ever so fine; and down by the village was the river, a whole mile broad, and awful still and grand. We went down the hill and found Joe Harper and Ben Rogers, and two or three more of the boys, hid in the old tanyard. So we unhitched a skiff and pulled down the river two mile and a half, to the big scar on the hillside, and went ashore.

We went to a clump of bushes, and Tom made everybody swear to keep the secret, and then showed them a hole in the hill, right in the thickest part of the bushes. We lit the candles and crawled in. After we went about two hundred yards the cave opened up. Tom poked about amongst the passages, and pretty soon we went along a narrow place and got into a kind of room, all damp and cold, and there we stopped.

Tom says, "Now, we'll start this band of robbers and call it Tom Sawyer's Gang. Everybody that wants to join has got to take an oath, and write his name in blood."

Everybody was willing. So Tom got out a sheet of paper that he had wrote the oath on, and read it. It swore every boy to stick to the band, and never tell any of the secrets; and if anybody done anything to any boy in the band, whichever boy was ordered to kill that person and his family must do it, and he mustn't eat or sleep till he had killed them and hacked a cross on their breasts, which was the sign of the band. And nobody that didn't belong to the band could use that mark, and if he did he must be sued; and if he done it again he must be killed. And if anybody that belonged to the band told the secrets, he must have his throat cut, and then have his carcass burnt up and the ashes scattered, and his name blotted off the list with blood and never mentioned again by the gang, but have a curse put on it and be forgot forever.

Everybody said it was a real beautiful oath, and asked Tom if he got it out of his own head. He said some of it, but the rest was out of pirate books and robber books, and every gang that was high-toned had it.

Some thought it would be good to kill the *families* of boys that told the secrets. Tom said it was a good idea and wrote it in. Then Ben Rogers says:

"Here's Huck Finn, he hain't got no family; what you going to do 'bout him?"

"Well, hain't he got a father?" says Tom Sawyer.

"Yes, he's got a father, but you can't never find him. He used to lay drunk with the hogs in the tanyard, but he hain't been seen in these parts for a year or more."

They talked it over, and they was going to rule me out, because they said every boy must have a family or somebody to kill, or else it wouldn't be fair and square for the others. I was most ready to cry; but all at once I thought of a way, and I offered them Miss Watson—they could kill her. Everybody said, "Oh, she'll do. That's all right. Huck can come in."

Then they all stuck a pin in their fingers to get blood to sign with, and I made my mark on the paper.

"Now," says Ben Rogers, "what's the line of business of this Gang?"

"Robbery and murder," Tom said. "We are highwaymen. We stop stages and carriages on the road, with masks on, and kill the people and take their watches and money."

"Must we always kill the people?"

"Oh, certainly. It's best—except some you bring to the cave here, and keep them till they're ransomed."

"Ransomed? What's that?"

"I don't know. But that's what they do. I've seen it in books; and of course that's what we've got to do."

"But how can we do it if we don't know what it is?"

"Why, blame it all, we've *got* to do it. Don't I tell you it's in the books?"

"That's all very fine to *say*, Tom Sawyer, but how in the nation are these fellows going to be ransomed if we don't know how to do it to them? What do you *reckon* it is?"

"Per'aps if we keep them till they're ransomed, it means that we keep them till they're dead."

"Now, that's something *like*. That'll answer. Why couldn't you said that before? We'll keep them till they're ransomed to death; and a bothersome lot they'll be too—eating up everything and always trying to get loose."

"How you talk, Ben Rogers. How can they get loose when there's a guard over them, ready to shoot them down if they move a peg?"

"A guard! So somebody's got to set up all night and never get any sleep, just so as to watch them! Why can't a body take a club and ransom them as soon as they get here?"

"Because it ain't in the books so—that's why. Now, Ben Rogers, do you want to do things regular, or don't you?"

"All right. But, say, do we kill the women, too?"

"Ben Rogers, if I was as ignorant as you I wouldn't let on. Kill the women? No; nobody ever saw anything in the books like that. You fetch them to the cave, and you're always as polite as pie to them; and by and by they fall in love with you, and never want to go home anymore."

"Well, if that's the way I'm agreed, but mighty soon we'll have a cave so cluttered up with women, and fellows waiting to be ransomed, that there won't be no place for the robbers. But go ahead, I ain't got nothing more to say."

Little Tommy Barnes was asleep now, and when they waked him up he was scared and cried, and said he wanted to go home to his ma. So they all called him crybaby, and that made him mad, and he said he would go straight and tell all the secrets. But Tom gave him five cents to keep quiet, and said we would all go home and meet next week, and rob somebody and kill some people.

Then we elected Tom Sawyer first captain and Joe Harper second captain of the Gang, and so started home.

I clumb up the shed and crept into my window just before day was breaking. My new clothes was all greased up and clayey, and I was dog-tired.

CHAPTER II

WELL, I GOT A GOOD GOING-OVER in the morning from old Miss Watson on account of my clothes; but the widow she didn't scold, but only looked so sorry that I thought I would behave awhile if I could. Then Miss Watson she took me in the closet and prayed, but nothing came of it. She told me to pray every day, and whatever I asked for I would get it. But it warn't so. I tried it. Once I got a fishline, but no hooks. It warn't any good to me without hooks. I tried for the hooks three or four times, but somehow I couldn't make it work. By and by, one day, I told the widow about it, and she said the thing a body could get by praying for it was "spiritual gifts." This was too many for me, but she told me what she meant—I must help other people, and do everything I could for other people, and look out for them all the time, and never think about myself. I went out in the woods and turned it over in my mind a long time, but I couldn't see no advantage about it—except for the other people; so at last I reckoned I wouldn't worry about it anymore, but just let it go.

Pap he hadn't been seen for more than a year, and that was comfortable for me. He used to always whale me when he was sober and could get his hands on me; though I used to take to the woods most of the time when he was around. But I warn't comfortable long, because I judged the old man would turn up again by and by, though I wished he wouldn't.

We played robber now and then about a month, and then I resigned. All the boys did. We hadn't robbed nobody, hadn't killed any people, but only just pretended. We used to hop out of the woods and go charging down on hog drivers and women in carts taking garden stuff to the market, but we never hived any of them. Tom Sawyer called the hogs "ingots," and he called the turnips and stuff "julery," and we would go to the cave and powwow over what we had done, and how many people we had killed. But I couldn't see no profit in it.

One time Tom sent a boy to run about town with a blazing stick, which was the sign for the Gang to get together, and then he said he had got news by his spies that next day a whole parcel of Spanish merchants and rich A-rabs was going to camp in Cave Hollow with two hundred elephants, and six hundred camels, and a thousand "sumter" mules, all loaded down with di'monds, and so we would lay in ambuscade, as he called it, and kill the lot and scoop the things. He said we must slick up our swords and guns, and get ready.

I didn't believe we could lick such a crowd, but I wanted to see the camels and elephants, so I was on hand next day, Saturday, in the ambuscade; and when we got the word we rushed out of the woods and down the hill. But there warn't no Spaniards and A-rabs; it warn't anything but a Sunday-school picnic, and only a primer class at that. We busted it up, and chased the children; but we never got anything but some doughnuts and jam, and then the teacher charged in, and made us drop everything and cut. I didn't see no di'monds, and I told Tom Sawyer so. He said there was loads of them there, anyway; and he said there was A-rabs there, too, and elephants and things. I said, why couldn't we see them, then? He said if I warn't so ignorant, I would know without asking it was all done by enchantment; but we had enemies which he called magicians, and they had turned the whole thing into an infant Sunday school, just out of spite. I said, all right; then the thing for us to do was to go for the magicians. Tom Sawyer said I was a numskull.

"Why," said he, "a magician could call up a lot of genies, and they would hash you up like nothing. They are as tall as a tree and as big round as a church."

"Well," I says, "s'pose we got some genies to help *us*—can't we lick the other crowd then?"

"How you going to get them?"

"I don't know. How do *they* get them?"

"Why, they rub an old tin lamp, and then the genies come tearing in, with the thunder and lightning a-ripping around, and the smoke a-rolling, and everything they're told to do they up and do it. Whoever rubs the lamp, they've got to do whatever he says. If he tells them to build a palace forty miles long out of di'monds, and fill it full of chewing gum, or whatever you want, they've got to do it."

"Well," says I, "I think they are a pack of flatheads for not keeping the palace themselves. And what's more—if I was one of them I would see a man in Jericho before I would drop my business and come to him for the rubbing of an old tin lamp."

"How you talk, Huck Finn. Why, you'd *have* to come when he rubbed it."

"What! And I as high as a tree and as big as a church?"

"Shucks, it ain't no use to talk to you, Huck Finn. You don't seem to know anything—perfect saphead."

I thought all this over for two or three days, and then I reckoned I would see if there was anything in it. I got an old tin lamp, and went out in the woods and rubbed and rubbed till I sweat like an Injun, calculating to build a palace and sell it; but it warn't no use, none of the genies come.

So then I judged that all that stuff was only just one of Tom Sawyer's lies. I reckoned he believed in the A-rabs and the elephants, but as for me I think different. It had all the marks of a Sunday school.

WELL, THREE OR FOUR MONTHS run along this way, and it was well into the winter now. I had been to school most all the time and could spell and read and write just a little, and could say the multiplication table up to six times seven is thirty-five. At first I hated the school, but by and by I got so I could stand it. I was getting sort of used to the widow's ways, too, and they warn't so raspy on me. Living in a house and sleeping in a bed pulled on me pretty tight mostly, but before the cold weather I used to slide out and sleep in the woods sometimes, and so that was a rest to me. The widow said I was coming along slow but sure, and doing very satisfactory. She said she warn't ashamed of me.

One morning I happened to turn over the salt at breakfast. I reached for some of it to throw over my left shoulder and keep off the bad luck, but Miss Watson was in ahead of me. She says, "Take your hands away, Huckleberry; what a mess you are always making!" So I started out, after breakfast, feeling worried and shaky, and wondering where the bad luck was going to fall on me, and what it was going to be.

I went down to the front garden and clumb over the stile where you go through the high board fence. There was an inch of new snow on the ground, and I seen somebody's tracks. They had come up from the quarry and stood around the stile awhile, and then went on around the garden fence. It was funny they hadn't come in, after standing around so. I couldn't make it out, and I stooped down to look at the tracks. I didn't notice anything at first, but next I did. There was a cross in the left bootheel made with big nails, to keep off the devil.

I was up in a second and shinning down the hill to Judge Thatcher's as quick as I could get there. He said:

"Why, my boy, you are all out of breath. Did you come for your interest?"

"No, sir," I says. "Is there some for me?"

"Yes, a half-yearly is in—a hundred and fifty dollars. Quite a fortune. You had better let me invest it along with your six thousand, because if you take it you'll spend it."

"No, sir," I says. "I don't want to spend it. I don't want it at all—nor the six thousand, nuther. I want you to take it; I want to give it to you—the six thousand and all."

He looked surprised, and then he says, "Why, what can you mean, my boy? Is something the matter?"

"Please take it," says I, "and don't ask me nothing—then I won't have to tell no lies."

He studied awhile, and then he says, "Oh-o! I think I see. You want to *sell* your property to me—not give it. That's the correct idea." Then he wrote something on a paper, and says, "There; you see it says 'for a consideration.' That means I have bought it and paid you for it. Here's a dollar for you. Now you sign it."

So I signed it, and left.

Miss Watson's nigger, Jim, had a hair ball as big as your fist, which had been took out of the fourth stomach of an ox, and he used to do magic with it. He said there was a spirit inside of it, and it knowed everything. So I went to him that night and told hirn Pap was here again, for I found his tracks in the snow. What I wanted to know was, what he was going to do, and was he going to stay? Jim got out his hair ball and said something over it, and then he dropped it on the floor. It fell pretty solid, and only rolled about an inch.

Jim got down on his knees, and put his ear against it and listened. But it warn't no use; he said it wouldn't talk. He said sometimes it wouldn't talk without money. I told him I had an old slick counterfeit quarter that warn't no good because the brass showed through the silver, but maybe the hair ball would take it, because it wouldn't know the difference. Jim smelt it and bit it and rubbed it, and said he would manage so the hair ball would think it was good.

Jim put the quarter under the hair ball, and got down and listened again. This time he said the hair ball was all right. He said it would tell me my whole fortune if I wanted it to. I says, go on. So the hair ball talked to him, and Jim told it to me. He says:

"Yo' ole father doan' know yit what he's a-gwyne to do. Sometimes he spec he'll go 'way, en den he spec he'll stay. De bes' way is to res' easy en let de ole man take his own way. Dey's two angels hoverin' roun' 'bout him. One uv 'em is white en shiny, en t'other one is black. De white one gits him to go right a little while, den de black one sails in en bust it all up. A body can't tell yit which one gwyne to fetch him at de las'. But you is all right. You gwyne to have considerable trouble in yo' life, en considerable joy. Dey's two gals flyin' 'bout you in yo' life. One uv 'em's light en t'other one is dark. One is rich en t'other is po'. You's gwyne to marry de po' one fust en de rich one by en by. You wants to keep 'way fum de water, en don't run no resk, 'kase it's down in de bills dat you's gwyne to git hung."

When I lit my candle and went up to my room that night there sat Pap—his own self!

CHAPTER III

I HAD SHUT THE DOOR TO. Then I turned around, and there he was.

He was most fifty, and he looked it. His hair was long and tangled and greasy. It was all black, no gray; so was his long whiskers. There warn't no color in his face, where his face showed; it was white—fish-belly white. As for his clothes—just rags, that was all. The boot on one foot was busted, and two of his toes stuck through. His hat was laying on the floor—an old black slouch with the top caved in, like a lid. He sat there a-looking at me, with his chair tilted back. I set the candle down. I noticed the window was up; so he had clumb in by the shed.

By and by he says, "Starchy clothes—very. Think you're a big-bug, *don't* you?"

"Maybe I am, maybe I ain't," I says.

"Don't give me none o' your lip," says he. "I'll take you down a peg before I get done. You're educated, too, they say—can read and write. Think you're better'n your father, now, don't you, because he can't? *I'll* take it out of you. Who told you you might meddle with such hifalut'n foolishness, hey? Who told you you could?"

"The widow. She told me."

"The widow, hey? I'll learn her to meddle! Looky here—you drop that school, you hear? I'll learn people to bring up a boy to put on airs over his own father and let on to be better'n what *he* is. I ain't the man to stand it—you hear? Say, lemme hear you read."

I took up a book and begun something about General Washington. When I'd read about a half minute, he fetched the book a whack and knocked it across the house. He says:

"It's so. You can do it. Now looky here; you stop that putting on frills. I'll lay for you, smarty; and if I catch you about that school I'll tan you good. First you know you'll get religion, too. I never see such a son."

He sat there a-mumbling and a-growling a minute, and then he says, "*Ain't* you a sweet-scented dandy, though? A bed, and a look'n-glass, and a piece of carpet on the floor—and they say you're rich. Hey—how's that?"

"They lie—that's how."

"Looky here—don't gimme no sass. I've been in town two days, and I hain't heard nothing but about you bein' rich. I heard about it down the river, too. That's why I come. You git me that money tomorrow—I want it."

"I hain't got no money."

"It's a lie. Judge Thatcher's got it. You git it."

"I hain't got no money, I tell you. You ask Judge Thatcher."

"All right; I'll ask him. Say, how much you got in your pocket? I want it."

"I hain't got only a dollar, and I want that to—"

"It don't make no difference what you want it for—shell it out."

He took it, and then he said he was going down to town to get some whiskey; said he hadn't had a drink all day. Then he went out over the shed.

Next day he was drunk, and he went to Judge Thatcher's and bullyragged him, and tried to make him give up the money; but he couldn't, and then he swore he'd make the law force him.

The judge and the widow went to law to get the court to take me away from him and let one of them be my guardian; but it was a new judge that had just come, and he didn't know the old man; so he said courts mustn't interfere and separate families if they could help it. So Judge Thatcher and the widow had to quit on the business.

That pleased the old man till he couldn't rest. He said he'd cow-hide me till I was black and blue if I didn't raise some money for him. I borrowed three dollars from Judge Thatcher, and Pap took it and got drunk, and went a-blowing around and whooping and carrying on; and he kept it up all over town, with a tin pan, till most midnight; then they jailed him, and the next day they had him before court, and jailed him for a week.

When he got out the new judge said he was a-going to make a man of him. So he took him to his own house, and dressed him up clean and nice, and had him to breakfast and dinner and supper with the family, and was just old pie to him, so to speak. And after supper he talked to him about temperance and such things till the old man cried, and said he'd been a fool, and fooled away his life; but now he was a-going to turn over a new leaf. And he rose up and held out his hand, and says:

"Look at it, gentlemen and ladies all; take a-hold of it; shake it. There's a hand that was the hand of a hog; but it ain't so no more; it's the hand of a man that's started in on a new life. It's a clean hand now; shake it—don't be afeard."

So they shook it, one after the other, all around, and cried. The judge's wife she kissed it. Then the old man he signed a pledge— made his mark. The judge said it was the holiest time on record, or something like that. Then they tucked the old man into a beautiful room, which was the spare room, and in the night sometime he got powerful thirsty and clumb out onto the porch roof and slid down a stanchion and traded his new coat for a jug of forty-rod, and clumb back again and had a good old time; and towards daylight he crawled out again, drunk as a fiddler, and rolled off the porch and broke his left arm in two places, and was most froze to death when somebody found him after sunup. And when they come to look at that spare room they had to take soundings before they could navigate it.

The judge he felt kind of sore. He said he reckoned a body could reform the old man with a shotgun, maybe, but he didn't know no other way.

WELL, PRETTY SOON THE OLD MAN was up and around again, and then he went for Judge Thatcher in the courts to make him give up that money, and he went for me, too, for not stopping school. He catched me a couple of times and thrashed me, but I went to school just the same; I didn't want to go to school much before, but I reckoned I'd go now to spite Pap. That law trial was a slow business—appeared like they warn't ever going to get started on it; so every now and then I'd borrow two or three dollars off of the judge for him, to keep from getting a cowhiding. Every time he got money he got drunk, and raised Cain; and every time he raised Cain he got jailed.

Then he got to hanging around the widow, and she told him at last that if he didn't quit she would make trouble for him. Well, *wasn't* he mad? He said he would show who was Huck Finn's boss. So he watched out for me one day in the spring, and catched me, and took me up the river alone three mile in a skiff, and crossed over to the Illinois shore where it was woody and there warn't no houses but an old log hut.

He kept me with him all the time, and I never got a chance to run off. We lived in that old cabin, and he always locked the door and put the key under his head nights. He had a gun, and we fished and hunted. Every little while he locked me in and went down to the store, three miles, to the ferry, and traded fish and game for whiskey, and fetched it home and got drunk. The widow she found out where I was by and by, and she sent a man to get me; but Pap drove him off with the gun, and it warn't long after that till I was used to being where I was, and liked it—all but the cowhide part.

It was kind of lazy and jolly, laying off all day, smoking and fishing, and no books nor study. Two months or more run along, and my clothes got to be all rags, and I didn't see how I'd ever got to like it so well at the widow's, where you had to wash, and eat on a plate.

But by and by Pap got too handy with his hick'ry, and I couldn't stand it. He got to going away so much, too, and locking me in. Once he locked me in and was gone three days. I judged he had got drowned, and I wasn't ever going to get out anymore. I was scared. I made up my mind I would fix up some way to leave there.

I had tried to get out of that cabin many a time, but I couldn't find no way. There warn't a window to it big enough for a dog to get through, and the door was thick oak slabs. Pap was pretty careful not to leave a knife or anything in the cabin when he was away; I reckon I had hunted the place over as much as a hundred times. But this time I found something at last: I found an old rusty wood saw without any handle; it was laid in between a rafter and the roof. I greased it up and went to work. There was an old horse blanket nailed against the logs at one end of the cabin behind the table, to keep the wind from blowing through the chinks and putting the candle out. I got under the table and raised the blanket, and went to work to saw out a section of the big bottom log. Well, it was a good long job, but I was getting towards the end of it when I heard Pap's gun in the woods. I got rid of the signs of my work, and pretty soon Pap came in.

Pap warn't in a good humor; he said he was down to town, and everything was going wrong. His lawyer said he reckoned he would win his lawsuit and get the money if they ever got started on the trial; but then there was ways to put it off a long time, and Judge Thatcher knowed how to do it. And he said people allowed there'd be another trial to get me away from him and give me to the widow, and they guessed it would win this time. This shook me up considerable, because I didn't want to go back to the widow's anymore and be so cramped up and sivilized. Then the old man said he would like to see the widow get me; he said if they tried to come any such game on him he knowed of a place six or seven mile off to stow me in, where they might hunt till they dropped and not find me. That made me pretty uneasy again, but only for a minute; I reckoned I wouldn't stay on hand till he got that chance.

The old man made me go to the skiff and fetch the things he had got. There was a fifty-pound sack of cornmeal, and a side of bacon, ammunition, and a four-gallon jug of whiskey. I toted up a load, and went back and sat down on the bow of the skiff to think it all over. I reckoned I would walk off with the gun, and take to the woods when I run away. I guessed I would tramp right across the country, mostly nighttimes, and hunt and fish to keep alive, and so get so far away that the old man nor the widow couldn't ever find me anymore. I judged I would saw out and leave that night if Pap got drunk enough. I got so full of it I didn't notice how long I was staying till the old man hollered and asked me whether I was asleep or drownded.

I got the things all up to the cabin, and then it was about dark. While I was cooking supper the old man took a swig or two and got sort of warmed up, and went to ripping again. He had been drunk over in town, and laid in the gutter all night, and he was a sight to look at, all mud. Whenever his liquor begun to work he most always went for the govment. This time he says:

"Call this a govment! Why, just look at it and see what it's like. Here's the law a-standing ready to take a man's son away from him—a man's own son, which he has had all the trouble and all the expense of raising. Yes, just as that man has got that son raised at last, and ready to go to work and begin to do suthin' for *him*, the law up and goes for him. And they call *that* govment! That ain't all, nuther. The law backs that old Judge Thatcher up and helps him to keep me out o' my property. The law takes a man worth six thousand dollars and up'ards, and jams him into an old trap of a cabin like this, and lets him go round in clothes that ain't fittin for a hog. They call that govment? Why, a man can't get his rights in a govment like this. Oh, yes, this is a wonderful govment, wonderful. Why, looky here. There was a free nigger there in town from Ohio. He had the whitest shirt on you ever see, and the shiniest hat; and a gold watch and chain, and a silver-headed cane. And what do you think? They said he was a p'fessor in a college, and could talk all kinds of languages, and knowed everything. And that ain't the wust. They said he could *vote* when he was at home. Well, that let me out. Thinks I, What is the country a-coming to? It was 'lection day, and I was just about to go and vote myself if I warn't too drunk to get there; but when they told me there was a state in this country where they'd let that nigger vote, I drawed out. I says the country may rot for all me—I'll never vote ag'in as long as I live!"

After supper Pap took the jug, and said he had enough whiskey there for two drunks and one delirium tremens. That was always his word. I judged he would be blind drunk in about an hour, and then I would steal the key, or saw myself out, one or t'other. He drank and drank, and tumbled down on his blankets by and by; but luck didn't run my way. He didn't go sound asleep, but groaned and moaned and thrashed around this way and that. At last I got so sleepy I couldn't keep my eyes open, and so before I knowed what I was about I was sound asleep, and the candle burning.

I don't know how long I was asleep, but all of a sudden there was an awful scream and I was up. There was Pap looking wild, and skipping around and yelling about snakes. I couldn't see no snakes, but he said they was crawling up his legs; and then he would give a jump and scream, and say one had bit him on the cheek. I never see a man look so wild. Pretty soon he was all fagged out, and fell down panting; then he rolled over and over, screaming and saying there was devils a-hold of him. He wore out by and by, and laid still awhile, moaning. Then he laid stiller, and didn't make a sound. I could hear the owls and the wolves away off in the woods, and it seemed terrible still. He was laying over by the corner. By and by he raised up partway and listened, with his head to one side. He says, very low:

"Tramp—tramp—tramp; that's the dead; tramp—tramp—tramp; they're coming after me; but I won't go. Oh, they're here! Don't touch me—don't! Hands off—they're cold; let go. Oh, let a poor devil alone!"

He rolled himself up in his blanket and went to crying. But by and by he rolled out and jumped up to his feet looking wild, and he see me and went for me. He chased me round and round the place with a clasp knife, calling me the Angel of Death, and saying he would kill me, and then I couldn't come for him no more. I begged, and told him I was only Huck; but he laughed *such* a screechy laugh, and roared and cussed, and kept on chasing me. Once when I turned short and dodged under his arm he got me by the jacket between my shoulders, and I thought I was gone; but I slid out of the jacket and saved myself. Pretty soon he was all tired out, and dropped down with his back against the door, and said he would rest a minute and then kill me. He put his knife under him, and pretty soon he dozed off.

By and by I got the old split-bottom chair and clumb up and got down the gun. I made sure it was loaded; and then I laid it across the turnip barrel, pointing towards Pap, and set down behind it to wait for him to stir.

Next thing I knew it was after sunup, and I had been sound asleep. Pap was standing over me looking sour—and sick, too. He says, "What you doin' with this gun?"

I judged he didn't know nothing about what he had been doing, so I says, "Somebody tried to get in, so I was laying for him."

"Why didn't you roust me out?"

"Well, I tried to, but I couldn't; I couldn't budge you."

"Well, all right. Don't stand there palavering all day, but out with you and see if there's a fish on the lines for breakfast. I'll be along in a minute."

He unlocked the door, and I cleared out up the riverbank. I noticed some pieces of limbs and things floating down; so I knowed the river had begun to rise. Over at the town the June rise used to be always luck for me; because as soon as that rise begins here comes cordwood floating down, and pieces of log rafts, so all you have to do is to catch them and sell them to the woodyards. I went along up the bank with one eye out for what the rise might fetch along, and all at once here comes a canoe; a beauty, too, about fourteen foot long, riding high like a duck. I shot head first off of the bank like a frog, clothes and all on, and struck out for it. It was a drift canoe sure enough, and I clumb in and paddled her ashore. Thinks I, The old man will be glad when he sees this—she's worth ten dollars. But when I got to shore Pap wasn't in sight yet, and I struck another idea: I judged I'd hide her, and then 'stead of taking to the woods when I run off, I'd go down the river fifty mile and camp in one place for good, and not have such a rough time tramping on foot.

I thought I heard the old man coming all the time; but I got her hid in a little creek all hung over with vines; and then I out and looked around a bunch of willows, and there was the old man down the path just drawing a bead on a bird with his gun. So he hadn't seen anything.

When he got along I was hard at it taking up a trotline. We got five catfish off the lines and went home.

While we laid off after breakfast to sleep up, both of us being about wore out, I got to thinking that if I could fix some way to keep Pap and the widow from trying to follow me, it would be a certainer thing than trusting to luck to get far enough off before they missed me. Well, I didn't see no way for a while, but by and by Pap raised up and says:

"Another time a man comes a-prowling round here you roust me out, you hear? That man warn't here for no good. I'd a shot him."

Then he dropped down and went to sleep again. What he had been saying give me the very idea I wanted. I says to myself, I can fix it now so nobody won't think of following me.

About twelve o'clock we turned out and went along up the bank. The river was coming up pretty fast, and lots of driftwood going by. By and by along comes part of a log raft—nine logs fast together. We towed it ashore with the skiff. Then we had dinner. Anybody but Pap would 'a' waited and seen the day through, so as to catch more stuff; but that warn't Pap's style. Nine logs was enough for one time; he must shove right over to town and sell. So he locked me in and took the skiff, and started off towing the raft about half past three. I judged he wouldn't come back that night. I waited till I reckoned he had got a good start; then I out with my saw, and went to work on that log again. Before he was t'other side of the river I was out of the hole; him and his raft was just a speck on the water away off yonder.

I took the sack of cornmeal to where the canoe was hid, and put it in; then I done the same with the side of bacon; then the whiskey jug. I took all the coffee and sugar there was, and all the ammunition; I took the bucket and a dipper and a tin cup, and my old saw and two blankets, and the skillet and the coffeepot. I took fishlines and matches and other things—everything that was worth a cent. I wanted an axe, but there was only the one at the woodpile, and I knowed why I was going to leave that. I fetched out the gun, and now I was done.

I had wore the ground a good deal crawling out of the hole and dragging out so many things. So I fixed that as good as I could from the outside by scattering dust; and then I fixed the piece of log back into its place. If you stood four or five foot away and didn't know it was sawed, you wouldn't never notice it; and besides, this was the back of the cabin.

It was all grass clear to the canoe, so I hadn't left a track. I stood on the bank and looked out over the river. All safe. So I took the gun and went a piece into the woods, and was hunting around for some birds when I see a wild pig. I shot him and took him into camp. Then I took the axe and smashed in the door. I fetched the pig in, and took him nearly to the table and hacked into his throat with the axe, and laid him down to bleed. Well, next I took an old sack and put a lot of big rocks in it, and I started it from the pig, and dragged it to the door and through the woods to the river and dumped it in. You could easy see that something had been dragged over the ground. I did wish Tom Sawyer was there; I knowed he would take an interest in this kind of business, and throw in the fancy touches. Nobody could spread himself like Tom Sawyer in such a thing as that.

Well, last I pulled out some of my hair, and blooded the axe good, and stuck it on the back side, and slung the axe in the corner. Then I took up the pig in my jacket (so he couldn't drip) till I got a good piece below the house and then dumped him into the river. Now I thought of something else. So I went and got the bag of meal out of the canoe, and fetched it to the house. I took the bag to where it used to stand and ripped a hole in the bottom of it. Then I carried the sack across the grass and through the willows east of the house, to a shallow lake that was five mile wide and full of rushes. There was a creek leading out of it on the other side that went miles away, I don't know where, but it didn't go to the river. The meal sifted out and made a little track all the way to the lake. I dropped Pap's whetstone there too, so as to look like it had been done by accident. Then I tied up the rip in the meal sack with a string, and took it to the canoe again.

It was about dark now; so I dropped the canoe down the river under some willows that hung over the bank, and waited for the moon to rise. I made fast to a willow; then I took a bite to eat, and by and by laid down in the canoe to smoke a pipe and lay out a plan. I says to myself, They'll follow the track of that sackful of rocks to the shore and then drag the river for me. And they'll follow that meal track to the lake and go browsing down the creek that leads out of it to find the robbers that killed me and took the things. They won't ever hunt the river for anything but my dead carcass. They'll soon get tired of that, and won't bother no more about me. All right; I can stop anywhere I want to. Jackson's Island is good enough for me; I know that island pretty well, and nobody ever comes there. And then I can paddle over to town nights, and slink around and pick up things I want. Jackson's Island's the place.

I was pretty tired, and the first thing I knowed I was asleep. When I woke up I didn't know where I was. I set up and looked around a little scared. Then I remembered. The river looked miles and miles across. The moon was so bright I could 'a' counted the drift logs that went a-slipping along, black and still, hundreds of yards out from shore. Everything was dead quiet, and it looked late, and *smelt late*. You know what I mean.

I took a good gap and a stretch, and was just going to unhitch and start when I heard a sound from oars working away over the water. I peeped out through the willow branches, and there it was—a skiff, away off. It kept a-coming, and I see there warn't but one man in it. Thinks I, Maybe it's Pap. By and by he came a-swinging up shore, and he went by so close I could 'a' reached out the gun and touched him. Well, it *was* Pap, sure enough—and sober, too, by the way he laid his oars.

I didn't lose no time. The next minute I was a-spinning down-stream soft, but quick, in the shade of the bank. I made two mile and a half, and then struck out towards the middle of the river, because pretty soon I would be passing the ferry landing, and people might see me. I got out amongst the driftwood, and then laid down in the bottom of the canoe and let her float till I was away below the ferry. Then I rose up, and there was Jackson's

Island, about two mile downstream, heavy-timbered and standing up out of the middle of the river, big and dark and solid, like a steamboat without any lights.

It didn't take me long to get there. I shot past the head in the current, and then I got into the dead water and landed on the side towards the Illinois shore. I run the canoe into a deep dent in the bank that I knowed about; I had to part the willow branches to get in; and when I made fast nobody could 'a' seen the canoe from the outside.

There was a little gray in the sky now; so I stepped into the woods, and laid down for a nap before breakfast.

CHAPTER IV

THE SUN WAS UP SO HIGH when I waked that I judged it was after eight o'clock. I laid there in the cool shade thinking, and feeling rested and ruther satisfied. Mostly it was big trees all about, and there was freckled places on the ground where the light sifted down through the leaves. A couple of squirrels set on a limb and jabbered at me very friendly.

I was powerful lazy and comfortable, and was dozing off again, when I thinks I hears a deep sound of *boom!* away up the river. I rouses up and listens; pretty soon I hears it again. I hopped up and went and looked out at a hole in the leaves at the head of the island and I see a bunch of smoke laying on the water near the ferry. And there was the ferryboat full of people floating along down. I knowed what was the matter now. *Boom!* I see the white smoke squirt out of the ferryboat's side. You see, they was firing cannon over the water, trying to make my carcass come to the top.

I was pretty hungry, but it warn't going to do for me to start a fire, because they might see the smoke. So I set there and watched the cannon smoke and listened to the boom. The river was a mile wide there, and it always looks pretty on a summer morning—so I was having a good enough time seeing them hunt for my remainders.

The ferryboat was floating with the current, and I allowed I'd have a chance to see who was aboard when she come along, because she would come in close, the way the current did. When she'd got pretty well along towards me, I went and laid down behind a log on the bank. Where the log forked I could peep through.

By and by she come along, and she drifted in so close that they could 'a' run out a plank and walked ashore. Most everybody was on the boat. Pap, and Judge Thatcher, and Bessie Thatcher, and Joe Harper, and Tom Sawyer, and his old Aunt Polly, and his half brother Sid, and plenty more. Everybody was talking about the murder, but the captain broke in and says:

"Look sharp, now; the current sets in close here, and maybe he's washed ashore and got tangled amongst the brush at the water's edge. I hope so, anyway."

They all leaned over the rails, nearly in my face, watching with all their might. I could see them first-rate, but they couldn't see me. Then the captain sung out, "Stand away!" and the cannon let off such a blast right before me that it made me deef. If they'd 'a' had some bullets in, I reckon they'd 'a' got the corpse they was after. Well, I see I warn't hurt, thanks to goodness. The boat floated on and went out of sight. I could hear the booming now and then, further and further off, and then after an hour they turned around the foot of the island and started up the channel on the Missouri side, booming once in a while. I crossed over to that side and watched them. When they got abreast the head of the island they quit shooting and dropped over to the Missouri shore and went home to the town.

I knowed I was all right now. I got my traps out of the canoe and made a nice camp in the woods, and I catched a catfish, and towards sundown I started my campfire and had supper. When it was dark I set by my campfire smoking; but by and by it got sort of lonesome, and so I went and set on the bank and listened to the current swashing along, and counted the stars and drift logs, and then went to bed; there ain't no better way to put in time when you are lonesome; you can't stay so, you soon get over it.

And so for three days and nights. No difference—just the same thing. But the next day I went exploring around down through the island. I was boss of it; it all belonged to me, so to say, and I wanted to know all about it. I found plenty strawberries, ripe and prime; and green summer grapes, and green razberries; and green blackberries was just beginning to show. They would all come handy by and by, I judged.

Well, I went fooling along in the deep woods till I judged I warn't far from the foot of the island. I clipped along, and all of a sudden I bounded right onto the ashes of a campfire that was all smoking.

My heart jumped up amongst my lungs. I never waited for to look further, but went sneaking back on my tiptoes as fast as ever I could. Every now and then I stopped a second amongst the thick leaves and listened, but my breath come so hard I couldn't hear nothing else.

When I got to camp I warn't feeling very brash, so I got all my traps into my canoe again, and I put out the fire and scattered the ashes around, and then I clumb a tree.

I reckon I was up in the tree two hours; but I didn't see nothing, didn't hear nothing—I only *thought* I heard and seen as much as a thousand things. Well, I couldn't stay up there forever; so at last I got down, but I kept in the thick woods and on the lookout all the time. All I could get to eat was berries and what was left over from breakfast.

When night come I reckoned I would sleep in the canoe. I didn't sleep much. I couldn't, somehow, for thinking. And every time I waked up I thought somebody had me by the neck. So the sleep didn't do me no good. By and by I says to myself, I can't live this way; I'm a-going to find out who it is that's here on the island with me. Well, I felt better right off.

So I took my paddle and slid out from shore, and then let the canoe drop along down amongst the shadows. When I was most down to the foot of the island I brung the canoe to shore. In a little while I see a pale streak over the treetops, and knowed the day was coming. Then I got my gun and slipped into the woods towards where I had run across the campfire. By and by, sure enough, I catched a glimpse of fire through the trees. I went for it cautious and slow, and there laid a man on the ground. It most give me the fantods. He had a blanket around his head, and his head was nearly in the fire. I set there behind a clump of bushes in about six foot of him, and kept my eyes on him steady. It was getting gray daylight now. Pretty soon he gapped and stretched himself and hove off the blanket, and it was Miss Watson's Jim! I bet I was glad to see him. I says, "Hello, Jim!" and skipped out.

He bounced up and stared at me wild. Then he drops down on his knees, and puts his hands together and says:

"Doan' hurt me—don't! I hain't ever done no harm to a ghos'. You go en git in de river ag'in, en doan' do nuffn to ole Jim, 'at 'uz alwuz yo' fren'."

Well, I warn't long making him understand I warn't dead. I was ever so glad to see Jim. I warn't lonesome now. I told him I warn't afraid of *him* telling the people where I was. Then I says, "It's daylight. Le's get breakfast. Make up your campfire good."

"What's de use er makin' up de campfire to cook strawbries en sich truck? But you got a gun, hain't you? Den we kin git sumfn better den strawbries."

"Strawberries and such truck," I says. "How long you been on the island, Jim?"

"I come heah de night arter you's killed."

"All that time? And ain't you had nothing but that kind of rubbage to eat?"

"No sah—nuffn else."

"Well, you must be most starved, ain't you?"

"I reck'n I could eat a hoss. How long you ben on de islan'?"

"Since the night I got killed."

"No! W'y, what has you lived on? Oh, you got a gun! Dat's good. Now you kill sumfn en I'll make up de fire."

While he built up the fire, I went over to the canoe, and fetched meal and bacon and coffee, and coffeepot and frying pan and cups. Jim was set back considerable, because he reckoned it was all done with witchcraft. I catched a good big catfish, too, and Jim cleaned him with his knife, and fried him. Then we lolled on the grass and eat breakfast smoking hot. When we had got pretty well stuffed, we laid off and lazied. By and by Jim says:

"But looky here, Huck, who wuz it dat 'uz killed in dat shanty ef it warn't you?"

Then I told him the whole thing, and he said it was smart. Then I says, "How do you come to be here, Jim, and how'd you get here?"

He looked pretty uneasy. "Maybe I better not tell," he says.

"Why, Jim?"

"Well, dey's reasons. But you wouldn' tell on me ef I 'uz to tell you, would you, Huck?"

"Blamed if I would, Jim."

"Well, I b'lieve you, Huck. I—I *run off*."

"Jim!"

"But mind, you said you wouldn' tell, Huck."

"Well, I did. I said I wouldn't, and I'll stick to it. Honest *injun*, I will, even if people call me a lowdown Abolitionist. So, now, le's know all about it."

"Well, you see, it 'uz dis way. Ole missus—dat's Miss Watson— she pecks on me all de time, en treats me pooty rough, but she awluz said she wouldn' sell me down to Orleans. But I noticed dey wuz a nigger trader roun' de place lately, en I begin to git oneasy. Well, one night de do' warn't quite shet, en I hear old missus tell de widder she gwyne to sell me down to Orleans. She didn' want to, but she could git eight hund'd dollars for me, en she couldn' resis'. I never waited to hear de res'. I lit out quick, I tell you. I shin down de hill, en 'spec to steal a skift 'long de sho', but dey wuz people a-stirring yit, so I hid in de ole tumbledown cooper shop on de bank to wait for everybody to go 'way. Well, I wuz dah all night. Dey wuz somebody roun' all de time. 'Long 'bout six in de mawnin' skifts begin to go by, en every skift wuz talkin' 'bout how yo' pap say you's killed. I 'uz powerful sorry you's killed, Huck, but I ain't no mo' now.

"I laid dah under de shavin's all day. I knowed ole missus en de widder wuz goin' to be gone to de camp meet'n', en so dey wouldn' miss me tell evenin'. When it come dark I tuck out up de river road, to whah dey warn't no houses. I'd made up my mine 'bout what I's a-gwyne to do. I says, a raff is what I's arter, en when I see a light a-comin' roun' de p'int bymeby, I wade' in en shove' a log ahead o' me en swum to de stern uv de raff en tuck a-holt. It 'uz pooty dark, so I clumb up en laid down on de planks. De men 'uz all 'way yonder in de middle, whah de lantern wuz. De river wuz a-risin', en dey wuz a good current; so I reck'n'd 'at by fo' in de mawnin' I'd be twenty-five mile down de river, en den I'd swim asho'.

"But I didn' have no luck. When we 'uz mos' down to de head er de islan' a man begin to come aft wid de lantern. So I slid overboard en swum to de islan'. I went into de woods en jedged I wouldn' fool wid raffs no mo', long as dey move de lantern roun' so. I had my pipe en some matches in my cap, en dey warn't wet, so I 'uz all right."

"And so you ain't had no meat nor bread all this time? Why didn't you get mud turkles?"

"How you gwyne to git 'm in de night? I warn't gwyne to show mysef on de bank in de daytime."

"Well, that's so. You've had to keep in the woods all the time, of course. Did you hear 'em shooting the cannon?"

"Oh, yes. I knowed dey was arter you. I see um go by heah—watched um thoo de bushes."

Some young birds come along, flying a yard or two at a time and lighting. Jim said it was a sign it was going to rain. I was going to catch some of them, but Jim wouldn't let me. He said it was a sign of death. And he said you mustn't count the things you are going to cook for dinner, because that would bring bad luck. The same if you shook the tablecloth after sundown. Jim knowed all kinds of signs. I said it looked to me like all the signs was about bad luck, and so I asked him if there warn't any good-luck signs. He says:

"Mighty few—an' *dey* ain't no use to a body. What you want to know when good luck's a-comin' for? Want to keep it off?" And he said, "Ef you's got hairy arms en a hairy breas', it's a sign dat you's a-gwyne to be rich."

"Have you got hairy arms and a hairy breast, Jim?"

"Don't you see I has?"

"Well, are you rich?"

"No, but I ben rich wunst, and gwyne to be rich ag'in. Wunst I had foteen dollars, but I tuck to specalat'n', en got busted out."

"What did you speculate in, Jim?"

"Why, livestock—cattle, you know. I put de money in a cow. But de cow up 'n' died on my han's."

"Well, it's all right, Jim, long as you're going to be rich again some time or other."

"Yes; en I's rich now, come to look at it. I owns mysef, en I's wuth eight hund'd dollars. I wisht I had de money, I wouldn' want no mo'."

I WANTED TO GO AND LOOK at a place right about the middle of the island that I'd found when I was exploring; so we started and soon got to it. This place was a tolerable long, steep ridge about forty foot high. We clumb all over it, and by and by found a good big cavern in the rock, most up to the top on the side towards Illinois. Jim said if we had the canoe hid and had all the traps in the cavern, we could rush there if anybody was to come to the island, and they would never find us. And, besides, he said them little birds had said it was going to rain, and did I want the things to get wet?

So we went back and lugged all the traps up there. Then we hunted up a place close by to hide the canoe in, amongst thick willows. We took some fish off of the lines and set them again, and begun to get ready for dinner.

The door of the cavern was big enough to roll a hogshead in, and on one side of the door the floor was flat and a good place to build a fire on. So we built it and cooked dinner.

We spread the blankets inside for a carpet, and eat our dinner in there. Pretty soon it darkened up, and begun to thunder and lighten; so the birds was right about it. Directly it begun to rain, and it rained like all fury, too. It was one of these regular summer storms. It would get so dark that it looked all blue-black outside, and lovely; and the rain would thrash by so thick that the trees off a little ways looked dim and spiderwebby; and here would come a blast of wind that would bend the trees down; and next, when it was just about the bluest and blackest—*fst!* it was as bright as glory; dark as sin again in a second, and you'd hear the thunder let go with an awful crash.

"Jim, this is nice," I says. "I wouldn't want to be nowhere else but here. Pass me along another hunk of fish."

"Well, you wouldn' 'a' ben here 'f it hadn' 'a' ben for Jim. You'd 'a' ben down dah in de woods widout any dinner. Birds knows when it's gwyne to rain, chile."

The river went on raising and raising for ten or twelve days, till at last it was over the banks. The water was three or four foot deep on the island in the low places.

Daytimes we paddled all over the island in the canoe. We went winding in and out amongst the trees, and sometimes the vines hung so thick we had to back away and go some other way. On every old broken-down tree you could see rabbits and snakes and such things; and after a day or two they got so tame, on account of being hungry, that you could put your hand right on them. We could 'a' had pets enough if we'd wanted them.

One night we catched a little section of a lumber raft—nice pine planks. It was twelve foot wide and about fifteen foot long. We could see sawlogs go by in the daylight sometimes, but we let them go; we didn't show ourselves in daylight.

Another night when we was up at the head of the island, just before daylight, here comes a frame house down. She was a two-story house, and tilted over considerable. We paddled out and got aboard, but it was too dark to see yet, so we made the canoe fast and set in her to wait for daylight.

The light begun to come before we got to the foot of the island. Then we looked in at the upstairs window. We could make out a bed, and a table, and two old chairs, and something laying on the floor in the corner that looked like a man. So Jim says:

"Hello, you!"

But it didn't budge. Then Jim says, "De man ain't asleep—he's dead. I'll go en see."

He went and looked, and says, "It's a dead man. Yes, indeedy; naked, too. He's ben shot in de back. I reck'n he's ben dead two er three days. Come in, Huck, but doan' look at his face—it's too gashly."

Jim throwed some old rags over him, but he needn't done it. I didn't look at him at all. There was heaps of old greasy cards scattered around over the floor, and old whiskey bottles; and all over the walls was the ignorantest kind of words and pictures made with charcoal. There was two old calico dresses and a sunbonnet hanging against the wall, and some men's clothing, too, and a boy's old speckled straw hat. We put the lot into the canoe— it might come good. The way things was scattered about we reckoned the people left in a hurry, and warn't fixed so as to carry off most of their stuff. Besides the clothes, we got an old tin lantern, and a bran-new Barlow knife, and a lot of candles, and a tin candlestick, and a cup, and a ratty old bedquilt, and a reticule with needles and pins and thread and such truck in it, and a hatchet and some nails, and a fishline with some hooks on it, and a roll of buckskin, and a dog collar, and a horseshoe.

And so, take it all around, we made a good haul.

When we was ready to shove off we was a quarter of a mile below the island, and it was pretty broad day; so I made Jim lay down in the canoe and cover up with the quilt, because if he set up people could tell he was a nigger a good ways off. I paddled back, and hadn't no accidents and didn't see nobody.

After breakfast I wanted to talk about the dead man and guess out how he come to be killed, but Jim didn't want to. He said it would fetch bad luck; and besides, he said, he might come and ha'nt us. That sounded pretty reasonable, so I didn't say no more, and we rummaged the clothes we'd got. We found eight dollars in silver sewed up in the lining of an old overcoat. Jim said he reckoned the people in that house stole the coat, because if they'd 'a' knowed the money was there they wouldn't 'a' left it. I said I reckoned they killed the dead man, too; but Jim didn't want to talk about that. I says:

"Now you think it's bad luck to talk about that man; but what did you say when I fetched in that snake skin I found yesterday? You said it was the worst bad luck in the world to touch a snake skin. Well, here's your bad luck! We've raked in all this truck and eight dollars besides. I wish we could have some bad luck like this every day, Jim."

"Don't you git too peart, honey. It's a-comin'."

It did come, too. It was Tuesday that we had that talk. Well, Friday night when we went to the cavern to sleep there was a rattlesnake in there. It was curled up on the foot of Jim's blanket, and when Jim flung himself down on the blanket while I was striking a light the snake bit him.

He jumped up yelling, and the first thing the light showed was the varmint curled up and ready for another spring. I laid him out with a stick, and Jim grabbed Pap's whiskey jug and begun to pour it down.

He was barefooted, and the snake bit him right on the heel. Jim told me to chop off the snake's head and throw it away, and then skin the body and roast a piece of it. I done it, and he eat it and said it would help cure him. He made me take off the rattles and tie them around his wrist, too. He said that would help. Then he sucked and sucked at the jug, and now and then he got out of his head and pitched around and yelled. His foot swelled up pretty big, and so did his leg; but by and by the drunk begun to come, and I judged he was all right; but I'd ruther been bit with a snake than Pap's whiskey.

Jim was laid up for four days and nights. Then the swelling was gone and he was around again. I made up my mind I wouldn't ever take a-holt of a snake skin again with my hands. Jim said he reckoned I would believe him next time. And he said that handling a snake skin was such awful bad luck that maybe we hadn't got to the end of it yet. He said he'd ruther see the new moon over his left shoulder as much as a thousand times than take up a snake skin in his hands.

Well, the days went along, and the river went down between its banks again. A day come when I said I was getting slow and dull, and I wanted to get a stirring-up someway. I said I reckoned I would slip over the river and find out what was going on. Jim liked that notion; but he said I must go in the dark and look sharp. Then he said, couldn't I put on some of them old things and dress up like a girl? That was a good notion. So we shortened up one of the calico gowns, and I turned my trouser legs to my knees and got into it, and it was a fair fit. I put on the sunbonnet and tied it under my chin, and then for a body to look in and see my face was like looking down a stovepipe. Jim said nobody would know me, even in the daytime, hardly. I practiced all day to get the hang of the things, and by and by I could do pretty well, only Jim said I didn't walk like a girl; and he said I must quit pulling up my gown to get at my britches pocket. I took notice, and done better.

I started up the Illinois shore in the canoe just after dark, crossed the river and fetched in at the bottom of the town. I tied up and started along the bank. There was a light burning in a little shanty that hadn't been lived in for a long time, and I slipped up and peeped in at the window. There was a woman about forty years old in there knitting by a candle that was on a pine table. I didn't know her face; she was a stranger, new to town. Now this was lucky, because I was weakening; I was getting afraid I had come; people might know my voice and find me out. But if this woman had been in such a little town two days she could tell me all I wanted to know; so I knocked at the door, and made up my mind I wouldn't forget I was a girl.

"Come in," says the woman, and I did. She says, "Take a cheer."

I done it. She looked me all over with her little shiny eyes, and says, "What might your name be?"

"Sarah Williams."

"Where'bouts do you live? In this neighborhood?"

"No'm. In Hookerville, seven miles below. I've walked all the way. My mother's down sick, and I come to tell my uncle Abner Moore. He lives at the upper end of the town, she says. Do you know him?"

"No; but I don't know everybody yet. I haven't lived here

quite two weeks. It's a ways to the upper end of the town. You better stay here all night. Take off your bonnet."

"No," I says; "I'll rest awhile, I reckon, and go on."

She said she wouldn't let me go by myself, but her husband would be in by and by, and she'd send him along with me. Then she got to talking about her husband, and about her relations up the river, and her relations down the river, and about how much better off they used to was, and so on and on, till I was afeard I had made a mistake coming to her; but by and by she dropped on to Pap and the murder, and then I was pretty willing to let her clatter right along. She told me about Tom Sawyer finding the twelve thousand dollars (only she got it twenty thousand) and all about Pap and what a hard lot he was, and what a hard lot I was, and at last she got down to where I was murdered. I says:

"Who done it? We've heard considerable in Hookerville, but we don't know who 'twas that killed Huck Finn."

"Well, there's a right smart chance of people *here* that'd like to know who killed him. At first most everybody thought old Finn done it himself. But before night they changed around and judged it was done by a runaway nigger named Jim."

"Why *he*—"

I stopped. I reckoned I better keep still. She run on, and never noticed I had put in at all:

"The nigger run off the very night Huck Finn was killed. So there's a reward out for him—three hundred dollars. And there's a reward out for old Finn, too—two hundred dollars. You see, he come to town the morning after the murder, and told about it. Before night they wanted to lynch him, but he was gone. Well, next day they found out the nigger was gone; so then they put the murder on him, you see; and while they was full of it, next day, back comes old Finn, and went boohooing to Judge Thatcher to get money to hunt for the nigger with. The judge gave him some, and that evening he got drunk, and was around with a couple of hard-looking strangers, and then went off with them. Well, he hain't come back sence, and they ain't looking for him back till this thing blows over, for people thinks now that he killed

35

his boy and fixed things so he'd get Huck's money without having to bother with a lawsuit. He's sly, I reckon. If he don't come back for a year he'll be all right. You can't prove anything on him; everything will be quieted down then, and he'll walk off with Huck's money as easy as nothing."

"I reckon so, 'm. I don't see nothing in the way of it. Has everybody quit thinking the nigger done it?"

"No, not everybody. A good many think he done it. But they'll get the nigger pretty soon now, and maybe they can scare it out of him."

"Why, are they after him yet?"

"Well, does three hundred dollars lay around every day for people to pick up? Some folks think the nigger ain't far from here. I'm one of them—but I hain't talked it around. A day ago I was talking with an old couple that lives next door, and they happened to say hardly anybody ever goes to that island yonder that they call Jackson's Island. 'Don't anybody live there?' says I. 'No, nobody,' says they. I didn't say any more, but I was near certain I'd seen smoke over there a day or two ago, so I says to myself, Like as not that nigger's hiding over there; anyway, says I, it's worth the trouble to give the place a hunt. So my husband's going over to see—him and another man."

I had got so uneasy I couldn't set still. I had to do something with my hands, so I took up a needle off of the table and went to threading it. My hands shook, and I was making a bad job of it. When the woman stopped talking I looked up, and she was looking at me, smiling a little. I put down the needle and thread, and let on to be interested—and I was, too—and says:

"Three hundred dollars is a power of money. I wish my mother could get it. Is your husband going over there tonight?"

"Yes. He went up to town with the man I was telling you of, to get a boat. They'll go over after midnight."

"Couldn't they see better if they was to wait till daytime?"

"Yes. And couldn't the nigger see better, too? After midnight he'll likely be asleep, and they can slip around through the woods and hunt up his campfire, if he's got one."

36

"I didn't think of that."

The woman kept looking at me pretty curious. Pretty soon she says, "What did you say your name was, honey?"

"M—Mary Williams."

Somehow it didn't seem to me that I said it was Mary before, so I didn't look up—I felt sort of cornered, and was afeard maybe I was looking it, too. The longer the woman set still the uneasier I was. But now she says:

"Honey, I thought you said it was Sarah when you come in?"

"Oh, yes'm, I did. Sarah Mary Williams. Sarah's my first name. Some calls me Sarah, some calls me Mary."

"Oh, that's the way of it?"

"Yes'm."

Well, the woman fell to talking then about how hard times was, and how poor they had to live, and how the rats was as free as if they owned the place, and I got to feeling better again. She was right about the rats. You'd see one stick his nose out of a hole in the corner every little while. She said she had to have things handy to throw at them, or they wouldn't give her no peace. She showed me a bar of lead twisted up into a knot, and said she was a good shot with it generly, but she'd wrenched her arm a day or two ago, and would I try for the next one that come out. I wanted to be getting away before the old man got back, but of course I didn't let on. I got the thing, and the first rat that showed his nose I let drive, and if he'd 'a' stayed where he was he'd 'a' been a tolerable sick rat. She said that was first-rate, and she reckoned I would hive the next one. She went and got the lump of lead and fetched it back, and brought along a hank of yarn which she wanted me to help her with. I held up my two hands and she put the hank over them, and went on talking about her arm and her husband's matters.

Then she said, "Keep your eye on the rats. You better have the lead in your lap, handy." She dropped the lump into my lap just at that moment, and I clapped my legs together on it and she went on talking. But only about a minute. Then she took off the hank and looked me straight in the face, and very pleasant, and says:

"Come, now, what's your real name?"

"Wh-hat, mum?"

"Is it Bill, or Tom, or Bob? Or what?"

I shook like a leaf, but I says:

"Please to don't poke fun at a poor girl like me, mum. If I'm in the way here, I'll—"

"No, you won't. Set down and stay where you are. I ain't going to tell on you. You just tell me your secret, and trust me. I'll keep it; and, what's more, I'll help you. You see, you're a runaway 'prentice, that's all. There ain't no harm in it. You've been treated bad, and you made up your mind to cut. Bless you, child, I wouldn't tell on you. Tell me all about it now, that's a good boy."

So I said it wouldn't be no use to try to play it any longer, and I would just tell her everything, but she mustn't go back on her promise. Then I told her my father and mother was dead, and the law had bound me out to a mean old farmer in the country thirty mile from the river, and he treated me so bad I couldn't stand it no longer; he went away to be gone a couple of days, and so I stole some of his daughter's clothes and cleared out, and I had been three nights coming the thirty miles. I said I believed my uncle Abner Moore would take care of me, and so that was why I struck out for this town of Goshen.

"Goshen, child? This ain't Goshen. This is St. Petersburg. Goshen's ten mile further up the river. Who told you this was Goshen?"

"Why, a man I met at daybreak this morning. He told me when the roads forked I must take the right hand, and five mile would fetch me Goshen."

"He was drunk, I reckon. He told you just exactly wrong."

"Well, he did act like he was drunk, but it ain't no matter now. I got to be moving along. I'll fetch Goshen before daylight."

"Hold on a minute. I'll put you up a snack to eat. You might want it."

So she put me up a snack, and says:

"Say, when a cow's laying down, which end of her gets up first? Answer prompt, now."

"The hind end, mum."

"Well, then, a horse?"

"The for-rard end, mum."

"Well, I reckon you *have* lived in the country. I thought you was trying to hocus me again. What's your real name, now?"

"George Peters, mum."

"Well, try to remember it, George. Don't forget and tell me it's Elexander before you go. And don't go about women in that old calico. You do a girl tolerable poor, but you might fool men, maybe. Bless you, child, when you set out to thread a needle don't hold the thread still and fetch the needle up to it; hold the needle still and poke the thread at it. And when you throw at a rat or anything, hitch yourself up a-tiptoe and fetch your hand up over your head as awkward as you can; throw stiff-armed from the shoulder, not from the wrist and elbow, with your arm out to one side, like a boy. And, mind you, when a girl tries to catch anything in her lap she throws her knees apart; she don't clap them together, the way you did when you catched the lump of lead. Why, I spotted you for a boy when you was threading the needle; and I contrived the other things just to make certain. Now, trot along to your uncle, Sarah Mary Williams George Elexander Peters, and if you get into trouble you send word to Mrs. Judith Loftus, which is me, and I'll do what I can to get you out of it."

I went up the road about fifty yards, and then I doubled on my tracks and slipped back to where my canoe was. I jumped in and was off in a hurry. I took off the sunbonnet, for I didn't want no blinders on then. When I was about the middle of the river, I heard the clock begin to strike, so I stops and listens; the sound come faint over the water but clear—eleven. When I struck the head of the island I never waited to blow, but I shoved right into the timber where my old camp used to be, and started a good fire there on a high and dry spot. Then I jumped in the canoe and dug out for our place, a mile and a half below. I landed, and slopped through the dark up the ridge and into the cavern. There Jim laid, sound asleep. I roused him out and says:

39

"Git up and hump yourself, Jim! They're after us!"

Jim never said a word; but the way he worked for the next half hour showed about how he was scared. By that time everything we had in the world was on our raft—that section of lumber raft we'd got off the river during the flood—and she was ready to be shoved out from the willow cove where she was hid. I took the canoe out from the shore a little piece, and took a look; but if there was a boat around I couldn't see it in the starlight. Then we got out the raft and slipped along down in the shade, past the foot of the island dead still—never saying a word.

CHAPTER V

IT MUST 'A' BEEN CLOSE ON to one o'clock when we got below the island at last, and the raft did seem to go mighty slow. If a boat was to come along we was going to take to the canoe and break for the Illinois shore; and it was well a boat didn't come, for we hadn't ever thought to put the gun in the canoe, or a fishing line, or anything to eat.

If the men went to the island I just expect they found the campfire I built, and watched it all night for Jim to come. Anyways, they stayed away from us, and if my building the fire never fooled them it warn't no fault of mine.

When the first streak of day began to show we tied up to a towhead in a big bend on the Illinois side. A towhead is a sandbar that has cottonwoods on it, as thick as harrow teeth. We hacked off cottonwood branches with the hatchet, and covered up the raft with them so she looked like there had been a cave-in in the bank there.

We had mountains on the Missouri shore and heavy timber on the Illinois side, and the channel was down the Missouri shore at that place, so we warn't afraid of anybody running across us. We laid there all day, and watched the rafts and steamboats spin down the Missouri shore, and I told Jim all about the time I had jabbering with that woman; Jim said she was a smart one.

When it was beginning to come on dark we poked our heads out of the cottonwood thicket, and looked up and down and across; nothing in sight; so Jim took up some of the top planks of the raft and built a snug wigwam to get under in blazing weather and rainy, and to keep the things dry. Jim made a floor for the wigwam, and raised it a foot or more above the level of the raft, so now the blankets and all the traps was out of reach of steamboat waves.

Right in the middle of the wigwam we made a layer of dirt about five or six inches deep with a frame around it; this was to build a fire on in sloppy weather or chilly; the wigwam would keep it from being seen. We made an extra steering oar, too, because one of the others might get broke; and we fixed up a forked stick to hang the old lantern on, because we must always light the lantern whenever we see a steamboat coming, to keep from getting run over.

This second night we run between seven and eight hours, with a current that was making over four mile an hour. We catched fish and talked, and we took a swim now and then to keep off sleepiness. It was kind of solemn, drifting down the big, still river, laying on our backs looking up at the stars, and we didn't ever feel like talking loud, and it warn't often that we laughed—only a little kind of low chuckle. We had mighty good weather as a general thing, and nothing ever happened to us at all—that night, nor the next, nor the next.

Every night we passed towns, some of them away up on black hillsides, nothing but just a shiny bed of lights. The fifth night we passed St. Louis, and it was like the whole world lit up. In St. Petersburg they used to say there was twenty or thirty thousand people in St. Louis, but I never believed it till I see that wonderful spread of lights at two o'clock that night. There warn't a sound there; everybody was asleep.

Every night now I used to slip ashore toward ten o'clock at some little village, and buy ten or fifteen cents' worth of meal or bacon or other stuff to eat; and sometimes I lifted a chicken that warn't roosting comfortable. Pap always said, take a chicken when you get a chance, because if you don't want him yourself you can easy find somebody that does, and a good deed ain't ever forgot. I never see Pap when he didn't want the chicken himself, but that is what he used to say, anyway. Mornings before daylight I slipped into cornfields and borrowed a watermelon, or a punkin, or some new corn, or things of that kind. And we shot a waterfowl now and then that got up too early in the morning. Take it all round, we lived pretty high.

The fifth night below St. Louis we had a big storm after midnight, with a power of thunder and lightning, and the rain poured down in a solid sheet. We stayed in the wigwam and let the raft take care of itself. When the lightning glared out we could see a big straight river ahead, and high rocky bluffs on both sides. By and by says I, "Hel-*lo*, Jim, looky yonder!" It was a steamboat that had killed herself on a rock. We was drifting straight down for her. The lightning showed her very distinct. She was leaning over, with part of her upper deck above water, and you could see every little chimbly guy clean and clear, and a chair by the big bell, when the flashes come.

Well, it being away in the night and stormy, and all so mysterious-like, I felt just the way any other boy would 'a' felt when I seen that wreck. I wanted to get aboard of her. So I says, "Le's land on her, Jim."

But Jim was dead against it at first. "I doan' want to go fool'n' 'long er no wrack," he says. "Like as not dey's a watchman on it."

"Watchman your grandmother," I says. "There ain't nothing to watch but the texas and the pilothouse; and do you reckon anybody's going to resk his life for a texas and a pilothouse such a night as this, when it's likely to break up any minute? And besides," I says, "we might borrow something worth having out of the captain's stateroom. Seegars, *I* bet you. Stick a candle in your pocket, Jim. Do you reckon Tom Sawyer would ever go by this thing? Not for pie, he wouldn't. He'd call it an adventure—and wouldn't he throw style into it? I wish Tom Sawyer *was* here."

Jim he grumbled a little, but give in. The lightning showed us the wreck again, and we fetched the stabboard derrick, and made fast there. Then we went sneaking down the slope of the deck in the dark, feeling our way slow with our feet and hands. Pretty soon we struck the forward end of the skylight, and clumb onto it; and the next step fetched us in front of the captain's door, which was open, and by Jimminy, away down through the texas hall we see a light! And all in the same second we hear voices!

Jim whispered he was feeling powerful sick, and told me to come along. I was going to start for the raft; but just then I heard a voice wail out:

"Oh, please don't, boys; I swear I won't ever tell!"

Another voice said, pretty loud, "It's a lie, Jim Turner. You've acted this way before. You always want more'n your share of the truck, and got it, too, because you've swore 't if you didn't you'd tell. But this time you've said it jest one time too many."

By this time Jim was gone for the raft. I was just a-biling with curiosity; and I says to myself, Tom Sawyer wouldn't back out now, and so I won't either. So I dropped on my hands and knees in the little passage, and crept aft in the dark till there warn't but one stateroom betwixt me and the cross hall of the texas. Then in there I see a man stretched on the floor and tied hand and foot, and two men standing over him, and one of them had a dim lantern in his hand, and the other one had a pistol. This one kept pointing the pistol at the man's head. But the man with the lantern said, "Put *up* that pistol, Bill."

Bill says, "I don't want to, Jake Packard. I'm for killin' him. Didn't he kill old Hatfield jist the same way—and don't he deserve it?"

"But I don't *want* him killed, and I've got my reasons."

"Bless yo' heart for them words, Jake Packard!" says the man on the floor, sort of blubbering.

Packard didn't take no notice of that, but hung up his lantern on a nail and started towards where I was, there in the dark, and motioned Bill to come. I crawfished as fast as I could about two yards, and to keep from getting catched I crawled into a stateroom. The man came a-pawing along in the dark, and when Packard got to my stateroom, he says:

"Here—come in here."

And in he come, and Bill after him. But before they got in I was up in the upper berth, cornered, and sorry I come. Then they stood there and talked. I couldn't see them, but I could tell where they was by the whiskey they'd been having. They talked low and earnest.

Bill wanted to kill Turner. He says, "He's said he'll tell, and he will. Shore's you're born, he'll turn state's evidence. I'm for putting him out of his troubles."

"So'm I," says Packard, very quiet.

"Blame it, I'd sorter begun to think you wasn't. Well, let's go and do it."

"Hold on a minute; I hain't had my say. You listen to me. Shooting's good, but there's quieter ways if the thing's *got* to be done. Now I say it ain't a-goin' to be more'n two hours befo' this wrack breaks up and washes off down the river. See? He'll be drownded, and won't have nobody to blame for it but his own self. I reckon that's a considerable sight better 'n killin' of him. Ain't I right?"

"Yes, I reck'n you are. But s'pose she *don't* break up and wash off?"

"Well, we can wait the two hours anyway and see, can't we?"

"All right, then; come along."

So they started, and I lit out, all in a cold sweat, and scrambled forward. It was dark as pitch there; but I said, in a kind of whisper, "Jim!" and he answered up, right at my elbow, with a sort of a moan, and I says:

"Quick, Jim, it ain't no time for fooling around and moaning; there's a gang of murderers in yonder, and if we don't hunt up their boat and set her drifting down the river so these fellows can't get away from the wreck there's one of 'em going to be in a bad fix. But if we find their boat we can put *all* of 'em in a bad fix—for the sheriff 'll get 'em. Quick—hurry! I'll hunt the labboard side, you hunt the stabboard. You start at the raft, and—"

"Oh, my lordy! *Raf'*? Dey ain' no raf' no mo'; she done broke loose en gone—en here we is!"

44

WELL, I CATCHED MY BREATH and most fainted. Shut up on a wreck with such a gang as that! But it warn't no time to be sentimentering. We'd *got* to find that boat now—for ourselves. So we went a-quaking and shaking down the stabboard side, and slow work it was, too—and no sign of a boat. Then we struck for the stern of the texas, and scrabbled forwards on the skylight, hanging on from shutter to shutter. When we got pretty close to the cross-hall door there was the skiff, sure enough! I felt ever so thankful. In another second I would 'a' been aboard of her, but just then the door opened. One of the men stuck his head out only a couple of foot from me, and I thought I was gone; but he jerked it in again, and says:

"Heave that blame lantern out o' sight, Bill!"

He flung a bag of something into the boat, and then got in himself and set down. It was Packard. Then Bill *he* come out and got in. Packard says, in a low voice, "All ready—shove off!"

I couldn't hardly hang on to the shutters, I was so weak. But Bill says, "Hold on—'d you go through him?"

"No. Didn't you?"

"No. So he's got his share o' the cash yet."

"Well, then, come along; no use to leave money."

So they got out and went back in, and in a half second I was in the boat, and Jim come tumbling after me. I out with my knife and cut the rope, and away we went!

We didn't touch an oar, and we didn't hardly even breathe. We went gliding along, dead silent, past the tip of the paddle box, and past the stern; then in a second or two more we was a hundred yards below the wreck, and the darkness soaked her up, every last sign of her, and we was safe, and knowed it.

When we was three or four hundred yards downstream we see the lantern show like a little spark at the texas door for a second, and we knowed by that that the rascals had missed their boat, and was beginning to understand that they was in just as much trouble now as Jim Turner was.

Then Jim manned the oars, and we took out after our raft. Now was the first time that I begun to worry about the men—I reckon

I hadn't had time to before. I begun to think how dreadful it was, even for murderers, to be in such a fix. So says I to Jim:

"The first light we see we'll land below it, and you hide there, and then I'll go and fix up some kind of a yarn, and get somebody to go for that gang and get them out of their scrape, so they can be hung when their time comes."

But that idea was a failure; for pretty soon it begun to storm again. The rain poured down, and never a light showed; everybody in bed, I reckon. We boomed along down the river, watching for lights and watching for our raft. After a long time the rain let up, but the clouds stayed, and the lightning kept whimpering, and by and by a flash showed us a black thing ahead, floating, and we made for it. It was the raft, and mighty glad was we to get aboard of it again.

We seen a light now away down to the right, on shore. So I said I would go for it. The skiff was half full of plunder which that gang had stole there on the wreck. We hustled it onto the raft in a pile, and I told Jim to float along down, and show a light when he judged he had gone about two mile, and keep it burning till I come; then I manned my oars and shoved for the light on the shore. As I got down towards it three or four more showed—up on a hillside. It was a village. I closed in above the shore light, and laid on my oars and floated. As I went by I see it was a lantern hanging on the jack staff of a double-hull ferryboat. I skimmed around for the watchman, a-wondering whereabouts he slept; and by and by I found him roosting on the bitts forward, with his head between his knees. I gave his shoulder two or three shoves, and begun to cry. He stirred up and took a good gap and stretch. Then he says:

"Hello, what's up? Don't cry, bub. What's the trouble?"

I says, "Pap, and Mam, and Sis, and—"

Then I broke down. He says, "Oh, dang it now, *don't* take on so; we all has our troubles, and this 'n 'll come out all right. What's the matter with 'em?"

"They're—they're—are you the watchman of the boat?"

"Yes," he says, well-satisfied like. "I'm the captain and the owner and the mate and the pilot and watchman; and sometimes I'm the freight and passengers. I ain't as rich as old Jim Hornback, and I can't slam around money the way he does; but I've told him a many a time 't I wouldn't trade places with him, not for all his spondulicks and much more. Says I—"

I broke in and says, "They're in an awful peck of trouble, and—"

"Who is?"

"Why, Pap and Mam and Sis and Miss Hooker; and if you'd take your ferryboat and go up there—"

"Up where? Where are they?"

"On the wreck."

"What! You don't mean they're on the *Walter Scott?*"

"Yes."

"Good land! What are they doin' *there*, for gracious sakes? Why, great goodness, they better git off mighty quick! How in the nation did they ever git into such a scrape?"

"Easy. Miss Hooker was a-visiting up there to the town—"

"Yes, Booth's Landing—go on."

"She was a-visiting there at Booth's Landing, and just in the edge of the evening she started over with her nigger woman in the horse ferry—and they lost their steering oar, and swung around and went a-floating down, stern first, and saddlebaggsed on the wreck, and the ferryman and the nigger woman and the horses was all lost, but Miss Hooker she made a grab and got aboard the wreck. Well, about an hour after dark we come along down in our trading scow, and it was so dark *we* saddlebaggsed; but all of us was saved but Bill Whipple—and oh, he was the best cretur! I most wish 't it had been me, I do."

"My George! And *then* what did you all do?"

"Well, we hollered, but nobody heard, so Pap said somebody got to get ashore and get help. I was the only one that could swim, so I made a dash for it, and Miss Hooker she said if I didn't strike help sooner, come here and hunt up her uncle. I made the land about a mile below, and been fooling along ever since, trying to get people to do something, but they said, 'What, in such a night and such a current? There ain't no sense in it; go for the steam ferry.' Now if you'll go and—"

"By Jackson, I'd *like* to, but who in the dingnation's a-going to *pay* for it? Do you reckon your pap—"

"Why, *that's* all right. Miss Hooker she tole me, *particular*, that her uncle Hornback—"

"Great guns! Is *he* her uncle? Looky here, you break for that light over yonder-way, and you'll come to the tavern; tell 'em to dart you out to Jim Hornback's, and he'll foot the bill. And don't you fool around any, because he'll want to know the news. Tell him I'll have his niece all safe before he can get to town. Hump yourself, now; I'm a-going up around the corner to roust out my engineer."

I struck for the light, but as soon as he turned the corner I went back and got into my skiff and bailed her out, and then pulled up shore in the easy water, and tucked myself in among some wood-boats; for I couldn't rest easy till I see the ferryboat start. Take it all around, I was feeling ruther comfortable on accounts of taking all this trouble for that gang. But before long here comes the wreck, dim and dusky, sliding along down! A kind of cold shiver went through me, and then I struck out for her. She was very deep, and I see in a minute there warn't much chance for anybody being alive in her. I pulled all around her and hollered, but there wasn't any answer; all dead still.

Then here comes the ferryboat, so I shoved for the middle of the river, and when I judged I was out of eye-reach I laid on my oars, and looked back and see her go and smell around the wreck for Miss Hooker's remainders, because the captain would know her uncle Hornback would want them; and pretty soon the ferryboat give it up and went for the shore, and I laid into my work and went a-booming down the river.

It did seem a powerful time before Jim's light showed up; and when it did show it looked like it was a thousand mile off. By the time I got there the sky was getting gray in the east; so we struck for an island, and hid the raft, and sunk the skiff, and turned in and slept like dead people.

CHAPTER VI

By AND BY, WHEN WE GOT UP, we turned over the truck the gang had stole off of the wreck, and found boots, and blankets, and clothes, and a lot of books, and three boxes of seegars. We hadn't ever been this rich before in neither of our lives. The seegars was prime. We laid off all the afternoon in the woods talking, and me reading the books, and having a general good time. I told Jim all about what happened inside the wreck, and I said these kinds of things was adventures; but he said he didn't want no more adventures. He said that when I went in the texas and he crawled back and found the raft gone he nearly died, because he judged it was all up with *him* any way it could be fixed; for if he didn't get saved he would get drownded; and if he did get saved, whoever saved him would send him back home, and then Miss Watson would sell him South, sure. Well, he was right; he was most always right; he had an uncommon level head for a nigger.

I read considerable to Jim about kings and dukes and earls and such, and how gaudy they dressed, and how much style they put on, and called each other your majesty, and your grace, and so on; and Jim's eyes bugged out, and he was interested. He says:

"I didn't know dey was so many un um. I hain't hearn 'bout none un um, skasely, but ole King Sollermun. How much do a king git?"

"Get?" I says. "Why, they get a thousand dollars a month if they want it; they can have just as much as they want."

"*Ain'* dat gay? En what dey got to do, Huck?"

"*They* don't do nothing! Why, they just set around."

"No; is dat so?"

"Of course. They just set around—except, maybe, when there's a war; then they go to the war. But other times they just lazy around; or go hawking; or when things is dull, they fuss with the parlyment; and if everybody don't go just so he whacks their heads off. But mostly they hang around the harem."

"Roun' de which?"

"Harem."

"What's de harem?"

"The place where he keeps his wives. Don't you know about the harem? Solomon had one; he had about a million wives."

"Why, yes, dat's so; I—I'd done forgot it. A harem's a bo'd'n-house, I reck'n. Mos' likely dey has rackety times in de nussery. En I reck'n de wives quarrels considable; en dat 'crease de racket. Yit dey say Sollermun de wises' man dat ever live'. I doan' take no stock in dat. Would a wise man want to live in de mids' er sich a blim-blammin' all de time? No—'deed he wouldn't."

"Well, but he *was* the wisest man, anyway; because the widow she told me so, her own self."

"I doan' k'yer what de widder say, he *warn't* no wise man nuther. Doan' talk to me 'bout Sollermun, Huck, I knows him by de back."

I never see such a nigger. He was sure down on Solomon. So I went on talking about other kings, and let Solomon slide. I told about Louis Sixteenth that got his head cut off in France long time ago; and about his little boy the dolphin, that would 'a' been king, but they took and shut him up in jail, and some say he died there.

"Po' little chap."

"But some says he got away, and come to America."

"Dat's good! But he'll be pooty lonesome—dey ain' no kings here, is dey, Huck?"

"No."

"Den he cain't git no situation. What he gwyne to do?"

"Well, I don't know. Some of them gets on the police, and some of them learns people how to talk French."

"Why, Huck, doan' de French people talk de same way we does?"

"*No*, Jim; you couldn't understand a word they said—not a single word."

"Well, now, I be ding-busted! How do dat come?"

"*I* don't know; but it's so. I got some of their jabber out of a book. S'pose a man was to come to you and say Polly-voo-franzy—what would you think?"

"I wouldn' think nuffn; I'd take en bust him over de head—dat is, if he warn't white. I wouldn' 'low no nigger to call me dat."

"Shucks, it ain't calling you anything. It's only saying, do you know how to talk French?"

"Well, den, why couldn't he say it?"

"Why, he *is* a-saying it. That's a Frenchman's *way* of saying it."

"Well, it's a blame ridicklous way, en I doan' want to hear no mo' 'bout it. Dey ain' no sense in it."

"Looky here, Jim; does a cat talk like we do?"

"No, a cat don't."

"Well, does a cow?"

"No, a cow don't, nuther."

"Does a cat talk like a cow, or a cow talk like a cat?"

"No, dey don't."

"It's natural and right for 'em to talk different from each other, ain't it?"

"Course."

"And ain't it natural and right for a cat and a cow to talk different from *us?*"

"Why, mos' sholy it is."

"Well, then, why ain't it natural and right for a *Frenchman* to talk different from us? You answer me that."

"Is a cat a man, Huck?"

"No."

"Well, den, dey ain't no sense in a cat talkin' like a man. Is a cow a man? Er is a cow a cat?"

"No, she ain't either of them."

"Well, den, she ain't got no business to talk like either one er the yuther of 'em. Is a Frenchman a man?"

"Yes."

"*Well*, den! Dad blame it, why doan' he *talk* like a man? You answer me *dat!*"

I see it warn't no use wasting words—you can't learn a nigger to argue. So I quit.

WE JUDGED THAT THREE NIGHTS more would fetch us to Cairo, at the bottom of Illinois, where the Ohio River comes in, and that was what we was after. We would sell the raft and get on a steamboat and go up the Ohio amongst the free states, and then be out of trouble.

Well, the second night a fog begun to come on, and we made for a towhead to tie to; but when I paddled ahead in the canoe, with the line to make fast, there warn't anything but little saplings to tie to. I passed the line around one of them, but there was a stiff current, and the raft come booming down so lively she tore it out by the roots and away she went. I see the fog closing down, and it made me so sick and scared I couldn't budge for most a half a minute—and then there warn't no raft in sight; you couldn't see twenty yards. I jumped into the canoe and grabbed the paddle and took out after the raft, hot and heavy, right down the towhead. But the towhead warn't sixty yards long, and the minute I flew by the foot of it I shot into solid white fog, and hadn't no more idea which way I was going than a dead man.

Thinks I, It won't do to paddle; I'll run into the bank or a towhead or something; I got to set still and float. I whooped and listened. Away down there somewheres I hears a small whoop, and up comes my spirits. I went tearing after it. The next time it come I warn't heading for it, but heading away to the right of it. And the next time I was heading away to the left of it—and not gaining on it much either, for I was flying around, this way and that, but it was going straight ahead all the time. Well, I fought along, and directly I hears the whoop *behind* me. I was tangled good now. That was somebody else's whoop, or else I was turned around.

I throwed the paddle down. I heard the whoop again; it was behind me yet, but a different place; it kept coming, and I kept answering, till by and by it was in front of me again, and I knowed the current had swung the canoe's head downstream, and I was all right if that was Jim and not some other raftsman hollering. I couldn't tell nothing about voices in a fog, for nothing don't sound natural in a fog.

The whooping went on, and in about a minute I come a-booming down on a cutbank with smoky ghosts of big trees on it, and the current throwed me off to the left and shot by amongst a lot of snags that fairly roared, the current was tearing by them so swift.

Then in a second or two it was solid white and still again. I set listening to my heart thump, and I reckon I didn't draw a breath while it thumped a hundred.

I just give up then. I knowed what the matter was. That cutbank was an island. It had the big timber of a regular island; it might be five or six miles long, and Jim had gone down t'other side of it.

I kept quiet, with my ears cocked, about fifteen minutes. I was floating along, of course, four or five miles an hour; but you *feel* like you are laying dead still on the water; and if a little glimpse of a snag slips by you catch your breath and think, My! How that snag's tearing along.

Next, for about a half an hour, I whoops now and then; at last I hears the answer a long ways off, and tries to follow it, but I couldn't do it, for directly I got into a nest of towheads. Well, I warn't long losing the whoops amongst the towheads. By and by I seemed to be in the open river again, but I still couldn't hear no sign of a whoop nowheres. I reckoned Jim had fetched up on a snag, maybe, and it was all up with him. I was good and tired, so I laid down in the canoe and said I wouldn't bother no more. I didn't want to go to sleep, of course; but I was so sleepy I couldn't help it; so I thought I would take jest one little catnap.

But I reckon it was more than a catnap, for when I waked up the stars was shining bright, the fog was all gone, and I was spinning down a big bend stern first.

It was a monstrous big river here, and with the tallest kind of timber on both banks; just a solid wall, as well as I could see by the stars. I looked away downstream, and seen a black speck on the water. I took after it; but when I got to it it warn't nothing but a couple of sawlogs made fast together. Then I see another speck, and chased that; then another, and this time it was the raft.

When I got to it Jim was setting there with his head down between his knees, asleep. The steering oar was smashed off, and the raft was littered up with leaves and branches and dirt. So she'd had a rough time.

I made fast and laid down under Jim's nose on the raft, and

began to gap, and stretch, and I says, "Hello, Jim, have I been asleep? Why didn't you stir me up?"

"Goodness gracious, is dat you, Huck? En you ain' dead—you ain' drownded—you's back ag'in? It's too good for true, honey, it's too good for true!"

"What's the matter with you, Jim? You been a-drinking?"

"Drinkin'? Has I ben a-drinkin'?"

"Well, then, what makes you talk so wild? What makes you talk as if I been gone away?"

"Huck—Huck Finn, you look me in de eye. *Hain't* you ben gone away? Didn't you tote out de line in de canoe fer to make fas' to de towhead?"

"No, I didn't. What towhead? I hain't seen no towhead."

"You hain't seen no towhead? Looky here, didn't de line pull loose en de raf' go down de river, en leave you behine in de fog?"

"What fog?"

"Why, *de* fog! De fog dat's been aroun' all night!"

"Well, this is too many for me, Jim. I hain't seen no fog. I been setting here talking with you all night till you went to sleep about ten minutes ago, and I reckon I done the same."

"Dad fetch it, how is I gwyne to dream all dat in ten minutes?"

"Well, hang it all, you did dream it, because there didn't any of it happen."

Jim didn't say nothing for about five minutes, but set there studying over it. Then he says:

"Well, den, I reck'n I did dream it, Huck; but dog my cats ef it ain't de powerfulest dream I ever see. En I hain't ever had no dream b'fo' dat's tired me like dis one."

"Oh, well, a dream does tire a body sometimes. But tell me all about it, Jim."

So Jim went to work and told me the whole thing right through, just as it happened. Then he said he must start in and "'terpret" it, because it was sent for a warning. He said the first towhead stood for a man that would try to do us some good, but the current was another man that would get us away from him. The whoops was warnings, and the other towheads was troubles we was going to get into with mean folks, but if we minded our business we would pull through and get out of the fog and into the big clear river, which was the free states, and wouldn't have no more trouble.

It had clouded up pretty dark just after I got onto the raft, but it was clearing up again now.

"Oh, well, that's all interpreted well enough as far as it goes, Jim," I says; "but what does *these* things stand for?"

It was the leaves and rubbish on the raft and the smashed oar. You could see them first-rate now.

Jim looked at the trash, and then at me, and back at the trash again. He had got the dream fixed so strong in his head that he couldn't seem to shake it loose. But when he did get the thing straightened around he looked at me steady without smiling, and says, "What do dey stan' for? I's gwyne to tell you. When I got all wore out wid work, en wid de callin' for you, en went to sleep, my heart wuz mos' broke bekase you wuz los', en I could 'a' got down on my knees en kiss yo' foot, I's so thankful. En all you wuz thinkin' 'bout wuz how you could make a fool uv ole Jim wid a lie. Dat truck is *trash;* en trash is what people is dat puts dirt on de head er dey fren's en makes 'em ashamed."

Then he got up slow and walked to the wigwam, and went in without saying anything but that. It made me feel so mean I could almost kissed *his* foot to get him to take it back.

It was fifteen minutes before I could work myself up to go and humble myself to him; but I done it, and I warn't ever sorry for it afterward. I didn't do him no more mean tricks, and I wouldn't done that one if I'd 'a' knowed it would make him feel that way.

WE SLEPT MOST ALL DAY, and started out at night, a little ways behind a monstrous long raft that was as long going by as a procession. She had four long sweeps at each end, so she carried as many as thirty men, likely. She had five big wigwams aboard, and an open campfire in the middle, and a tall flagpole at each end. There was a power of style about her. It *amounted* to something being a raftsman on such a craft as that.

We went drifting down into a big bend, and the night clouded up and got hot. The river was very wide, and was walled with solid timber on both sides; you couldn't see a break in it hardly ever, or a light. We talked about Cairo, and wondered whether we would know it when we got to it. I said I had heard say there warn't but a dozen houses there, and if they didn't have them lit up, how was we going to know we was passing a town? Jim said if the two big rivers joined together there, that would show. But I said maybe we might think we was just passing the foot of an island. That disturbed Jim—and me too. But there warn't nothing to do now but to look out sharp for the town, and not pass it without seeing it. Jim said he'd be mighty sure to see it, because he'd be a free man the minute he seen it, but if he missed it he'd be in a slave country again and no more show for freedom. Every little while he jumps up and says, "Dah she is!"

But it warn't. It was jack-o'-lanterns, or lightning bugs; so he sat down again. He said it made him all over trembly and feverish to be so close to freedom. Well, I can tell you it made me all over trembly and feverish, too, to hear him, because I begun to get it through my head that he *was* most free—and who was to blame for it? Why, *me*. I couldn't get that out of my conscience, no how nor no way. I tried to make out to myself that *I* warn't to blame, because *I* didn't run Jim off from his rightful owner; but it warn't no use, conscience up and says, every time, But you knowed he was running for his freedom, and you could 'a' paddled ashore and told somebody. That was so—I couldn't get around that. Conscience says to me, What had poor Miss Watson done to you that you could see her nigger go off right under your eyes and never say one single word? What did that poor old woman do to you that you could treat her so mean? Why, she tried to learn you your book, and your manners; she tried to be good to you every way she knowed how. *That's* what she done.

I got to feeling so mean and so miserable I most wished I was dead. I fidgeted up and down the raft, abusing myself to myself, and Jim was fidgeting up and down past me. He talked out loud all the time while I was talking to myself. He was saying how the first thing he would do when he got to a free state he would go to saving up money, and when he got enough he would buy his wife, which was owned on a farm close to where Miss Watson lived; and then they would both work to buy the two children, and if their master wouldn't sell them, they'd get an Ab'litionist to go and steal them.

It most froze me to hear such talk. Here was this nigger, which I had as good as helped to run away, coming right out flat-footed and saying he would steal his children—children that belonged to a man that hadn't ever done me no harm. My conscience got to stirring me up worse than ever, until at last I says to it, Let up on me—it ain't too late yet—I'll paddle ashore at the first light and tell. I felt easy and happy right off. All my troubles was gone and I went to looking out sharp for a light. By and by one showed. Jim sings out:

"We's safe, Huck, we's safe! Dat's Cairo at las'. I jis' knows it!"

I says, "I'll take the canoe and go and see, Jim. It mightn't be, you know."

He jumped and got the canoe ready, and as I shoved off, he says, "Pooty soon I'll be a-shout'n' for joy, en I'll say, it's all on accounts o' Huck; I's a free man, en Huck done it. Jim won't ever forget you, Huck; you's de bes' fren' Jim's ever had; en you's de *only* fren' ole Jim's got now."

I was paddling off, all in a sweat to tell on him; but when he says this, it seemed to kind of take the tuck all out of me. I went along slow then, and when I was fifty yards off, along comes a skiff with two men in it with guns. They stopped and I stopped. One of them says, "What's that yonder?"

"A piece of a raft," I says.

"Do you belong on it?"

"Yes, sir."

"Any men on it?"

"Only one, sir."

"Well, there's five niggers run off tonight up yonder, above the bend. Is your man white or black?"

I didn't answer up prompt. I tried to, but the words wouldn't come. I tried for a second or two to brace up and out with it, but I warn't man enough—hadn't the spunk of a rabbit; so I just give up trying, and says, "He's white."

"I reckon we'll go and see for ourselves."

"I wish you would," says I, "because it's Pap, and maybe you'd help me tow the raft ashore where the light is. He's sick—and so is Mam and Mary Ann."

"Oh, the devil! We're in a hurry, boy. But I s'pose we've got to. Come, let's get along."

We had made a stroke or two, when I says, "Pap 'll be much obleeged to you, I can tell you. Everybody goes away when I want them to help me tow the raft ashore, and I can't do it by myself."

"Well, that's odd. Say, boy, what's the matter with your father?"

"It's the—a—the—well, it ain't anything much."

They stopped pulling. It warn't but a little ways to the raft now. One says, "Boy, that's a lie. What *is* the matter with your pap? Answer up square."

"I will, sir, honest—but don't leave us, please. It's the—Gentlemen, if you'll only pull ahead, and let me heave you the headline, you won't have to come a-near the raft—please."

"Set her back, John!" says one. They backed water. "Keep away, boy, keep to looard. Confound it, I expect the wind has blowed it to us. Your pap's got the smallpox, and you know it. Why didn't you come out and say so?"

"Well," says I, a-blubbering, "I've told everybody before, and they just went away and left us."

"Poor devil, there's something in that. We are right down sorry for you, but we—well, hang it, we don't want the smallpox, you see. Look here, I'll tell you what to do. You float along down about twenty miles, and you'll come to a town on the left-hand side of the river. Tell them your folks are down with chills and fever. Don't be a fool again, and let people guess what is the matter. Say, I reckon your father's poor, and I'm bound to say he's in hard luck. Here, we'll each put a twenty-dollar gold piece on this board, and you get them when it floats by. I feel mighty mean to leave you; but my kingdom, it won't do to fool with smallpox! Good-by, boy; if you see any runaway niggers get help and nab them, and you can make some money by it."

They went off and I got aboard the raft, feeling bad and low, because I knowed I had done wrong, and I see it warn't no use for me to try to learn to do right; a body that don't get *started* right when he's little ain't got no show. Then I thought a minute, and says to myself, Hold on; s'pose you'd 'a' done right and give Jim up, would you felt better than what you do now? No, says I, I'd feel bad—I'd feel just the same way I do now. Well, then, says I, what's the use you learning to do right when it's troublesome to do right and ain't no trouble to do wrong, and the wages is just the same? I couldn't answer that. So I reckoned I wouldn't bother no more about it, but after this always do whichever come handiest at the time.

I went into the wigwam; Jim warn't there. I says, "Jim!"

"Here I is, Huck. Is dey out o' sight yit? Don't talk loud."

He was in the river under the stern oar, with just his nose out. I told him they were out of sight, so he come aboard. He says, "I was a-listenin' to de talk, en I was gwyne to shove off if dey come aboard. But lawsy, how you did fool 'em, Huck! Dat *wuz* de smartes' dodge! I tell you, chile, I 'spec it save' ole Jim—ole Jim ain't going to forgit you for dat, honey."

Then we talked about the money. It was a pretty good raise—twenty dollars apiece. Jim said we could take deck passage on a steamboat now, and the money would last us as far as we wanted to go in the free states.

Towards daybreak we tied up, hiding the raft good. Then Jim worked all day fixing things in bundles, and getting all ready to quit rafting.

That night about ten we hove in sight of the lights of a town down in a left-hand bend.

I went off in the canoe to ask about it. Pretty soon I found a man out in a skiff, setting a trotline, and I says, "Mister, is that town Cairo?"

"Cairo? No. You must be a blame' fool."

"What town is it, mister?"

"If you want to know, go find out. If you stay here botherin' me a minute longer you'll get something you won't want."

I paddled to the raft. Jim was awful disappointed, but I said never mind, Cairo would be the next place, I reckoned.

We passed another town before daylight, and I was going out again; but it was high ground, so I didn't go. No high ground about Cairo, Jim said. I had forgot it. We laid up for the day on a towhead. I begun to suspicion something. So did Jim. I says, "Maybe we went by Cairo in the fog that night."

He says, "Doan' le's talk about it, Huck. I alwuz 'spected dat rattlesnake skin warn't done wid its work."

When it was daylight, here was the clear Ohio water inshore, sure enough, and outside was the old regular Muddy! So it was all up with Cairo.

We talked it all over. We couldn't take the raft up the stream, of course; and it wouldn't do to take to the shore. There warn't no way but to wait for dark, and start back in the canoe. So we slept all day, so as to be fresh for the work, and when we went back to the raft about dark the canoe was gone!

We didn't say a word for a good while. We both knowed well enough it was some more work of the rattlesnake skin; so what was the use to talk about it? But by and by we talked about what we better do, and found there warn't no way but just to go along down with the raft till we got a chance to buy a canoe to go back in.

So we shoved out after dark on the raft.

Anybody that don't believe yet that it's foolishness to handle a snake skin, after all that that snake skin done for us, will believe it now if they read on and see what more it done.

The place to buy canoes is off of rafts laying up at shore. But we didn't see no rafts; so we went along three hours and more. Well, the night got gray and ruther thick, which is the next meanest thing to fog. It got to be very late and still, and then along comes a steamboat up the river. We lit the lantern, and judged she would see it. We could hear her pounding along, but we didn't see her good till she was close. She aimed right for us. Often they do that and try to see how close they can come without touching; and then the pilot sticks his head out and laughs, and thinks he's mighty smart. Well, here she comes, and we said she was going to try and shave us; but she didn't seem to be sheering off a bit. She was a high one, and she was coming in a hurry, too, looking like a black cloud with rows of glowworms around it; but all of a sudden she bulged out, big and scary, with her monstrous bows and guards hanging right over us. There was a yell at us, and a jingling of bells, a powwow of cussing and whistling of steam—and as Jim went overboard on one side and I on the other, she came smashing straight through the raft.

I dived—and I aimed to find the bottom, too, for a thirty-foot wheel had to go over me. I could always stay under water a minute; this time I reckon I stayed under a minute and a half. Then I bounced for the top in a hurry, popping out to my armpits and blowing the water out of my nose. Of course there was a booming current; and of course that boat started her engines again ten seconds after she stopped them, for they never cared much for raftsmen; so now she was churning along up the river, out of sight in the thick weather.

I sung out for Jim about a dozen times, but I didn't get any answer; so I grabbed a plank that touched me and struck out for shore, shoving it ahead of me. I was a good long time in getting there, but I made a safe landing. I couldn't see only a little ways, but I went poking along over rough ground for a quarter of a mile, and then I run across a big old-fashioned log house. I was going to rush by, but a lot of dogs jumped out and went to howling and barking at me, and I knowed better than to move another peg.

CHAPTER VII

In about a minute somebody spoke out of a window and says, "Be done, boys! Who's there?"

I says, "It's me."

"Who's me?"

"George Jackson, sir."

"What are you prowling around here for—hey?"

"I warn't prowling around, sir; I only want to go along by; I fell overboard off of the steamboat."

"Oh, you did, did you? Strike a light there, somebody. What did you say your name was?"

"George Jackson, sir. I'm only a boy."

"Look here, if you're telling the truth you needn't be afraid—nobody 'll hurt you. Is there anybody with you?"

"No, sir, nobody."

I heard people stirring around in the house now, and see a light. The man sung out, "Bob, if you and Tom are ready, take your places."

"All ready."

"Now, George Jackson, do you know the Shepherdsons?"

"No, sir. I never heard of them."

"Well, step forward, George Jackson. And mind, come mighty slow. If there's anybody with you, let him keep back—if he shows himself he'll be shot. Come along now; push the door open yourself—just enough to squeeze in, d'you hear?"

I took one slow step at a time and there warn't a sound, only I thought I could hear my heart. The dogs were as still as the humans, but they followed a little behind me. When I got to the three log doorsteps I heard them unlocking and unbolting. I put my hand on the door and pushed it till somebody said, "There, that's enough—put your head in." I done it, but I judged they would take it off.

A candle was on the floor, and there they all was, looking at me, and me at them. Three big men with guns pointed at me; the oldest, gray and about sixty, the other two thirty or more—all of them fine and handsome—and the sweetest old gray-headed lady, and back of her two young women. The old gentleman says:

"There; I reckon it's all right. Come in."

As soon as I was in the old gentleman he locked the door and bolted it. They took a good look at me, and all said, "Why, *he* ain't a Shepherdson—no, there ain't any Shepherdson about him."

Then the old man told me to make myself at home, and tell all about myself; but the old lady says:

"Why, bless you, Saul, the poor thing's as wet as he can be; and don't you reckon maybe he's hungry?"

"True for you, Rachel—I forgot."

So the old lady says, "Betsy," (this was a nigger woman) "you fly around and get him something to eat, poor thing; and one of you girls wake up Buck—oh, here he is himself. Buck, take this little stranger and get the wet clothes off from him and dress him up in some of yours that's dry."

Buck looked about as old as me—thirteen or fourteen. He hadn't on anything but a shirt, and he came in gaping and digging one fist into his eyes, and he was dragging a gun along with the other one. He says, "Ain't they no Shepherdsons around?"

They said, no, 'twas a false alarm.

"Well," he says, "if they'd 'a' ben some, I reckon I'd 'a' got one."

They all laughed, and Bob says, "Why, Buck, they might have scalped us all, you've been so slow in coming."

"Well, nobody come after me, and it ain't right. I'm always kept down; I don't get no show."

"Never mind, Buck, my boy," says the old man, "you'll have show enough, all in good time. Go 'long now, and do as your mother told you."

When we got upstairs to his room he got me a shirt and pants of his, and I put them on. While I was at it he asked what my name was, but before I could tell him he started to tell me about a blue jay he had catched day before yesterday, and he asked me where Moses was when the candle went out. I said I didn't know.

"Well, guess," he says.

"How'm I going to guess," says I, "when I never heard tell of it before?"

"But you can guess, can't you? It's just as easy."

"*Which* candle?" I says.

"Why, any candle," he says.

"I don't know where he was," says I. "Where was he?"

"Why, he was in the *dark!* That's where he was!"

"Well, if you knowed where he was, what did you ask me for?"

"Why, blame it, it's a riddle! Say, how long are you going to stay here? You got to stay always. We can just have booming times. Do you own a dog? I've got a dog—and he'll go in the river and bring out chips that you throw in. Do you like to comb up Sundays, and that kind of foolishness? I don't, but Ma she makes me. Confound these britches! I reckon I'd better put 'em on, but I'd ruther not, it's so warm. Are you all ready? All right. Come along, old hoss."

Cold corn pone, corn beef, butter and buttermilk—that is what they had for me down there, and there ain't nothing better that ever I've come across yet. While I eat they all asked me questions, and I told them how Pap and me and all the family was living on a little farm in Arkansaw, and my sister Mary Ann run off and got married and never was heard of no more, and Bill went to hunt them and he warn't heard of no more, and Tom and Mort died, and then there warn't nobody but me and Pap left, and he was just trimmed down to nothing, on account of his troubles; so when he died I took what there was left, and started up the river, deck passage, and fell overboard; and that was how I come to be here. So they said I could have a home there as long as I wanted it. Then everybody went to bed, and I went to bed with Buck, and when I waked up in the morning, drat it all, I had forgot what my name was. So I laid there trying to think, and when Buck waked up I says:

"Can you spell, Buck?"

"Yes," he says.

"I bet you can't spell my name," says I.

"I bet you what you dare I can," says he.

"All right," says I, "go ahead."

"G-e-o-r-g-e J-a-x-o-n—there now," he says.

"Well," says I, "you done it, but I didn't think you could."

I set it down, private, because somebody might want *me* to spell it next, and so I wanted to be handy with it.

It was a mighty nice family, and a mighty nice house, too. I hadn't seen no house out in the country before that was so nice and had so much style. It didn't have an iron latch on the front door, but a brass knob to turn, the same as houses in town. There was a big fireplace that was bricked on the bottom, with big brass dog irons that could hold up a sawlog. There was a clock on the middle of the mantelpiece, with a picture of a town painted on the bottom half of the glass front. It was beautiful to hear that clock tick; and sometimes when one of these peddlers had been along and scoured her up and got her in good shape, she would start in and strike a hundred and fifty before she got tuckered out. They wouldn't took any money for her.

Well, there was a big outlandish parrot on each side of the clock, made of something like chalk, and painted up gaudy. By one of the parrots was a cat made of crockery, and a crockery dog by the other; and when you pressed down on them they squeaked, but didn't open their mouth nor look different nor interested. They squeaked through underneath. On the table in the middle of the room was a kind of crockery basket that had apples and peaches and grapes piled up in it, which was much redder and yellower and prettier than real ones, but they warn't real because you could see where pieces had got chipped off and showed the white chalk, or whatever it was, underneath.

This table had a cover made out of beautiful oilcloth, with a red and blue spread eagle painted on it. There was some books, too, piled up exact, on each corner of the table. One was a big family Bible full of pictures. One was *Pilgrim's Progress*, about a man that left his family, it didn't say why. I read considerable in it now and then. There was a hymnbook, too, and a lot of other books. And there was nice split-bottom chairs, and perfectly sound, too—not bagged down in the middle and busted, like an old basket.

And they had pictures hung on the walls—mainly Washingtons and Lafayettes, and battles, and Highland Marys, and one called "Signing the Declaration." There was some that they called crayons, which one of the daughters which was dead made her own self when she was only fifteen years old. They was different from any pictures I ever see before—blacker, mostly, than is common. One was a woman in a slim black dress, belted small under the armpits, with bulges like a cabbage in the middle of the sleeves, and white slim ankles crossed about with black tape, and very wee black slippers, like a chisel, and she was leaning pensive on a tombstone on her elbow, under a weeping willow, and underneath the picture it said, "Shall I Never See Thee More Alas." Another one was a young lady with her hair all combed up straight to the top of her head, and she was crying into a handkerchief and had a dead bird lying on its back in her other hand with its heels up, and underneath the picture it said, "I Shall Never Hear Thy Sweet Chirrup More Alas." There was one where a young lady was at a window looking up at the moon, and tears running down her cheeks; and she had an open letter in one hand with black sealing wax on it, and she was mashing a locket against her mouth, and underneath the picture it said, "And Art Thou Gone Yes Thou Art Gone Alas."

These was all nice pictures, I reckon, but I didn't somehow take to them, because if ever I was down a little they always give me the fantods. Everybody was sorry she died, and a body could see by what she had done what they had lost. But I reckoned that with her disposition she was having a better time in the graveyard. She was at work on what they said was her greatest picture when she took sick, and every day and every night it was her prayer to be allowed to live till she got it done, but she never got the chance. It was a picture of a young woman, standing on the rail of a bridge all ready to jump off, with her hair all down her back, and looking up to the moon, with the tears running down her face, and she had two arms folded across her breast, and two arms stretched out in front, and two more reaching up toward the moon—and the idea was to see which pair would look best, and then scratch out all the other arms; but, as I was saying, she died before she got her mind made up, and now they kept this picture over her bed, and every time her birthday come they hung flowers on it. The young woman in the picture had a kind of a sweet face, but there was so many arms it made her look too spidery, seemed to me.

This young girl had kept a scrapbook, and used to paste obituaries and accidents and cases of patient suffering in it, and write poetry after them out of her own head. This is what she wrote about a boy that fell down a well and was drownded:

ODE TO STEPHEN DOWLING BOTS, DEC'D

And did young Stephen sicken,
    And did young Stephen die?
And did the sad hearts thicken,
    And did the mourners cry?

No; such was not the fate of
    Young Stephen Dowling Bots;
Though sad hearts round him thickened,
    'Twas not from sickness' shots.

No whooping cough did rack his frame,
    Nor measles drear with spots;
Not these impaired the sacred name
    Of Stephen Dowling Bots.

O no. Then list with tearful eye,
    Whilst I his fate do tell.
His soul did from this cold world fly
    By falling down a well.

They got him out and emptied him;
    Alas it was too late;
His spirit was gone for to sport aloft
    In the realms of the good and great.

If Emmeline Grangerford could make poetry like that before she was fourteen, there ain't no telling what she could 'a' done by and by. Buck said she could rattle off poetry like nothing. She didn't ever have to stop to think. Every time a man died, or a woman, or a child, she would be on hand with her "tribute" before he was cold. The neighbors said it was the doctor first, then Emmeline, then the undertaker. The undertaker never got in ahead of Emmeline but once, and then she hung fire on a rhyme for the dead person's name, which was Whistler. She warn't ever the same after that; she never complained, but she kinder pined away and did not live long. They kept her room trim and nice, and all the things fixed in it just the way she liked to have them when she was alive. The old lady took care of the room herself, and she sewed there a good deal and read her Bible there mostly.

Well, as I was saying about the parlor, there was beautiful curtains on the windows: white, with pictures painted on them of castles with vines, and cattle coming down to drink. There was a little old piano too. The walls of all the rooms was plastered, and most had carpets on the floors, and the whole house was whitewashed on the outside. It was a cool, comfortable place. Nothing couldn't be better. And warn't the cooking good, and just bushels of it too!

Colonel Grangerford was a gentleman, you see. He was wellborn, as the saying is. He was very tall and very slim, and had a darkish-paly complexion; he was clean-shaved every morning all over his thin face, and he had the thinnest kind of lips, and a high nose, and the blackest kind of eyes, sunk so deep they seemed like they was looking out of caverns at you. His hair was gray and straight and hung to his shoulders. His hands was long and thin, and every day of his life he put on a clean shirt and a suit made out of white linen; and on Sundays he wore a blue tailcoat with brass buttons. There warn't no frivolishness about him, not a bit, and he warn't ever loud. He was as kind as he could be—you could feel that, you know, and so you had confidence. When him and the old lady come down in the morning all the family got out of their chairs and give them good-day, and didn't set down again till they had set down. Then Tom and Bob went to the sideboard and mixed a glass of bitters and handed it to him, and he held it and waited till Tom's and Bob's was mixed, and then they bowed and said, "Our duty to you, sir and madam," and *they* bowed and said thank you, and so they drank, all three, and Bob and Tom poured a spoonful of water on the sugar and the mite of whiskey in the bottom of their tumblers, and give it to me and Buck, and we drank to the old people too.

Bob was the oldest and Tom next—tall, beautiful men with

broad shoulders and long black hair and black eyes. They dressed in white linen, like the old gentleman, and wore broad Panama hats.

Then there was Miss Charlotte; she was twenty-five, and tall and proud and grand, but as good as she could be when she warn't stirred up. She was beautiful. So was her sister, Miss Sophia, but it was a different kind. She was gentle and sweet like a dove, and she was only twenty.

Each person had their own nigger to wait on them—Buck too. My nigger had a monstrous easy time, because I warn't used to having anybody do anything for me, but Buck's was on the jump most of the time.

This was all there was of the family now, but there used to be more—three sons, they got killed; and Emmeline that died.

The old gentleman owned a lot of farms and over a hundred niggers. Sometimes a stack of people would come there, horseback, from miles around, and stay five or six days, and have such junketings round about, dances and picnics daytimes and balls nights. These people was mostly kinfolks of the family. It was a handsome lot of quality, I tell you.

There was another clan of aristocracy around there—five or six families—mostly of the name of Shepherdson. They was as high-toned and rich as the Grangerfords. The Shepherdsons and Grangerfords used the same steamboat landing, two mile above our house; so sometimes when I went up there with our folks I used to see the Shepherdsons there on their fine horses.

One day Buck and me was in the woods hunting, and heard a horse coming. We was crossing the road. Buck says, "Quick! Jump for the woods!"

We done it, and then peeped down the woods through the leaves. Pretty soon a splendid young man came galloping down the road. He had his gun across his pommel. I had seen him before. It was young Harney Shepherdson. I heard Buck's gun go off at my ear, and Harney's hat tumbled off from his head. He grabbed his gun and rode straight to the place where we was hid. We didn't wait, but run. The woods warn't thick, so I looked over my shoulder to dodge the bullet, and twice I seen Harney cover Buck with his gun; and then he rode away the way he come—to get his hat, I reckon. We never stopped running till we got home. The old gentleman's eyes blazed a minute—'twas pleasure, mainly, I judged—and then he says, kind of gentle:

"I don't like that shooting from behind a bush. Why didn't you step into the road, my boy?"

"The Shepherdsons don't, Father. They always take advantage."

Miss Charlotte she held her head up like a queen, and her nostrils spread and her eyes snapped. The two young men looked dark, but never said nothing. Miss Sophia she turned pale, but the color come back when she found the man warn't hurt.

Soon as I got Buck by ourselves, I says, "Did you want to kill him, Buck?"

"Well, I bet I did."

"What did he do to you?"

"Him? He never done nothing to me."

"Well, then, what did you want to kill him for?"

"Why, nothing—only it's on account of the feud."

"What's a feud?"

"Why, where was you raised?" says Buck. "Don't you know what a feud is? A man has a quarrel with another man, and kills him; and then that other man's brother kills *him;* then the other brothers, on both sides, goes for one another; then the *cousins* chip in—and by and by everybody's killed, and there ain't no more feud. But it's kind of slow."

"Has this one been going on long, Buck?"

"Well, I *reckon!* It started thirty years ago, or som'ers along there. There was trouble 'bout something, and then a lawsuit to settle it; and the suit went agin one of the men, and so he up and shot the man that won the suit."

"Well, who done the shooting? Was it a Grangerford or a Shepherdson?"

"Laws, how do *I* know? It was so long ago."

"Don't anybody know?"

"Oh, yes, Pa knows, I reckon, and the other old people; but they don't know now what the row was about in the first place."

"Has there been many killed, Buck?"

"Yes; right smart chance of funerals."

"Has anybody been killed this year?"

"Yes; we got one and they got one. 'Bout three months ago my cousin Bud, fourteen year old, was riding through the woods and didn't have no weapon with him, and he hears a horse a-coming behind him, and sees old Baldy Shepherdson a-linkin' after him with his gun in his hand and his white hair a-flying; and 'stead of taking to the brush, Bud 'lowed he could outrun him; so they had it, nip and tuck, for five mile, the old man a-gaining all the time; so at last Bud stopped and faced around so as to have the bullet holes in front, you know, and the old man shot him down. But he didn't git much chance to enjoy his luck, for inside of a week our folks laid *him* out."

Next Sunday we all went to church, about three mile, everybody a-horseback. The men took their guns along, so did Buck, and kept them between their knees. The Shepherdsons done the same. It was pretty ornery preaching—all about brotherly love; but everybody said it was a good sermon, and they all talked it over going home, and had such a powerful lot to say about faith and grace and preforeordestination, that it did seem to me to be one of the roughest Sundays I had run across yet.

About an hour after dinner everybody was dozing around, and it got to be pretty dull. Buck and a dog was stretched out on the grass sound asleep. I went up to our room, and judged I would take a nap myself. I found that sweet Miss Sophia standing in her door, and she took me in her room and shut the door very soft; and she asked me if I would do something for her and not tell anybody, and I said I would. Then she said she'd forgot her Testament, and left it in the seat at church, and would I go fetch it, and not say nothing to nobody. I said I would. So I slid out and slipped off up the road to the church. Says I to myself, Something's up; it ain't natural for a girl to be in such a sweat about a Testament. So I give it a shake, and out drops a little piece of paper with *Half past two* wrote on it. I couldn't make anything out of that, so I put the paper in the book again, and when I got home and upstairs there was Miss Sophia in her door, waiting for me. She pulled me in and shut the door; then she looked in the Testament till she found the paper, and as soon as she read it her eyes lighted up, and she looked glad and grabbed me and give me a squeeze, and said I was the best boy in the world, and not to tell anybody.

I was a good deal astonished, but when I got my breath I asked her what the paper was about, and she asked me if I had read it, and I said no, and then she said the paper warn't anything but a bookmark, and I might go and play now.

I went off down to the river, studying over this thing, and pretty soon I noticed that my nigger was following. When we was out of sight of the house he comes a-running, and says:

"Mars Jawge, if you'll come into de swamp I'll show you a stack o' water moccasins."

Thinks I, That's mighty curious; he said that yesterday. He oughter know a body don't love water moccasins that much. What's he up to, anyway? But I says, "All right; trot ahead."

I followed a half a mile; then he struck out over the swamp till we come to a little flat piece of land which was dry and thick with trees and bushes. He says, "Right in dah, Mars Jawge; dah's whah I's seed 'm befo'; I don't k'yer to see 'em no mo'."

Then he slopped away, and I poked into the place a ways and pretty soon I come to a little open patch and found a man lying there asleep—and, by jings, it was my old Jim!

I waked him up, and I reckoned it was going to be a grand surprise to him to see me again, but it warn't. He nearly cried he was so glad, but he warn't surprised. Said he swum along behind me that night, and heard me yell every time, but dasn't answer, because he didn't want anybody to pick *him* up and take him into slavery again. Says he:

"I got hurt a little, so I wuz a considerable ways behine you towards de las'; when you landed I reck'ned I could ketch up wid you on de lan', but when I see dat house I go slow. I 'uz off too fur to hear what dey say to you—I wuz 'fraid o' de dogs; but when it 'uz all quiet ag'in I knowed you's in de house, so I struck out for de woods. Early in de mawnin' some er de niggers come along, en dey tuk me en showed me dis place, whah de dogs can't track me on account o' de water, en dey brings me truck to eat every night, en tells me how you's a-gittin' along."

"Why didn't you tell my Jack to fetch me here sooner, Jim?"

"'Twarn't no use to 'sturb you, Huck, tell we could do sumfn—but we's all right now. I ben a-buyin' pots en vittles, as I got a chanst, en a-patchin' up de raf'—"

"*What* raft, Jim?"

"Our ole raf'."

"You mean to say our old raft warn't smashed all to flinders?"

"No, she warn't. She was tore up a good deal—one en' of her was; but dey warn't no great harm done, on'y our traps was mos' all los'. Some er de niggers foun' her ketched on a snag along heah in de ben', en dey hid her in de willows, en dey wuz so much jawin' 'bout which un 'um she b'long to dat I heah 'bout it, so I ups en settles de trouble by tellin' 'um she b'long to you en me; en I ast 'm if dey gwyne to grab a young white genlman's propaty, en git a hid'n for it? Den I gin 'em ten cents apiece, en dey 'uz mighty satisfied, en wisht some mo' raf's 'ud come along en make 'm rich ag'in. Dey's mighty good to me, dese niggers, en whatever I wants 'm to do I doan' have to ast 'm twice, honey. Dat Jack's a good nigger, en pooty smart."

"Yes, he is. He ain't ever told me you was here; told me to come, and he'd show me a lot of water moccasins. If anything happens *he* ain't mixed up in it. He can say he never seen us together, and it'll be the truth."

I DON'T WANT TO TALK much about the next day. I reckon I'll cut it pretty short. I waked up about dawn, and was a-going to go to sleep again when I noticed how still it was. Next I noticed that Buck was up and gone. Well, I gets up, a-wondering, and goes downstairs—nobody around. Thinks I, What does it mean? Down by the woodpile I comes across my Jack, and says, "What's it all about?"

Says he, "Don't you know, Mars Jawge? Miss Sophia's run off! She run off in de night to get married to dat young Harney

Shepherdson. De fambly foun' it out 'bout half an hour ago—en' I *tell* you dey warn't no time los'. De womenfolks has gone for to stir up de relations, en ole Mars Saul en de boys tuck dey guns en rode up de river road for to try to ketch dat young man en kill him 'fo' he kin git acrost de river wid Miss Sophia. I reck'n dey's gwyne to be rough times."

"Buck went off 'thout waking me up."

"Well, I reck'n he *did!* Dey warn't gwyne to mix you up in it. Mars Buck he loaded up his gun en 'lowed he's gwyne to fetch home a Shepherdson or bust."

I took up the river road as hard as I could put. By and by I heard a gun a good ways off. When I come in sight of the log store and the woodpile where the steamboats lands I worked along under the trees and brush, and then I clumb up into a cottonwood, and watched. There was a wood-rank four foot high a little ways in front of the tree, and first I was going to hide behind that; but maybe it was luckier I didn't.

There was four or five men cavorting around on their horses in the open place before the store, cussing and yelling, and trying to get a couple of young chaps that was squatting behind the wood-rank alongside the steamboat landing. But they couldn't come it, so by and by the men stopped cavorting around and started riding towards the store. Then up gets one of the boys, draws a steady bead and drops one man out of his saddle. All the men jumped off of their horses and grabbed the hurt one to carry him to the store; and that minute the two boys started on the run. They got halfway to the tree I was in before the men noticed. Then the men see them, and jumped on their horses and took out after them. They gained on the boys, but it didn't do no good; the boys got to the woodpile that was in front of my tree, and slipped in behind it, and so they had the bulge on the men again. One of the boys was Buck, and the other was a slim young chap about nineteen years old.

The men ripped around awhile, and then rode away. As soon as they was out of sight I sung out to Buck. He didn't know what to make of my voice coming out of the tree at first. He was awful

74

surprised. He told me to watch out sharp and let him know when the men come in sight again; said they must be up to some devilment or other. I wished I was out of that tree, but I dasn't come down. Buck begun to cry and rip, and 'lowed that him and his cousin Joe (that was the other young chap) would make up for this day yet. He said his father and his two brothers was killed, and two or three of the enemy. Said the Shepherdsons laid for them in ambush. I asked him what was become of young Harney and Miss Sophia. He said they'd got across the river and was safe. I was glad of that, but the way Buck did take on because he didn't manage to kill Harney that day he shot at him—I hain't ever heard anything like it.

All of a sudden, *bang! bang!* goes three or four guns—the men had slipped around through the woods and come in from behind without their horses! The boys jumped for the river—both of them hurt—and as they swum down the current the men run along the bank shooting at them and singing out, "Kill them, kill them!" It made me so sick I most fell out of the tree. I wished I hadn't ever come ashore that night to see such things. I ain't ever going to get shut of them—lots of times I dream about them.

I stayed in the tree till it begun to get dark, afraid to come down. Sometimes I heard guns away off, and I seen little gangs of men gallop past the log store; so I reckoned the trouble was still a-going on. I was mighty downhearted. I made up my mind I wouldn't ever go anear the house again, because I reckoned I was to blame, somehow. I judged that that piece of paper meant that Miss Sophia was to meet Harney somewheres at half past two and run off; and I judged I ought to told her father about that paper, and then maybe he would 'a' locked her up, and this awful mess wouldn't ever happened.

When I got down out of the tree I crept along down the riverbank a piece, and found the two bodies laying in the edge of the water. I covered up their faces, and got away as quick as I could. I cried when I was covering up Buck's face, for he was mighty good to me.

It was dark now. I never went near the house, but made for

the swamp. Jim warn't on his island, so I tramped off in a hurry for the crick, and crowded through the willows, red-hot to jump aboard the raft and get out of that awful country. I couldn't find it, and at last I raised a yell. A voice not twenty-five foot from me says, "Good lan'! Is dat you, honey? Doan' make no noise."

It was Jim's voice—nothing ever sounded so good before. I run along the bank and got aboard, and Jim he hugged me, he was so glad to see me. He says:

"Laws bless you, chile, I 'uz right down sho' you's dead ag'in. Jack's been heah; he says he reck'n you's ben shot, kase you didn' come home no mo'. Lawsy, I's glad to git you back ag'in, honey!"

I says, "All right—that's mighty good; they'll think I've been killed, and floated down the river—so don't you lose no time, Jim, but shove off fast as you can."

I never felt easy till the raft was two miles below there and in the middle of the Mississippi. Then we hung up our signal lantern, and judged that we was free and safe once more. I hadn't had a bite to eat since yesterday, so Jim he got out some corn dodgers and buttermilk, and whilst I eat my supper we talked and had a good time. I was powerful glad to get away from the feuds, and so was Jim to get away from the swamp. We said there warn't no home like a raft, after all. Other places do seem so cramped up and smothery, but a raft don't. You feel mighty free and easy and comfortable on a raft.

CHAPTER VIII

TWO OR THREE DAYS AND NIGHTS went by; I reckon I might say they swum by, they slid along so quiet and smooth and lovely. It was a monstrous big river down there—sometimes a mile and a half wide; we run nights, and laid up and hid daytimes. Soon as night was most gone we stopped navigating and tied up—nearly always in the dead water under a towhead; and then cut young cottonwoods, and hid the raft with them. Then we set out the lines. Next we slid into the river and had a swim; then we set down where the water was about knee-deep, and watched the daylight come. The first thing to see, looking away over the water, was a kind of dull line—that was the woods on t'other side; then a pale place in the sky; then more paleness spreading around; then the river softened up and warn't black anymore, but gray; and by and by the mist curls up off the water, and the east reddens up, and the river; then the nice breeze springs up, and comes fanning you, so cool and fresh and sweet to smell on account of the woods and the flowers; but sometimes not that way, because they've left dead fish laying around; and next you've got the full day, and everything smiling in the sun, and the songbirds just going it!

A little smoke couldn't be noticed now, so we would take some fish off of the lines and cook up a hot breakfast. And afterwards we would watch the lonesomeness of the river, and kind of lazy along, and by and by lazy off to sleep. Wake up by and by, and look, and maybe see a steamboat coughing along upstream, or a raft sliding by away off yonder. So we would put in the day, lazing around, listening to the stillness.

Soon as it was night out we shoved; when we got the raft out to about the middle of the river we let her alone, and let her float wherever the current wanted her to; then we lit the pipes, and dangled our legs in the water, and talked about all kinds of things— we was always naked, day and night, whenever the mosquitos would let us—the new clothes Buck's folks made for me was too good to be comfortable, and besides I didn't go much on clothes, nohow.

Sometimes we'd have that whole river all to ourselves for the longest time. Yonder was the banks and the islands, across the water; and maybe a spark—which was a candle in a cabin window; and sometimes on the water you could see a spark or two—on a raft or a scow; and maybe you could hear a fiddle or a song coming from one of them crafts. It's lovely to live on a raft. We had the sky up there, all speckled with stars, and we used to lay on our backs and look up at them, and discuss about whether they was made or only just happened. Jim he allowed they was made, but I allowed they happened; I judged it would have took too long to *make* so many. Jim said the moon could 'a' *laid* them; well, that looked kind of reasonable, so I didn't say nothing against it, because I've seen a frog lay most as many, so of course it could be done.

After midnight the people on shore went to bed, and then for two or three hours the shores was black—no more sparks in the cabin windows. These sparks was our clock—the first one that showed again meant morning was coming, so we hunted a place to hide and tie up right away.

One morning about daybreak I found a canoe and crossed over to the main shore and paddled about a mile up a crick to see if I couldn't get some berries. Just as I was passing a place where a kind of cowpath crossed the crick, here comes a couple of men tearing up the path. They sung out and begged me to save their lives— said they hadn't been doing nothing, and was being chased for it—said there was men and dogs a-coming. They wanted to jump right in, but I says:

"Don't you do it. I don't hear the dogs yet; you've got time to crowd through the brush and get up the crick a little ways; then you take to the water and wade down to me—that'll throw the dogs off the scent."

They done it, and soon as they was aboard I lit out. In about five minutes we heard the dogs and the men away off, shouting. We heard them come along towards the crick, but couldn't see them; they seemed to stop and fool around awhile; then, as we got further away all the time, we couldn't hardly hear them at all; and when we struck the river, everything was quiet, and we paddled over to the towhead and hid in the cottonwoods and was safe.

One of these fellows was about seventy or upwards, and had a bald head and very gray whiskers. He had an old battered-up slouch hat on, and a greasy blue woolen shirt, and ragged blue jeans stuffed into his boot tops, and home-knit galluses—no, he only had one. The other fellow was about thirty, and dressed about as ornery. Both of them had big, fat, ratty-looking carpetbags.

After breakfast we laid off and talked, and the first thing that come out was that these chaps didn't know one another.

"What got you into trouble?" says the baldhead to t'other.

"Well, I'd been selling an article to take the tartar off the teeth—and it does take it off, too, and generly the enamel with it—but I stayed about one night longer than I ought to, and was just in the act of sliding out when I ran across you on the trail, and you told me they were coming, and begged me to help you to get off. So I told you I was expecting trouble myself, and would scatter out *with* you. That's the whole yarn—what's yourn?"

"Well, I'd been a-runnin' a little temperance revival thar 'bout a week, and was the pet of the womenfolks, big and little, for I was makin' it mighty warm for the rummies and takin' as much as five dollars a night—ten cents a head, children free—when somehow or another a little report got around last night that I was puttin' in my time with a private jug on the sly. A nigger rousted me out this mornin', and told me the people was getherin' on the quiet with their dogs and horses, and they'd be along pretty soon and give me 'bout half an hour's start, and then run me down; and if they got me they'd tar and feather me and ride me on a rail, sure. I didn't wait for no breakfast—I warn't hungry."

"Old man," said the young one, "I reckon we might double-team it together; what do you think?"

"I ain't undisposed. What's your line—mainly?"

"Printer by trade; do a little patent medicines; theater actor—tragedy, you know; sling a lecture sometimes—oh, I do lots of things, so it ain't work. What's your lay?"

"I've done considerable in the doctoring way in my time. Layin' on o' hands is my best holt—for cancer and paralysis, and sich things; and I k'n tell a fortune pretty good when I've got somebody along to find out the facts for me. Preachin's my line, too, and missionaryin' around."

Nobody never said anything for a while; then the young man hove a sigh and says, "Alas!"

"What 're you alassin' about?" says the baldhead.

"To think I should have lived to be leading such a life, and be degraded down in such company." And he begun to wipe the corner of his eye with a rag.

"Dern your skin, ain't the company good enough for you?" says the baldhead, pretty pert and uppish.

"Yes, it *is* good enough for me; it's as good as I deserve; for who fetched me so low when I was so high? *I* brought myself down. I don't blame *you*, gentlemen—far from it; I don't blame anybody. One thing I know—there's a grave somewhere for me. The world may go on just as it's always done, and take everything from me—loved ones, property, everything; but it can't take that. Someday I'll lie down in it and forget it all, and my poor broken heart will be at rest." He went on a-wiping.

"Drot your pore broken heart," says the baldhead. "Who brought you down from whar? An' whar was you brought down from?"

"Ah, you would not believe me; let it pass—'tis no matter. The secret of my birth—"

"The secret of your birth! Do you mean to say—"

"Gentlemen," says the young man, very solemn, "I will reveal it to you, for I feel I may have confidence in you. By rights I am a duke!"

Jim's eyes bugged out; and I reckon mine did, too. Then the baldhead says, "No! You can't mean it?"

"Yes. My great-grandfather, eldest son of the Duke of Bridgewater, fled to this country about the end of the last century, to breathe the pure air of freedom; married here, and died, leaving a son, his own father dying about the same time. The second son of the late duke seized the titles and estates—the infant real duke was ignored. I am the lineal descendant of that infant—I am the rightful Duke of Bridgewater; and here am I, forlorn, torn from my high estate, ragged, worn, heartbroken, and degraded to the companionship of felons on a raft!"

Jim pitied him ever so much and so did I. We tried to comfort him, but he said it warn't much use; said if we was a mind to acknowledge him, that would do him more good than most anything else; so we said we would, if he would tell us how. He said we ought to bow when we spoke to him, and say, "Your Grace," or "Your Lordship"—and he wouldn't mind it if we called him plain "Bridgewater," which, he said, was a title, and not a name; and one of us ought to wait on him at dinner, and do any little thing for him he wanted done.

Well, that was all easy, so we done it. All through dinner Jim stood around and waited on him, and says, "Will yo' Grace have some o' dis or some o' dat?" But the old man got pretty silent by and by—didn't look comfortable over all that petting that was going on around that duke. Along in the afternoon he says:

"Looky here, Bilgewater," he says, "I'm nation sorry for you, but you ain't the only person that's had troubles."

"No?"

"No, you ain't. You ain't the only person that's ben snaked down wrongfully out'n a high place. You ain't the only person that's had a secret of his birth." And by jinks, *he* begins to cry.

"Hold! What do you mean?"

"Bilgewater, kin I trust you?" says the old man, still sobbing.

"To the bitter death!" He took the old man by the hand. "That secret of your being: speak!"

"Bilgewater, I am the late Dauphin!"

You bet you, Jim and me stared this time. Then the duke says, "You are what?"

"Yes, my friend, it is true—your eyes is lookin' at this very moment on the pore disappeared Dauphin, Looy the Seventeen, son of Looy the Sixteen and Marry Antonette. Yes, gentlemen, you see before you, in blue jeans and misery, the wanderin', exiled, rightful King of France."

Well, he cried and took on so that me and Jim didn't know hardly what to do, we was so sorry. So we set in, like we done before with the duke, and tried to comfort *him*. But he said it warn't no use, nothing but to be dead and done with it all could do him any good; though he said it often made him feel better for a while if people treated him according to his rights, and got down on one knee to speak to him, and called him "Your Majesty," and waited on him first at meals, and didn't set down in his presence till he asked them. So Jim and me set to majestying him, and doing this and that for him, and standing up till he told us we might set down. This done him heaps of good, and so he got cheerful. But the duke kind of soured on him, and didn't look a bit satisfied with the way things was going, and he stayed huffy a good while, till by and by the king says:

"Like as not we got to be together a blamed long time on this h'yer raft, Bilgewater, and so what's the use o' your bein' sour? It ain't my fault I warn't born a duke, it ain't your fault you warn't born a king—so what's the use to worry? This ain't no bad thing that we've struck here—so come, give us your hand, Duke, and le's all be friends."

The duke done it, and Jim and me was glad to see it. It would 'a' been a miserable business to have any unfriendliness on the raft; for what you want, above all things, on a raft, is for everybody to be satisfied, and feel right and kind towards the others.

It didn't take me long to make up my mind that these liars warn't no kings nor dukes at all, but just low-down humbugs and frauds. But I never let on; kept it to myself; it's the best way; then you don't get into no trouble. If I never learned nothing else out of Pap, I learned that the best way to get along with his kind of people is to let them have their own way.

IN THE MEANTIME they asked us considerable many questions; wanted to know what we covered up the raft that way for, and laid by in the daytime—was Jim a runaway nigger? Says I, "Goodness sakes! Would a runaway nigger run *south*?"

No, they allowed he wouldn't. I had to account for things some ways, so I says:

"My folks was living in Pike County, Missouri, and they all died off but me and Pa and my brother Ike. Pa, he 'lowed he'd go live with Uncle Ben, who's got a little place on the river forty-four mile below Orleans. Pa was pretty poor; so when he'd squared up his debts there warn't nothing left but sixteen dollars and our nigger, Jim. That warn't enough to take us fourteen hundred mile, so Pa ketched this piece of a raft; and we reckoned we'd go to Orleans on it. But a steamboat run over the raft, and we all went overboard; Jim and me come up all right, but Pa was drunk, and

Ike was only four years old, so they never come up no more. Well, for the next day or two we had considerable trouble, because people was always trying to take Jim away from me, saying they believed he was a runaway nigger. We don't run daytimes no more now; nights they don't bother us."

The duke says, "Leave me alone to cipher out a way so we can run in the daytime. I'll invent a plan that'll fix it. We'll let it alone for today, because of course we don't want to go by that town yonder in daylight—it mightn't be healthy."

Towards night it begun to darken up and look like rain; the heat lightning was squirting around in the sky; but we got away anyway as soon as it was good and dark. The king told us to stand well out towards the middle of the river, and not show a light till we got below the town. We come in sight of the little bunch of lights by and by—that was the town—and slid by, all right. When we was three-quarters of a mile below we hoisted up our signal lantern; and about ten o'clock it come on to rain and blow and thunder like everything; so the king told us to both stay on watch till the weather got better; then him and the duke crawled into the wigwam and turned in for the night on Jim's and my tick beds. It was my watch below till twelve, but I wouldn't 'a' turned in anyway if I'd had a bed, because a body don't see such a storm as that every day in the week. My souls, how the wind did scream! And every second or two there'd come a glare that lit up the whitecaps for a half a mile around; then comes a *h-whack!—bum! bumble-umble-um-bum-bum-bum-bum*—and the thunder would go grumbling away, and quit—and then *rip* comes another flash and another sockdolager. The waves most washed me off the raft sometimes, but I hadn't any clothes on, and didn't mind.

I had the middle watch, you know, but I was pretty sleepy by that time, so Jim he said he would stand the first half of it for me; he was always mighty good that way, Jim was. I crawled into the wigwam, but the king and the duke had their legs sprawled around so there warn't no show for me; so I laid outside—I didn't mind the rain, because it was warm, and the waves warn't running so high now. About two I took the watch, and Jim he laid down and snored away; and by and by the storm let up; and the first cabin light that showed I rousted him out, and we slid the raft into hiding quarters for the day.

The king got out an old ratty deck of cards after breakfast, and him and the duke played seven-up awhile. Then they got tired of it, and allowed they would "lay out a campaign," as they called it. The duke went down into his carpetbag, and fetched up a lot of printed bills and read them out loud. One bill said, "The celebrated Dr. Armand de Montalban, of Paris," would "lecture on the Science of Phrenology," at such and such a place, on the blank day of blank, at ten cents admission, and "furnish charts of character at twenty-five cents apiece." The duke said that was *him*. In another bill he was the "world-renowned Shakespearian tragedian, Garrick the Younger, of Drury Lane, London." In other bills he had a lot of other names and done other wonderful things, like finding water and gold with a "divining rod," "dissipating witch spells," and so on. By and by he says, "But the histrionic muse is the darling. Have you ever trod the boards, Royalty?"

"No," says the king.

"You shall then, before you're three days older, Fallen Grandeur," says the duke. "The first good town we come to we'll hire a hall and do the sword fight in *Richard Third*, and the balcony scene in *Romeo and Juliet*. How does that strike you?"

"I'm in, up to the hub, for anything that will pay, Bilgewater; but, you see, I don't know nothing about playactin'. Do you reckon you can learn me?"

"Easy!"

"All right. Le's commence."

So the duke he told him all about who Romeo was and who Juliet was, and said he was used to being Romeo, so the king could be Juliet.

"But if Juliet's such a young gal, Duke, my peeled head and my white whiskers is goin' to look oncommon odd on her."

"No, don't you worry; these country jakes won't ever think of that. Besides, you'll be in costume, and that makes all the difference. Juliet's in a balcony, enjoying the moonlight before she goes to bed, and she's got on her nightgown and her ruffled nightcap. Here are the costumes." He got out two or three curtain-calico suits, which he said was meedyevil armor for Richard III and t'other chap, and a long white cotton nightshirt and a ruffled nightcap. The king was satisfied; so the duke got out his book and read the parts over in the most splendid spread-eagle way, prancing around to show how it had got to be done; then he gives the book to the king and told him to get his part by heart.

There was a little one-horse town about three miles down the bend, and after dinner the duke said he had ciphered out his idea about how to run in daylight without it being dangersome for Jim; so he allowed he would go down to the town and fix that thing. The king allowed he would go too. We was out of coffee, so Jim said I better go along with them in the canoe and get some.

When we got there, there warn't nobody stirring; streets empty and still, like Sunday. We found a sick nigger sunning himself, and he said everybody was gone to camp meeting, about two mile back in the woods. The king got the directions, and allowed he'd go and work that camp meeting, and I might go too.

The duke said what he was after was a printing office. We found it up over a carpenter shop—carpenters and printers all gone to the meeting, and no doors locked. It was a littered-up place, and had ink marks and handbills about runaway niggers all over the walls. The duke said he was all right now. So me and the king lit out for the camp meeting.

We got there fairly dripping, for it was an awful hot day. There was as much as a thousand people there from twenty mile around. The woods was full of teams and wagons, hitched everywhere, stomping to keep off the flies. There was sheds made out of poles and roofed with branches, where they had lemonade and ginger-bread to sell, and piles of watermelons and corn and suchlike truck. The preaching was going on in the same kinds of sheds, only they was bigger and held crowds of people.

The first shed we come to the preacher was lining out a hymn. He lined out two lines, and everybody sung it, and it was kind of grand to hear it; then he lined out two more for them to sing—and so on. The people sung louder and louder; and towards the end some begun to groan, and some begun to shout. Then the preacher begun to preach, and went weaving first to one side of the platform and then the other, and then a-leaning down over the front of it, shouting with all his might; and every now and then he would hold up his Bible, crying, "Look upon it and live!" And the people would shout, "Glory—A-a-*men!*" And so he went on, and the people groaning and saying amen:

"Oh, come to the mourners' bench! (*Amen!*) Come, black with sin! (*Amen!*) Come, lame and halt and blind! (*Amen!*) Come, pore and needy, sunk in shame! (*A-a-men!*) Come, all that's worn and soiled and suffering! The door of heaven stands open—oh, enter and be at rest!" (*A-a-men! Glory, glory hallelujah!*)

And so on. You couldn't make out what the preacher said anymore, on account of the shouting and crying. Folks got up in the crowd, and worked their way to the mourners' bench with the tears running down their faces, and when they had got there they sung and shouted, just crazy and wild.

Well, the first I knowed the king got a-going and you could hear him over everybody; and next he went a-charging up onto the platform, and the preacher he begged him to speak to the people, and he done it. He told them he was a pirate—been a pirate for thirty years out in the Indian Ocean—and his crew was thinned out considerable last spring in a fight, and he was home now to take out some fresh men, and thanks to goodness he'd been robbed last night and put ashore off a steamboat without a cent, and he was glad of it; it was the blessedest thing that ever happened to him, because he was a changed man now, and happy for the first time in his life; and now he was going to work his way back to the Indian Ocean, and put in the rest of his life trying to turn the pirates into the true path; for he could do it better than anybody, being acquainted with all pirate crews in that ocean; and though it would take him a long time to get there without money, he would get there, and every time he convinced a pirate he would say to him, "Don't you thank me, don't you give me no credit; it all belongs to them dear people in Pokeville camp meeting, natural brothers and benefactors, and that dear preacher there, the truest friend a pirate ever had!"

And then he busted into tears, and so did everybody. Then somebody sings out, "Take up a collection for him!" Well, half a dozen made a jump to do it, but somebody sings out, "Let *him* pass the hat around!" Then everybody said it, the preacher too.

So the king went all through the crowd with his hat, swabbing his eyes and blessing the people; and every little while the prettiest girls, with the tears running down their cheeks, would up and ask to kiss him; and he always done it; and he was invited to stay a week; and everybody wanted him to live in their houses; but he said as this was the last day of the camp meeting he couldn't do no good, and besides he was in a sweat to get to the Indian Ocean right off and go to work on the pirates.

When we got back to the raft and the king come to count up he found he had collected eighty-seven dollars and seventy-five cents. And he said, take it all around, it laid over any day he'd ever put in in the missionarying line. He said it warn't no use talking, heathens don't amount to shucks alongside of pirates to work a camp meeting with.

The duke was thinking *he'd* been doing pretty well till the king come to show up, but after that he didn't think so so much. He had set up and printed off two little jobs for farmers in that printing office—and took the money, four dollars. And he had got in ten dollars' worth of advertisements for the paper, which he said he would put in for four dollars if they would pay in advance—so they done it. The price of the paper was two dollars a year, but he took in three subscriptions for half a dollar apiece on condition of them paying cash in advance. He set up a little piece of poetry, which he made himself, out of his own head—three verses—kind of sweet and saddish—the name of it was, "Yes, crush, cold world, this breaking heart"—and he left that all set up and ready to print in the paper, and didn't charge nothing for it. Well, he took in nine dollars and a half, and said he'd done a square day's work for it.

Then he showed us another little job he'd printed and hadn't charged for, because it was for us. It had a picture of a runaway nigger with a bundle on a stick over his shoulder, and "$200 reward" under it. The reading was all about Jim and described him to a dot. It said he run away from St. Jacques's plantation, forty mile below New Orleans, and likely went north, and whoever would catch him and send him back he could have the reward and expenses.

"Now," says the duke, "after tonight we can run in the daytime if we want to. Whenever we see anybody coming we can tie Jim with a rope, and show this handbill and say we captured him up the river and are going down to get the reward."

We all said the duke was pretty smart, and there couldn't be no trouble about running daytimes. We judged we could make miles enough that night to get out of the reach of the powwow we reckoned the duke's work in the printing office was going to make in that little town; then we could boom right along if we wanted to. We laid low and never shoved out till nearly ten o'clock; then we slid by, wide away from the town, and didn't hoist our lantern till we was clear out of sight of it.

When Jim called me to take the watch at four in the morning, he says, "Huck, does you reck'n we gwyne to run acrost any mo' kings on dis trip?"

"No," I says, "I reckon not."

"Well," says he, "dat's all right, den. I doan' mine one er two kings, but dat's enough. Dis one's powerful drunk, en de duke ain' much better."

I found Jim had been trying to get him to talk French, so he could hear what it was like; but he said he had been in this country so long, and had so much trouble, he'd forgot it.

CHAPTER IX

IT WAS AFTER SUNUP NOW, but we went right on and didn't tie up. The king and the duke turned out by and by looking pretty rusty; but after they'd jumped overboard and took a swim it chippered them up. After breakfast the king he rolled up his britches, and let his legs dangle in the water, so as to be comfortable, and went to getting his *Romeo and Juliet* by heart. When he had got it pretty good him and the duke begun to practice it together. The duke learned him how to say every speech; and he made him sigh, and put his hand on his heart, and after a while he said he done it pretty well.

"Only," the duke says, "you mustn't bellow out *Romeo!* that way, like a bull. You must say it soft and sick and languishy, so—R-o-o-meo! For Juliet's a dear sweet mere child, and she doesn't bray like a jackass."

Well, next they got out a couple of long swords that the duke made out of laths, and begun to practice the sword fight. The duke called himself Richard III; and the way they laid on and pranced around the raft was grand to see. But by and by the king tripped and fell overboard, and after that they took a rest. Then after dinner the duke says:

"Well, King, we'll want to make this a first-class show, you know, so I guess we'll add a little more to it. We want a little something to answer encores with, anyway."

"What's onkores, Bilgewater?"

The duke told him, and then says, "I'll answer by doing the Highland fling, and you—well, let me see—oh, I've got it—you can do Hamlet's soliloquy."

"Hamlet's which?"

"Hamlet's soliloquy, you know; the most celebrated thing in Shakespeare. Ah, it's sublime, sublime! I haven't got it in the book—but I reckon I can piece it out from memory. I'll just walk up and down a minute, and see if I can call it back from recollection's vaults."

So he went to marching up and down, thinking, and frowning horrible every now and then; then he would squeeze his hand on his forehead and stagger and kind of moan; next he would sigh, and drop a tear. It was beautiful to see him. By and by he got it. He told us to give attention. Then he strikes a most noble attitude, with one leg shoved forwards, and his arms stretched up, and his head tilted back, looking up at the sky; and then he begins to rip and rave. This is the speech—I learned it, easy, while he was learning it to the king:

> To be, or not to be; that is the bare bodkin
> That makes calamity of so long life;
> For who would fardels bear, till Birnam Wood do
>   come to Dunsinane,
> But that the fear of something after death
> Murders the innocent sleep,
> And makes us rather sling the arrows of outrageous
>   fortune
> Than fly to others that we know not of.
> There's the respect must give us pause:
> Wake Duncan with thy knocking! I would thou couldst;
> For who would bear the whips and scorns of time,
> The oppressor's wrong, the proud man's contumely,
> In the dead waste and middle of the night,
> But that the undiscovered country from whose bourne no
>   traveler returns,
> Breathes forth contagion on the world,
> And thus the native hue of resolution, like the poor
>   cat i' the adage,
> Is sicklied o'er with care,
> And loses the name of action.
> But soft, the fair Ophelia:
> Ope not thy ponderous and marble jaws,
> But get thee to a nunnery—go!

Well, the old man he liked that speech, and he mighty soon got it so he could do it first-rate. It was lovely the way he would rip and tear and rair up behind when he was getting it off.

The first chance we got the duke he had some showbills printed; and after that, for two or three days, the raft was a most uncommon lively place, for there warn't nothing but rehearsing going on all the time.

One morning, when we was pretty well down the state of Arkansaw, we come in sight of a little one-horse town in a big bend, so we tied up about a mile above it, in the mouth of a crick

I made sure it was loaded; and then I laid it across the turnip barrel, pointing towards Pap, and set down behind it to wait for him to stir.

When she'd (the ferryboat) got pretty well along towards me, I went and laid down behind a log on the bank. Where the log forked I could peep through.

Then he strikes a most noble attitude, with one leg shoved forwards, and his arms stretched up, and his head tilted back, looking up at the sky; and then he begins to rip and rave.

And when they got there they looked in the coffin, and then they bust out a-crying so you could 'a' heard them to Orleans, most; and then for three minutes, or maybe four, I never see two men leak the way they done.

They gripped up all, me and the four men, and marched us right along for the graveyard, a mile and a half down the river, and the whole town at our heels, for we made noise enough.

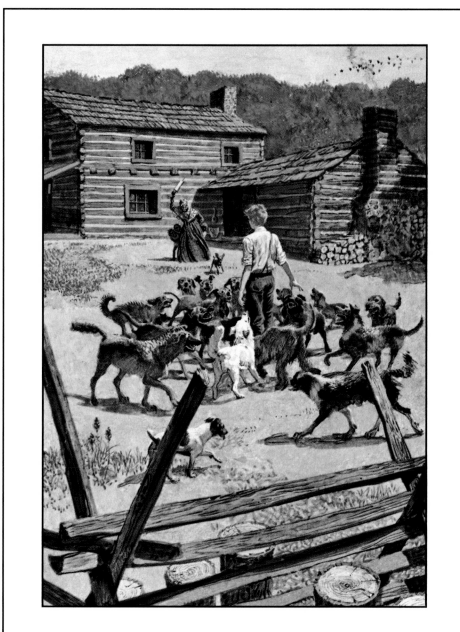

In a quarter of a minute I was a kind of hub of a wheel—spokes made out of dogs—circle of fifteen of them packed together around me a-barking and howling.

So I started for town in the wagon, and when I was halfway I see a wagon coming, and sure enough it was Tom Sawyer.

And the third time I waked up at dawn, and slid down, and she was there yet, and her old gray head was resting on her hand, and she was asleep.

which was shut in like a tunnel by the cypress trees, and all of us but Jim took the canoe and went down there to see if there was any chance in that place for our show.

We struck it lucky; there was going to be a circus there that afternoon, and the country people was already beginning to come in, in all kinds of shackly wagons, and on horses. The circus would leave before night, so our show would have a pretty good chance. The duke he hired the courthouse, and we went around and stuck up our bills. They read like this:

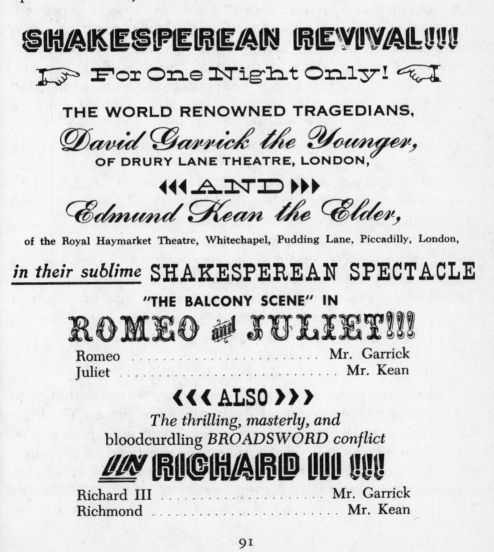

SHAKESPEREAN REVIVAL!!!!

☞ For One Night Only! ☜

THE WORLD RENOWNED TRAGEDIANS,

David Garrick the Younger,
OF DRURY LANE THEATRE, LONDON,

◀◀AND▶▶

Edmund Kean the Elder,
of the Royal Haymarket Theatre, Whitechapel, Pudding Lane, Piccadilly, London,

in their sublime SHAKESPEREAN SPECTACLE

"THE BALCONY SCENE" IN

ROMEO and JULIET!!!

Romeo . . . . Mr. Garrick
Juliet . . . . Mr. Kean

◀◀◀ ALSO ▶▶▶

The thrilling, masterly, and
bloodcurdling *BROADSWORD conflict*

IN RICHARD III !!!!

Richard III . . . . Mr. Garrick
Richmond . . . . Mr. Kean

ALSO: (by Special Request)

HAMLET'S IMMORTAL SOLILOQUY!!

By the Illustrious KEAN!

Done by him 300 consecutive nights in PARIS!
ADMISSION 25 cents; children and servants, 10 cents.

Then we went loafing around town. The stores and houses was most all old, shackly frame concerns that hadn't ever been painted; they was set up three or four foot above ground on stilts, so as to be out of reach of the water when the river was overflowed. The houses had little gardens around them, but they didn't seem to raise hardly anything in them but jimpsonweeds, and ash piles, and old curled-up shoes. The fences was made of different kinds of boards, nailed on at different times; and they leaned every which way. There was generly hogs in the garden, and people driving them out.

All the stores was along one street. They had awnings in front, and the country people hitched their horses to the awning posts. There was empty dry-goods boxes under the awnings, and loafers roosting on them all day long, whittling with their Barlow knives; and chawing tobacco, and gaping and yawning and stretching—a mighty ornery lot. There was as many as one loafer leaning up against every awning post, and he most always had his hands in his britches pockets, except when he fetched them out to scratch. What a body was hearing amongst them all the time was:

"Gimme a chaw 'v tobacker, Hank."

"Cain't; I hain't got but one chaw left. Ask Bill."

All the streets and lanes was just mud; they warn't nothing else *but* mud—mud nigh about a foot deep in some places. The hogs loafed and grunted around everywheres. You'd see a muddy sow and a litter of pigs come lazying along the street and whollop herself right down in the way, and she'd stretch out and shut her eyes and wave her ears whilst the pigs was milking her, and look as happy as if she was on salary. And pretty soon you'd hear a loafer sing out, "Hi! *So* boy! Sick him, Tige!" And away the sow would go, squealing most horrible, with a dog or two swinging to each ear, and three or four dozen more a-coming; and then you would see all the loafers get up and watch the thing out of sight, and laugh and look grateful for the noise. Then they'd settle back again till there was a dogfight. There couldn't anything wake them up all over, and make them happy all over, like a dogfight.

The nearer it got to noon that day the thicker and thicker was the wagons and horses in the streets, and more coming all the time. Families fetched their dinners with them from the country, and eat them in the wagons. At last it was time for the circus. I went, and loafed around the back side till the watchman went by, and then dived in under the tent. I ain't opposed to spending money on circuses when there ain't no other way, but there ain't no use in *wasting* it on them.

It was a real bully circus. All through it they done the most astonishing things; and all the time there was a clown that carried on in the funniest way so it most killed the people. But the splendidest sight ever was when they all came riding in on horses, two and two, gentleman and lady, side by side, the men just in their drawers and undershirts, and no shoes nor stirrups, and resting their hands on their thighs easy and comfortable—there must 'a' been twenty of them—and every lady perfectly beautiful, and looking just like a gang of queens, and dressed in clothes that cost millions of dollars, and just littered with diamonds. And then one by one they got up and stood, and went a-weaving around the ring so gentle and wavy and graceful, the men looking ever so tall and airy and straight.

And faster and faster they went, all of them dancing, first one foot out in the air and then the other, the horses leaning more and more, and the ringmaster going round and round the center pole, cracking his whip and shouting, "Hi! Hi!" and the clown cracking jokes behind him; and by and by all hands dropped the reins, and every lady put her knuckles on her hips and every gentleman folded his arms, and then how the horses did lean over and hump themselves! And so one after the other they all skipped off into the ring, and made the sweetest bow I ever see, and then scampered out, and everybody clapped their hands and went just about wild.

I don't know; there may be bullier circuses than what that one was, but I never struck them yet. Anyways, it was plenty good enough for *me*.

Well, that night we had *our* show; but there warn't only about twelve people there. And they laughed all the time, and that made the duke mad; and everybody left before the show was over, but one boy which was asleep. So the duke said these Arkansaw lunkheads couldn't come up to Shakespeare; what they wanted was low comedy—and maybe something worse. So next morning he got some big sheets of wrapping paper and some black paint, and drawed off some handbills, and stuck them up all over the village. The bills said:

At The court house For 3 Nights Only!
The world - reNowned tragedians
DAVID GARRICK THE YOUNGER!
and
EDMUND KEAN THE ELDER!
In their THRILLING Tragedy of
THE KINGS CAMELEOPARD
OR
THE ROYAL NONESUCH !!
Admission 50¢

Then at the bottom was the biggest line of all, which said:

LAdies AND CHILDREN NOT AdmiTTed

"There," says he, "if that line don't fetch them, I don't know Arkansaw!"

Well, all day him and the king was hard at it, rigging up a stage and a curtain, and candles for footlights; and that night the house was jam full of men in no time. When the place couldn't hold no more, the duke he quit tending the door and come and stood up before the curtain and made a little speech, and praised up this tragedy, and said it was the most thrillingest one that ever was; and at last when he'd got everybody's expectations up high, he rolled up the curtain, and the next minute the king come a-prancing out on all fours, naked; and he was painted all over, ring-streaked-and-striped, all sorts of colors, as splendid as a rainbow. And—but never mind the rest of his outfit; it was just wild, but it was awful funny. The people most killed themselves laughing; and when the king got done capering and capered off, they roared and clapped and haw-hawed till he come back and done it over again, and after that they made him do it another time. Well, it would make a cow laugh to see the shines that old idiot cut.

Then the duke he lets the curtain down, and bows to the people, and says the great tragedy will be performed only two nights more, on account of pressing London engagements; and then he makes them another bow, and says if he has succeeded in pleasing them, he will be deeply obleeged if they will mention it to their friends.

Twenty people sings out, "What, is it over? Is that *all?*"

The duke says yes. Then there was a fine time. Everybody sings out, "Sold!" and rose up mad, and was a-going for that stage and them tragedians. But a big, fine-looking man jumps up on a bench and shouts:

"Hold on! Just a word, gentlemen." They stopped to listen. "We are sold—mighty badly. But we don't want to be the laughing-stock of this whole town, I reckon. *No.* What we want is to go out of here quiet, and talk this show up, and sell the *rest* of the town! Then we'll all be in the same boat. Ain't that sensible?" ("You bet it is!" "The jedge is right!" everybody sings out.) "All right, then, go along home, and advise everybody to come and see the tragedy."

Next day you couldn't hear nothing around that town but how splendid that show was. House was jammed again that night, and we sold this crowd the same way. When me and the king and the duke got home to the raft we all had supper; and by and by they made Jim and me back the raft out and float her down the river, and hide her about two mile below town.

The third night the house was crammed again—and they warn't

newcomers this time, but people that was at the show the other two nights. I stood by the duke at the door, and I see that every man that went in had his pockets bulging, or something muffled up under his coat—and it warn't no perfumery, neither. I smelt sickly eggs by the barrel, and rotten cabbages; and if I know the signs of a dead cat being around there was sixty-four of them went in. Well, when the place couldn't hold no more people the duke he give a fellow a quarter and told him to tend door for him a minute, and then he started for the stage door, I after him; but the minute we turned the corner and was in the dark he says:

"Walk fast now till you get away from the houses, and then shin for the raft like the dickens was after you!"

I done it, and he done the same. We struck the raft at the same time, and in less than two seconds we was gliding downstream, all dark and still. I reckoned the poor king was in for a gaudy time of it with the audience, but nothing of the sort; soon he crawls out from the wigwam. He hadn't been up to town at all.

We never showed a light till we was about ten mile below the village. Then we lit up and had a supper. Them rapscallions had took in four hundred and sixty-five dollars in that three nights, and the king and the duke fairly laughed their bones loose over the way they'd served them people.

By and by, when they was asleep and snoring, Jim says:

"Don't it s'prise you de way dem kings carries on, Huck?"

"No," I says, "it don't."

"Why don't it, Huck?"

"Well, it don't, because it's in the breed. I reckon they're all alike; all kings is mostly rapscallions, as fur as I can make out. You read about them, you'll see. Look at Henry the Eight; this 'n' 's a Sunday-school superintendent to *him*. And look at Charles Second, and Louis Fourteen, and Louis Fifteen, and Richard Third, and forty more. My, you ought to seen old Henry the Eight when he was in bloom. He *was* a blossom. He used to marry a new wife every day, and chop off her head next morning. He would do it just as indifferent as if he was ordering up eggs. You don't know kings, Jim, but I know them; and this old rip of ourn is one of the cleanest I've struck in history. Kings is kings, and you got to make allowances. It's the way they're raised."

"But dis one do *smell* so, Huck."

"Well, they all do, Jim."

"Now de duke, he's a tolerble likely man in some ways."

"Yes, a duke's different. But not very. This one's a middling hard lot for a duke. When he's drunk there ain't no nearsighted man could tell him from a king."

"Well, anyways, I doan' hanker for no mo' un um, Huck. Dese is all I kin stan'."

"It's the way I feel, too, Jim. Sometimes I wish we could hear of a country that's out of kings."

What was the use to tell Jim these warn't real kings and dukes? It wouldn't 'a' done no good; and, besides, it was just as I said: you couldn't tell them from the real kind.

I went to sleep, and Jim didn't call me when it was my turn. He often done that. When I waked up just at daybreak he was sitting there with his head down, moaning and mourning to himself. I knowed he was thinking about his wife and his children, away up yonder, and he was low and homesick; and I do believe he cared just as much for his people as white folks does for their'n. He was often mourning that way nights, when he judged I was asleep, and saying, "Po' little 'Lizabeth! Po' little Johnny! I spec' I ain't ever gwyne to see you no mo'!" But this time I somehow got to talking to him about his wife and young ones; and by and by he says:

"What makes me feel so bad dis time 'uz bekase I 'uz thinkin' er de time I treat my little 'Lizabeth so ornery. She warn't on'y 'bout fo' year ole, en she tuck de sk'yarlet fever; but she got well, en one day she was a-stannin' aroun', en I says to her, I says, 'Shet de do'.'

"She never done it; jis stood dah, kiner smilin' up at me. It make me mad; en I says ag'in, mighty loud, 'Doan' you hear me? Shet de do'!' She jis stood de same way, kiner smilin' up. I was a-bilin'! I says, 'I lay I *make* you mine!' En wid dat I fetch' her a slap side de head dat sont her a-sprawlin'. Den I went into de yuther room; en when I come back dah was dat do' a-stannin' open *yit*, en dat chile stannin' mos' right in it, a-lookin' down and mournin', en de tears runnin' down. My, but I *wuz* mad. I was a-gwyne for de chile, but jis' den, 'long come de wind en slam dat do' to, behine de chile, ker-*blam!* En my lan', de chile never move'! My breff mos' hop outer me; en I feel so—so—I doan' know *how* I feel. I crope out, all a-tremblin', en crope aroun' en open de do' easy en slow, en poke my head in behine de chile, en all uv a sudden I says *pow!* jis' as loud as I could. *She never budge!* Oh, Huck, I bust out a-cryin' en grab her up in my arms, en say, 'Oh, de po' little thing! De Lord God fogive ole Jim, kaze he never gwyne to fogive hisself as long's he live!' Oh, she was plumb deef en dumb from the fever, Huck, deef en dumb—en I'd ben a-treat'n her so!"

CHAPTER X

NEXT DAY, TOWARDS NIGHT, we laid up under a little willow towhead out in the middle, where there was a village on each side of the river, and the duke and the king begun to lay out a plan for working them towns. Jim he spoke to the duke, and said he hoped it wouldn't take but a few hours, because it got mighty tiresome to him to lay all day in the wigwam tied with the rope. You see, when we left him alone we had to tie him, because if anybody happened on to him not tied it wouldn't look much like he was a runaway nigger. So the duke said he'd cipher out some way to get around it, and he soon struck it. He dressed Jim up in King Lear's outfit—it was a long calico gown, and a white wig and whiskers; and then he took his theater paint and painted Jim's face and hands and ears and neck all over a dead, dull solid blue, like a man that's been drownded nine days. Then the duke wrote a sign on a shingle:

Sick Arab—but harmless when not out of his head.

He nailed that shingle to a lath, and stood the lath up in front of the wigwam. And he told Jim if anybody come meddling around, he must hop out of the wigwam, and carry on a little, and fetch a howl or two, and he reckoned they would light out and leave him alone. Which was sound enough; but you take the average man, he wouldn't wait for him to howl. Why, Jim didn't only look like he was dead, he looked considerable more than that.

Then the duke said he reckoned he'd see if he couldn't put up something on the Arkansaw village; and the king he allowed he would drop over to t'other village. We had all bought store clothes where we stopped last; and now the king put his'n on, and he told me to put mine on. I done it, of course. The king's duds was all black. I never knowed how clothes could change a body before; he looked that grand and pious that you'd say he had walked right out of the ark. Jim cleaned up the canoe, and I got my paddle ready. There was a big steamboat lying at the shore, about three mile above the town, taking on freight. Says the king:

"Seein' how I'm dressed, I reckon I better arrive from St. Louis or Cincinnati, or some other big place. Go for the steamboat, Huckleberry; we'll come down to the village on her."

I fetched the shore a half a mile above the village, and then went scooting along the bank in the easy water. Pretty soon we come to a nice innocent-looking young country jake setting on a log swabbing the sweat off of his face; and he had a couple of big carpetbags by him.

"Run inshore," says the king. I done it. "Wher' you bound for, young man?"

"For the steamboat; going to Orleans."

"Git aboard," says the king. "My servant 'll he'p you with them bags. He'p the gentleman, Adolphus," meaning me, I see.

I done so, and then we all three started on again. The young chap was mighty thankful. He asked the king where he was going, and the king told him he'd landed at the other village this morning, and now he was going up a few mile to see an old friend. The young fellow says, "When I first see you I says to myself, 'It's Mr. Wilks, sure, and he come mighty near getting here in time.' But you *ain't* him, are you?"

"No, my name's Blodgett—Reverend Elexander Blodgett. I'm one o' the Lord's poor servants. But I'm sorry for Mr. Wilks for not arriving in time, if he's missed anything by it."

"Well, he don't miss any property by it; he'll get that all right; but he's missed seeing his brother Peter die. Peter never talked about nothing else all these three weeks; hadn't seen Harvey since they was boys together—and hadn't ever seen his brother William at all—that's the deef and dumb one—William ain't more than thirty-five. Peter and George were the only ones that come out here; George was the married brother; him and his wife both died last year. Harvey and William's the only ones that's left now; and, as I was saying, they haven't got here in time."

"Did anybody send 'em word?"

"Oh, yes; a month or two ago, when Peter was first took. You see, he was pretty old, and he most desperately wanted to see Harvey—and William, too, for that matter—because he was one of them kind that can't bear to make a will. He left a letter behind for Harvey, and said he'd told in it where his money was hid, and how he wanted the property divided up so George's g'yirls would be all right. That letter was all they could get him to put a pen to."

"Why do you reckon Harvey don't come? Wher' does he live?"

"Oh, he lives in England—Sheffield—preaches there. He hasn't had any too much time to get here."

"Too bad, poor soul. You going to Orleans, you say!"

"Yes, but that ain't only a part. I'm going in a ship, Wednesday, for Ryo Janeero, where my uncle lives."

"It's a long journey. But it'll be lovely; I wisht I was a-going. How old is the girls?"

"Mary Jane the redheaded one's nineteen, Susan's fifteen, and Joanna's about fourteen—that's the one that has a harelip."

"Poor things, to be left alone in the cold world so!"

"Well, they could be worse off. Peter had friends who ain't going to let them come to no harm. There's Hobson, the Babtis' preacher; and Deacon Hovey, and Abner Shackleford, and Levi Bell, the lawyer; and Dr. Robinson."

Well, the old man went on asking questions till he just fairly emptied that young fellow. Blamed if he didn't inquire about Peter's business—which was a tanner; and about Harvey's—which was a dissentering minister; and how much property Peter left;

and so on and so on. And finally he asks, "When did you say he died?"

"I didn't say, but it was last night."

"Well, it's all terrible sad; but we've all got to go, sometime. So what we want to do is to be prepared."

"Yes, sir. Ma used to always say that."

When we struck the boat she was about done loading, and pretty soon she got off. The king never said nothing more about going aboard. When the boat was gone the king made me paddle up to a lonesome place, and then he got ashore and says, "Now hustle back and fetch the duke up here, and the new carpetbags. Shove along, now."

I see what *he* was up to; but I never said nothing, of course. When I got back with the duke they set down on a log, and the king told him everything, just like the young fellow had said it. And all the time he was a-doing it he tried to talk like an Englishman; and he done it pretty well, too. I can't imitate him, and so I ain't a-going to try. Then he says:

"How are you on the deef and dumb, Bilgewater?"

The duke said he had played a deef and dumb person on the histrionic boards. So we hid the canoe, and then they waited for a steamboat. At last about the middle of the afternoon there was a big one, and they hailed her. She sent out her yawl, and we went aboard, and she was from Cincinnati; and when they found we only wanted to go four or five mile they was booming mad. But the king offered to pay a dollar a mile apiece for us, so they softened down and said it was all right; and when we got to the village they yawled us ashore. About two dozen men flocked down when they see the yawl a-coming, and when the king says, "Kin any of you gentlemen tell me wher' Mr. Peter Wilks lives?" they give a glance at one another. Then one of them says, kind of gentle:

"I'm sorry, sir, but the best we can do is to tell you where he *did* live yesterday evening."

Sudden as winking the ornery old cretur went all to smash, and fell up against the man, and put his chin on his shoulder, and cried down his back, and says:

"Alas, alas, our brother—gone! Oh, it's *too* hard!"

Then he turns around, blubbering, and makes a lot of idiotic signs to the duke on his hands, and blamed if *he* didn't drop a carpetbag and bust out a-crying. If they warn't the beatenest lot, them two frauds, that ever I struck! It was enough to make a body ashamed of the human race.

The news was all over town in two minutes, and you could see the people tearing down on the run from every which way. When we got to the house the street in front of it was packed, and the three girls was standing in the door. Mary Jane *was* redheaded and she was most awful beautiful, and her eyes was all lit up like glory, she was so glad her uncles was come. The king he spread his arms, and Mary Jane she jumped for them, and the harelip jumped for the duke. Everybody most, leastways women, cried for joy to see them meet at last.

Then the king he hunched the duke private—I see him do it—and then he looked around and see the coffin, over in the corner on two chairs; so then him and the duke, with a hand across each other's shoulder, and t'other hand to their eyes, walked over there, everybody dropping back to give them room. And when they got there they looked in the coffin, and then they bust out a-crying so you could 'a' heard them to Orleans, most; and then for three minutes, or maybe four, I never see two men leak the way they done. Then they kneeled down and rested their foreheads on the coffin, and let on to pray all to themselves. Well, when it come to that it worked the crowd like anything, and everybody went to sobbing right out loud.

Well, by and by the king he gets up and slobbers out a speech, all full of tears and flapdoodle, about its being a sore trial for him and his poor brother to lose the diseased, but it's a trial that's sweetened and sanctified by this dear sympathy and these holy tears, and all that kind of rot and slush, till it was just sickening. Then he says how him and his nieces would be glad if a few of the main principal friends of the family would take supper here with them this evening, and help set up with the diseased; and says if his poor brother laying yonder could speak he knows who he would name; and so he will name the same, to wit, as follows, viz.: Rev. Mr. Hobson, and Deacon Hovey, and Abner Shackleford, and Levi Bell, and Dr. Robinson.

Rev. Hobson and Dr. Robinson was down to the end of the town with a sick man. Lawyer Bell was up to Louisville on business. But the others was on hand, and so they come and thanked the king; and then they shook hands with the duke whilst he made all sorts of signs with his hands and said "Goo-goo-goo-goo-goo" all the time, like a baby.

Then Mary Jane she fetched the letter her father left, and the king he read it out loud. It give the dwelling house and three thousand dollars in gold to the girls; and it give the tanyard along with some other houses and land (worth about seven thousand), and three thousand dollars in gold to Harvey and William, and told where the six thousand cash was hid down cellar. So these two frauds said they'd go and fetch it, and told me to come with a candle. We shut the cellar door behind us, and when they found the bag they spilt it out on the floor, and it was a lovely sight, all them yaller boys. My, the way the king's eyes did shine! He slaps the duke on the shoulder and says, "Oh, ain't *this* bully! Why, Biljy, it beats the Nonesuch, *don't* it?"

The duke allowed it did. They pawed the yaller boys and let them jingle down on the floor. "Say," says the duke, "I got an idea. Le's go upstairs and count this money, and then *give it to the girls*."

"Good land, Duke, lemme hug you! Oh, this is the boss dodge! This 'll lay 'em out."

When we got upstairs the king he counted the money and stacked it up in elegant little piles on the table, and everybody looked hungry at it. Then they raked it into the bag again, and the king says, "Friends, my poor brother that lays yonder has done generous by them that's left behind in the vale of sorrers. He has done generous by these pore little lambs that he loved. Yes, and we that knowed him knows that he would 'a' done *more* generous by 'em if he hadn't ben afeard o' woundin' his dear William and me. Now, *wouldn't* he? Well, then, what kind o' brothers would it be that 'd stand in his way at sech a time? And what kind o' uncles would it be that 'd rob—yes, *rob*—sech poor sweet lambs as these at sech a time?" Then the king says, "Here, Mary Jane, Susan, Joanner, William 'n' I want you to take the money—take it *all*. It's the gift of him that lays yonder, cold but joyful."

Mary Jane she went for him, Susan and the harelip went for the duke, and then such another hugging and kissing I never see yet. And everybody crowded up and most shook the hands off of them frauds, saying all the time, "You *dear* good souls! How *lovely*! How *could* you!"

Well, then, pretty soon all hands got to talking about the diseased again; and before long a big iron-jawed man worked himself in from outside, and stood a-listening, not saying anything. The king was saying—in the middle of something he'd started in on—

"—they bein' partikler friends o' the diseased who's invited here this evenin'; but tomorrow we want *all* to come—everybody; for he respected everybody, he liked everybody, and so it's fitten that his funeral orgies sh'd be public."

And so he went a-mooning on, and every little while he fetched in his funeral orgies again, till the duke he couldn't stand it; so he writes on a scrap of paper, "*Obsequies*, you old fool," and folds it up, and goes to goo-gooing and reaching it over people's heads to him. The king he reads it, and says:

"Poor William, his *heart's* aluz right. Asks me to invite everybody to the funeral. But he needn't 'a' worried." Then he weaves along again, perfectly ca'm, and goes to dropping in his funeral orgies again, and then he says, "I says orgies, not because it's the common term, because it ain't—obsequies bein' the common term—but because orgies is the right term. Obsequies ain't used in England no more—we say orgies now in England. Orgies is a word that's made up out'n the Greek *orgo*, outside, open; and the Hebrew *jeesum*, to plant, cover up; hence in*ter*. So, you see, funeral orgies is an open er public funeral."

He was the *worst* I ever struck. Well, the iron-jawed man he laughed right in his face. Everybody was shocked. Everybody says, "Why, *Doctor!*" and Abner Shackleford says, "Why, Robinson, hain't you heard the news? This is Harvey Wilks."

The king he smiled eager, and shoved out his flapper, and says, "*Is* it my brother's dear friend and physician? I—"

"Keep your hands off me!" says the doctor. "*You* talk like an Englishman, *don't* you? It's the worst imitation I ever heard. You're a fraud, that's what you are!"

Well, how they all took on! They crowded around the doctor and tried to quiet him down, and tried to explain to him how Harvey's showed in forty ways that he *was* Harvey. But it warn't no use. All of a sudden the doctor turns on the girls, and he says:

"I was your father's friend, and I'm your friend; and I warn you, *as* one that wants to protect you, to turn your backs on that scoundrel. He has come here with a lot of empty names and facts which he picked up somewheres; and you take them for *proofs*. Mary Jane Wilks, you know me for your friend. Listen to me; turn this rascal out—I *beg* you. Will you?"

Mary Jane straightened up, and my, but she was handsome! She says, "*Here* is my answer." She hove up the bag of money and put it in the king's hands, and says, "Take this six thousand dollars, and invest it for me and my sisters, and don't give us no receipt."

Then everybody clapped their hands and stomped like a perfect storm. The doctor says, "All right; I wash *my* hands of the matter. But I warn you all, a time's coming when you're going to feel sick when you think of this day."

"All right, Doctor," says the king, kinder mocking him; "we'll try and get 'em to send for you"; which made them all laugh, and they said it was a prime good hit.

CHAPTER XI

WELL, WHEN THEY WAS ALL GONE the king he asks Mary Jane how they was off for spare rooms, and she said she had one spare room, which would do for Uncle William, and she'd give her own room to Uncle Harvey, and turn into the room with her sisters; and up garret was a little cubby, with a pallet in it. The king said the cubby would do for his valley—meaning me. So Mary Jane took us up, and she showed them their rooms, which was plain but nice. She said she'd have her frocks took out of her room if they was in Uncle Harvey's way, but he said they warn't. The frocks was behind a calico curtain that hung down to the floor. The duke's room was pretty small, but plenty good enough, and so was my cubby.

That night they had a big supper, and all them men and women was there, and I stood behind the king and the duke's chairs and waited on them, and the niggers waited on the rest.

When it was all done me and the harelip had supper in the kitchen, and the harelip she got to pumping me about England. She says, "Did you ever see the king?"

"Who? William Fourth? Well, I bet I have—he goes to our church."

"What—regular?"

"Yes—regular. His pew's right over opposite ourn."

"I thought he lived in London?"

"Well, he does. Where *would* he live?"

"But I thought *you* lived in Sheffield."

I see I was up a stump. I had to let on to get choked with a chicken bone, so as to get time to think. Then I says, "I mean he goes to our church regular when he's in Sheffield. That's only in the summertime, when he comes there to take the sea baths."

"Why, how you talk—Sheffield ain't on the sea."

"Well, who said it was?"

"Why, you did."

"I *didn't*, nuther. I said he come to take the sea *baths*. He don't have to go to the sea to get a sea bath."

"How does he get it, then?"

"Gets it in barrels. In the palace at Sheffield they've got furnaces, and he wants his water hot. They can't bile that amount of water away off there at the sea. They haven't got no conveniences for it."

"Oh, I see. You might 'a' said that in the first place and saved time."

When she said that I see I was out of the woods again, and so I was glad. Next, she says, "Do you go to church, too?"

"Yes—regular."

"Where do you set?"

"Why, in our pew—your Uncle Harvey's."

"His'n? What does *he* want with a pew?"

"Wants it to set in. What did you *reckon* he wanted with it?"

"Why, I thought he'd be in the pulpit."

Rot him, I forgot he was a preacher. I see I was up a stump again, so I played another chicken bone. Then I says, "Blame it, do you suppose there ain't but one preacher to a church?"

"Why, what do they want with more?"

"What—to preach before a king? I never did see such a girl as you. They don't have no less than seventeen."

"Seventeen! My land! Why, I'd *never* set out such a string as that. It must take 'em a week."

"Shucks, they don't *all* of 'em preach the same day—only *one*."

"Well, then, what does the rest of 'em do?"

"Oh, loll around, pass the plate—one thing or another. But mainly they don't do nothing."

"Well, then, what are they *for?*"

"Why, they're for *style*."

I see she still warn't satisfied. She says, "Honest injun, hain't you been telling me a lot of lies?"

"Honest injun," says I, "not a lie in it."

"Lay your hand on this book and say it."

It warn't nothing but a dictionary, so I laid my hand on it and said it. So then she says, "Well, then, I'll believe some of it; but I hope to gracious if I'll believe the rest."

"What is it you won't believe, Jo?" says Mary Jane, stepping in. "It ain't right nor kind for you to talk so to him, and him a stranger and so far from his people."

"I hain't done nothing to him, Maim. He's told some stretchers, I reckon, and I said I wouldn't swallow it all; but I reckon he can stand a little thing like that, can't he?"

"I don't care whether 'twas little or whether 'twas big; he's here in our house and a stranger. It don't make no difference what he said. The thing is for you to treat him *kind*."

I says to myself, *This* is a girl that I'm letting that old reptile rob her of her money!

Then Susan *she* waltzed in; and if you'll believe me, she too give Harelip hark from the tomb!

Says I to myself, And this is *another* one that I'm letting him rob her of her money!

When they both got done there warn't hardly anything left o' poor Harelip. So she hollered.

"All right," says the other girls, "you just ask his pardon."

She done it, too; and she done it beautiful. She done it so beautiful I wished I could tell her a thousand lies, so she could do it again. I says to myself, This is *another* one that I'm letting him rob her of her money. And I felt so ornery and mean that I says to myself, My mind's made up; I'll hive that money for them or bust.

So then I lit out—for bed, I said. When I got by myself I went to thinking the thing over. I says to myself, Shall I go to that doctor, private, and blow on these frauds? No, he might tell who told him; then the king and the duke would make it warm for me. Shall I go private, and tell Mary Jane? No, her face would give them a hint, sure; they've got the money, and they'd slide right out and get away with it. No; there ain't no good way but one. I got to steal that money, somehow, and hide it; and by and by, when I'm away down the river, I'll write and tell Mary Jane where it's hid.

So, thinks I, I'll go and search them rooms. Upstairs the hall was dark, but I found the king's room, and begun to paw around there. But I see I couldn't do nothing without a candle, and I dasn't light one. So I judged I'd lay for them and eavesdrop. About that time I hears their footsteps coming, and was going to skip under the bed when I touched the curtain that hid Mary Jane's frocks, so I jumped in behind that and snuggled in amongst the gowns, and stood there perfectly still. They come in and shut the door; and the first thing the duke done was to look under the bed. Then they sets down, and the king says:

"Well, what is it? Cut it short, because it's better for us to be down there a-whoopin' up the mournin' than up here givin' 'em a chance to talk us over."

"Well, this is it, King. That doctor lays on my mind. I've got a notion that we better glide out of this before morning, and clip it down the river with what we've got."

The king rips out and says, "What! And not sell out the rest o' the property?"

The duke he grumbled; said the bag of gold was enough, and he didn't want to rob a lot of orphans of *everything* they had.

"Why, how you talk!" says the king. "We shan't rob 'em of nothing but jest this money. The people that *buys* the property is the suff'rers; because as soon 's it's found out 'at we didn't own it—after we've slid—the sale won't be valid. These yer orphans 'll get their house back ag'in."

Well, at last the duke said all right, and they got ready to go downstairs again. The duke says, "I don't think we put that money in a good place."

That cheered me up. I'd begun to think I warn't going to get a hint of no kind of help. The king says, "Why?"

"Because Mary Jane 'll be in mourning; and first you know the nigger that does up the rooms will get an order to box these duds up; and do you reckon a nigger can run across money and not borrow some of it?"

"Your head's level ag'in, Duke," says the king; and he comes a-fumbling under the curtain two or three foot from where I was. I kept mighty still, though quivery; and I wondered what them fellows would say if they catched me. But the king he got the bag before I could think more than half a thought, and he never sus-picioned I was around. They shoved the bag through a rip in the straw tick that was under the featherbed, and said it warn't in no danger of getting stole now.

But I knowed better. I had it out of there before they was half-way downstairs. I groped along up to my cubby, and hid it there till I could get a chance to do better. I judged I better hide it outside of the house somewheres, because if they missed it they would give the house a good ransacking; I knowed that very well. Then

I turned in, with my clothes all on; but I couldn't 'a' gone to sleep if I'd 'a' wanted to.

By and by I heard the king and the duke come up. Still I held on till all sounds had quit; and then I rolled off my pallet and slipped down the ladder and downstairs.

There warn't a sound anywheres. I peeped through the dining-room door, and see the men that was watching the corpse all sound asleep on their chairs. The door was open into the parlor, where the corpse was laying, and there was a candle in both rooms. I see there warn't anybody in the parlor but the remainders of Peter; so I shoved on by; but the front door was locked, and the key wasn't there. Just then I heard somebody coming down the stairs behind me. I run in the parlor and took a swift look, and the only place I see to hide the bag was in the coffin. The lid was shoved along about a foot, showing the dead man's face. I tucked the moneybag in under the lid, just down beyond where his hands was crossed, which made me creep, they was so cold, and then I run back across the room and in behind the door.

The person coming was Mary Jane. She went to the coffin, very soft, and kneeled down and looked in; then she put up her hand-kerchief and begun to cry. Her back was to me so I slid out. Then I slipped up to bed, feeling ruther blue, on accounts of the thing playing out that way after I had took so much trouble about it. Says I, If it could stay where it is, all right; because when we get down the river I could write back to Mary Jane, and she could dig him up again and get it; but that ain't the thing that's going to happen; the money'll be found when they come to screw on the lid, and the king 'll get it again. Of course I *wanted* to slide down and get it out of there, but I dasn't try it. Every minute it was get-ting earlier now, and I might get catched—catched with six thou-sand dollars that nobody hadn't hired me to take care of. I didn't wish to be mixed up in no such business as that.

When I got downstairs in the morning the parlor was shut up, and the watchers was gone. There warn't nobody around but the family and our tribe. I watched their faces to see if anything had been happening, but I couldn't tell.

Towards the middle of the day the undertaker come with his man, and they set the coffin in the middle of the room, and then set all our chairs in rows, and borrowed more from the neighbors till the hall and the parlor was full. I see the coffin lid was the way it was before, but I dasn't go look under it.

Then people begun to flock in, and for a half an hour they filed around slow, and looked down at the dead man's face, and some dropped in a tear, and it was all very still and solemn, only the girls sobbing a little into their handkerchiefs.

When the place was packed full the undertaker he slid around in his black gloves with his softy soothering ways, getting people seated, and making no more sound than a cat. He was the softest, glidingest, stealthiest man I ever see; and there warn't no more smile to him than there is to a ham.

They had borrowed a melodeum—a sick one; and when everything was ready a young woman set down and worked it, and it was pretty skreeky and colicky, but everybody joined in and sung. Then the Reverend Hobson opened up, slow and solemn, and begun to talk; and straight off the most outrageous row busted out in the cellar a body ever heard; it was only one dog, but he made a most powerful racket; the parson he had to stand there, over the coffin, and wait—you couldn't hear yourself think, and nobody didn't seem to know what to do. But pretty soon that long-legged undertaker made a sign to the preacher as much as to say, "Don't you worry—just depend on me." Then he stooped down and begun to glide along the wall, just his shoulders showing over the people's heads. So he glided along, and the powwow and racket getting more and more outrageous all the time; and at last, when he had gone around two sides of the room, he disappears down the cellar. Then in about two seconds we heard a whack, and the dog he finished up with a most amazing howl or two, and then everything was dead still, and the parson begun his solemn talk where he left off. In a minute or two here comes this undertaker's back and shoulders gliding along the wall again; and so he glided and glided around three sides of the room, and then rose up, and shaded his mouth with his hands, and stretched his neck out towards the preacher, over the people's heads, and says, in a kind of coarse whisper, "*He had a rat!*" Then he dropped down and glided along the wall again to his place. You could see it was a great satisfaction to the people, because naturally they wanted to know. A little thing like that don't cost nothing, and it's just the little things that makes a man to be looked up to and liked. There warn't no more popular man in town than what that undertaker was.

Well, the funeral sermon was good, though pison long; but at last the job was through, and the undertaker sneaked up on the coffin with his screwdriver. I was in a sweat then; but he just slid the lid along and screwed it down. So there I was! I didn't know whether the money was in there or not. Says I, S'pose somebody has hogged that bag on the sly? Now how do *I* know whether to write to Mary Jane? S'pose she dug him up and didn't find nothing? Blame it, I says, maybe I'd better not write at all; the thing's awful mixed now; and I wish I'd just let it alone, dad fetch the whole business!

They buried him, and we come back home. After that the king he visited around and made himself friendly to everybody; and he give out the idea that his congregation over in England would be in a sweat about him, so he must hurry and settle up the estate and leave for home. And he said of course him and William would take the girls home with them; and that pleased everybody; because then the girls would be well fixed and amongst their own relations; and it pleased the girls, too—tickled them so they told him to sell out as quick as he wanted to.

Well, blamed if the king didn't bill the house and the niggers and all the property for auction straight off—sale two days after the funeral; but anybody could buy private beforehand if they wanted to.

So the next day after the funeral, along about noontime, the girls' joy got the first jolt. A couple of nigger-traders come along, and the king sold them the niggers reasonable, and away they went, the two sons up the river to Memphis, and their mother down the river to Orleans. I thought them poor girls and them niggers would break their hearts for grief; they cried so it most made me sick to see it. The girls said they hadn't ever dreamed of seeing the family separated or sold away from the town; and I reckon I couldn't 'a' stood seeing them cry if I hadn't knowed the sale warn't no account and the niggers would be back home in a week or two.

Next day was auction day. In the morning the king and the duke come up in the garret and woke me up, and I see by their look that there was trouble. The king says, "Was you in my room night before last?"

"No, your majesty"—which was the way I always called him when nobody warn't around—"I hain't been a-near your room since Mary Jane showed it to you."

The duke says, "Have you seen anybody else go in there?"

I studied awhile and see my chance; then I says, "Well, I see the niggers go in there several times."

Both of them gave a little jump, and looked like they hadn't expected it, and then like they *had*. The duke says, "What, *all* of them?"

"No—leastways, not all at once—that is, I don't think I ever see them all come *out* at once but just one time."

"Hello! When was that?"

"The day we had the funeral. In the morning. It warn't early, because I overslept, and I was just starting down the ladder, and I see them."

"Well, go on, *go* on! What did they do? How'd they act?"

"They didn't do nothing. They tiptoed away; so I seen, easy enough, that they'd shoved in there to do up your majesty's room, or something, and found you warn't up, and so they was hoping to slide out without waking you."

"Great guns, *this* is a go!" says the king; and both of them looked pretty silly. Then the duke he bust into a little raspy chuckle, and says:

"It does beat all how neat the niggers played their hand. They let on to be *sorry* they was going out of this region!"

Says I, kind of timid-like, "Is something gone wrong?"

The king whirls on me. "None o' your business! Keep your

head shet, and mind y'r own affairs." Then he says to the duke, "We got to jest swaller it and say noth'n': mum's the word."

So they went off down the ladder; and I felt dreadful glad I worked it all off onto the niggers, and yet hadn't done the niggers no harm by it.

BY AND BY IT WAS GETTING-UP TIME, so I started for downstairs; but as I come to the girls' room the door was open, and I see Mary Jane setting by her trunk, crying. I felt awful bad to see it; and I went in and says:

"Miss Mary Jane, you can't a-bear to see people in trouble, and *I* can't—most always. Tell me about it."

So she done it. And it was the niggers—I just expected it. She said the beautiful trip to England was about spoiled for her; and then she busted out bitterer than ever, "Oh, dear, dear, to think that that mother and her children ain't *ever* going to see each other any more!"

"But they *will*—and inside two weeks—I *know* it!" says I.

Laws, it was out before I could think! And she throws her arms around my neck and told me to say it *again*, say it *again!* I see I had said too much, and was in a close place. I asked her to let me think a minute, and she set there, very impatient and excited and handsome. So I went to studying it out. I says to myself, I reckon a body that ups and tells the truth when he is in a tight place is taking considerable many resks; but here's a case where I'm blest if it don't look to me like the truth is better and actuly *safer* than a lie. So I says to myself at last, I'm a-going to chance it; and then I says:

"Miss Mary Jane, is there any place out of town a little ways where you could go and stay three or four days?"

"Yes; Mr. Lothrop's. Why?"

"Never mind why yet. If I'll tell you how I know the niggers will see each other again—will you go to Mr. Lothrop's and stay four days?"

"Four days!" she says. "I'll stay a year!"

"All right," I says, "I don't want nothing more than just your word—I'd ruther have it than another man's kiss-the-Bible." She smiled and reddened up very sweet, and I says, "If you don't mind it, I'll shut the door—and bolt it."

Then I come back and set down again, and says, "Don't you holler now. Just set still. I got to tell the truth, and you want to brace up, Miss Mary, because it's going to be hard to take. These uncles of yourn ain't no uncles at all; they're a couple of frauds— regular deadbeats. There, now we're over the worst of it; you can stand the rest middling easy."

It jolted her up like anything, of course; but I was over the shoal water now, so I went right along, and told her every blame thing clear through—and then up she jumps, with her face afire like sunset, and says:

"The brutes! Come, don't waste a *second*—we'll have them tarred and feathered, and flung in the river!"

Says I, "Cert'nly. But do you mean *before* you go to Mr. Lothrop's, or—"

"Oh," she says, "what am I *thinking* about!" she says, and sets down again. "I never thought, I was so stirred up," she says, laying her hand on mine. "Now go on, and I won't do so any more; just you tell me what to do."

"Well," I says, "it's a rough gang, them two frauds, and I got to travel with them a while longer—I'd ruther not tell you why; and if you was to blow on them *I'd* be all right; but there'd be another person that you don't know about who'd be in big trouble. Well, we got to save *him*."

Saying them words put an idea in my head. I see how maybe I could get me and Jim rid of the frauds; get them jailed here, and then leave. But I didn't want to run the raft in the daytime; so I didn't want the plan to begin working till late tonight. I says, "Miss Mary Jane, I'll tell you what we'll do, and you won't have to stay at Mr. Lothrop's so long, nuther. How fur is it?"

"Four miles—right out in the country, back here."

"Well, now you go along out there, and lay low till nine tonight, and then get them to fetch you home again. If you get here before eleven put a candle in this window, and if I don't turn up wait *till* eleven, and *then* if I don't turn up it means I'm gone, and safe.

Then you come out and spread the news around, and get these beats jailed."

"Good," she says, "I'll do it."

"And if it happens that I don't get away, but get took up along with them, you must up and say I told you the whole thing beforehand, and stand by me all you can."

"Stand by you! Indeed I will!" she says, and I see her eyes snap when she said it.

"If I get away I shan't be here," I says, "to prove these rapscallions ain't your uncles, and I couldn't do it if I *was* here. I could swear they was beats and bummers, that's all. Well, there's others can do that better than what I can. I'll tell you how to find them. Gimme a pencil and a piece of paper. There—'Royal Nonesuch, Bricksville.' Put it away and don't lose it. When the court wants to find out something about these two, let them send up to Bricksville and say they've got the men that played the 'Royal Nonesuch,' and ask for some witnesses—why, you'll have that entire town down here before you can hardly wink, Miss Mary. They'll come a-biling, too."

I judged we had got everything fixed now. So I says, "Just let the auction go along, and don't worry. Nobody don't have to pay for the things they buy till a whole day after the auction on accounts of the short notice, and them two frauds ain't going out of this till they get that money. And the way we've fixed it the sale ain't going to count; it's just like the way it was with the niggers—it warn't no sale, and the niggers will be back before long."

"Well," she says, "I'll run down to breakfast now, and then I'll start straight for Mr. Lothrop's."

"'Deed, *that* ain't the ticket, Miss Mary Jane," I says, "by no manner of means. Go *before* breakfast."

"Why?"

"What did you reckon I wanted you to go at all for, Miss Mary? It's because there ain't no better book than what your face is. A body can set down and read it off like coarse print. Do you reckon you can go and face your uncles when they come to kiss you good-morning, and never—"

"There, there, don't! Yes, I'll go before breakfast. And leave my sisters with them?"

"Yes; never mind about them. They've got to stand it yet awhile. They might suspicion something if all of you was to go. No, you go right along, Miss Mary Jane, and I'll fix it with them and say you've went away for a few hours." Then I says, "There's one more thing—the bag of money."

"Well, they've got that; and it makes me feel pretty silly to think *how* they got it."

"No, you're out, there. They hain't got it, because I stole it from them! I stole it to give to you; and I know where I hid it, but I'm afraid it ain't there no more. I'm just as sorry as I can be, Miss Mary Jane, but I done the best I could; I did honest. And I'd ruther not *tell* you where I put it; but I'll write it for you on a piece of paper, and you can read it along the road to Mr. Lothrop's. Do you reckon that'll do?"

"Oh, yes."

So I wrote: "I put it in the coffin. It was in there when you was crying there, way in the night. I was behind the door, and I was mighty sorry for you, Miss Mary Jane."

It made my eyes water to remember her crying there; and when I folded it up and give it to her I see the water come into her eyes, too; and she shook my hand, hard, and says:

"*Good*-by. I'm going to do everything just as you've told me; and if I don't ever see you again, I shan't ever forget you, and I'll *pray* for you, too!" And she was gone.

Pray for me! I reckoned if she knowed me she'd take a job that was more nearer her size. But I bet she done it, just the same—she was just that kind. In my opinion she had more sand in her than any girl I ever see. I hain't ever seen her since that time that I see her go out of that door; but I reckon I've thought of her a million times, and of her saying she would pray for me; and if ever I'd 'a' thought it would do any good for me to pray for *her*, blamed if I wouldn't 'a' done it or bust.

Well, Mary Jane she lit out the back way, I reckon; because nobody see her go. When I struck Susan and the harelip, I says,

"What's the name of them people on t'other side of the river that you all goes to see sometimes?"

They says, "There's several; but it's the Proctors, mainly."

"That's the name," I says. "Well, Miss Mary Jane she told me to tell you she's gone over there in a dreadful hurry—one of them's sick."

"Sakes alive, I hope it ain't *Hanner?*"

"I'm sorry to say it," I says, "but Hanner's the very one. They set up with her all night, Miss Mary Jane said."

"Only think of that, now! What's the matter with her?"

I couldn't think of anything reasonable, right off, so I says, "Mumps."

"Mumps, your granny! They don't set up with people that's got mumps."

"These mumps is different. It's a new kind, Miss Mary Jane said, because it's all mixed up with measles, and whooping cough, and consumption, and janders, and brain fever, and I don't know what all."

"Well, what in the nation do they call it the *mumps* for?"

"Why, because it *is* the mumps. That's what it starts with."

"Well, ther' ain't no sense in it," says the harelip. "A body might stump his toe, and take pison, and fall down the well, and break his neck, and bust his brains out, and somebody come along and ask what killed him, and some numskull up and say, 'Why, he stumped his *toe*.' Would ther' be any sense in that? *No.* And ther' ain't no sense in *this*, nuther. It's awful, *I* think. I'll go to Uncle Harvey and—"

"Oh, yes," I says. "Of *course*. I wouldn't lose no time."

"Well, why wouldn't you?" says Susan.

"Just look a minute. Hain't your uncles obleeged to get along home to England as fast as they can? And do you reckon they'd be mean enough to go off and leave you to go all that journey by yourselves? *You* know they'll wait for you. So fur, so good. Your Uncle Harvey's a preacher, ain't he? Very well, then; is a *preacher* going to deceive a *steamboat clerk* so as to get them to let Miss Mary Jane go aboard? *You* know he ain't. What *will* he do, then? Why, he'll say, 'It's a great pity, but my church matters has got to get along the best way they can; for my niece has been exposed to the dreadful pluribus-unum mumps, and so it's my bounden duty to set here and wait the three months it takes to show on her if she's got it.' But never mind, if you think it's best to tell your Uncle Harvey—"

"Shucks, and stay fooling around here when we could all be having good times in England? Why, you talk like a muggins. Ther' ain't no way but just to not tell anybody at all."

"Well, maybe you're right—yes, I judge you are right."

"But I reckon we ought to tell Uncle Harvey she's gone out awhile, anyway, so he won't be uneasy about her?"

"Yes, Miss Mary Jane she wanted you to do that. She says, 'Tell them to give Uncle Harvey and William my love, and say I've run over to see Mr—Mr.—what is the name of that rich family over the river?"

"Why, you must mean the Apthorps, ain't it?"

"Of course. Yes, she said, say she has run over for to ask the Apthorps to be sure and come to the auction and buy this house; and she's going to stick to them till they say they'll come, and then, if she ain't too tired, she's coming home; and if she is, she'll be home in the morning."

"All right," they said, and cleared out to lay for their uncles and tell them the message.

Everything was all right now. The girls wouldn't say nothing because they wanted to go to England; and the king and the duke would ruther Mary Jane was off working for the auction than around in reach of Doctor Robinson. I felt good; I judged I had done it pretty neat—I reckoned Tom Sawyer couldn't 'a' done it no neater himself.

Well, they held the auction in the public square in the afternoon, and the old man he was up there longside of the auctioneer, and chipping in a little Scripture now and then, and the duke was around goo-gooing and just spreading himself generly. By and by everything was sold—everything but a little old lot in the grave-yard. So they was working that off when a steamboat landed, and in about two minutes up comes a crowd a-whooping and laughing, and singing out:

"*Here's* your opposition line! Here's two sets o' heirs to old Peter Wilks—you pays your money and you takes your choice!"

THEY WAS FETCHING A NICE-LOOKING old gentleman along, and a nice-looking younger one, with his right arm in a sling. I reckoned the duke and the king'd at least turn pale. But no. The duke he never let on he suspicioned what was up, but just went on a goo-gooing around; and as for the king, he just gazed and gazed down sorrowful on them newcomers like it give him the stomach ache in his very heart to think there could be such frauds and rascals in the world. As for that old gentleman that had just come, he looked all puzzled to death. Pretty soon he begun to speak, and I see straight off he pronounced *like* an Englishman. I can't give his words nor imitate him; but he turned to the crowd, and says, about like this:

"This is a surprise to me, and I'll acknowledge, candid, I ain't well fixed to meet it; for my brother and me has had misfortunes; he's broke his arm and our baggage got put off at a town above here by mistake. I am Peter Wilks's brother Harvey, and this is his brother William, which can't hear nor speak—and can't even make signs to amount to much, now't he's only got one hand to work with. We are who we say we are; and in a day or two, when I get the baggage, I can prove it. But up till then I won't say no more, but go to the hotel and wait."

So him and the new dummy started off; and the king he laughs, and blethers out, "Broke his arm—*very* convenient, *ain't* it, for a fraud that's got to make signs! Lost their baggage! That's *mighty* ingenious—under the *circumstances!*"

So he laughed again; and so did everybody else, except maybe half a dozen. One of these was that doctor; another one was a sharp-looking gentleman that had just come off the steamboat—it was Levi Bell, the lawyer that was gone up to Louisville; and another one was a big rough husky. When the king got done this husky up and says:

"Say, looky here; if you are Harvey Wilks, when'd you come to this town?"

"The day before the funeral, friend, in the afternoon," says the king.

"How'd you come?"

"I come down on the *Susan Powell* from Cincinnati."

"Well, then, how'd you come to be up at the Pint in the *mornin'*— in a canoe?"

"I warn't up at the Pint in the mornin'."

"It's a lie."

Several of them jumped for him and begged him not to talk that way to an old man and a preacher.

"Preacher be hanged, he's a fraud. He was up at the Pint that mornin'. I live up there, don't I? Well, I *see* him there. He comes in a canoe, along with Tim Collins and a boy."

The doctor he says, "Would you know the boy again, Hines?"

"I reckon I would. Why, yonder he is, now!"

It was me he pointed at. The doctor says:

"Neighbors, I don't know whether the new couple is frauds or not, but if *these* two ain't frauds, I am an idiot. I think it's our duty to see that they don't get away from here till we've looked into this thing. Come along, Hines; come along, the rest of you. We'll take these fellows to the tavern and affront them with t'other couple, and I reckon we'll find out *something* before we get through."

It was nuts for the crowd, so we all started. It was about sundown. The doctor he led me by the hand, and was plenty kind enough, but he never *let go* my hand.

We all got in a big room in the hotel, and lit up some candles, and fetched in the new couple.

Then they sailed in on a general investigation. It *was* the worst mixed-up thing you ever see. They made the king tell his yarn, and they made the old gentleman tell his'n; and by and by they had me up to tell what I knowed. The king he give me a left-handed look, out of the corner of his eye, and so I knowed enough to talk on the right side.

I begun to tell about Sheffield and how we lived there, and all about the English Wilkses, and so on; but I didn't get fur till the doctor began to laugh; and Levi Bell, the lawyer, says:

"Set down, my boy. I reckon you ain't used to lying; what you want is practice. You do it pretty awkward."

I didn't care nothing for the compliment, but I was glad to be let off, anyway.

Well, what do you think? That mule-headed old fool the king wouldn't give in *then!* He went warbling right along till he was actuly beginning to believe what he was saying *himself;* but pretty soon the new gentleman broke in, and says:

"I've thought of something. Is there anybody here that helped to lay out my br—helped to lay out the late Peter Wilks for burying?"

"Yes," says somebody, "me and Ab Turner done it. We're both here."

Then the old man turns towards the king, and says, "Perhaps this gentleman can tell me what was tattooed on his breast?"

It took the king sudden, and it was mighty still in there, and everybody bending fowards and gazing at him. Says I to myself, *Now* he'll throw up the sponge. Well, did he? A body can't hardly believe it, but he didn't. He begun to smile, and says, "Mf! It's a *very* tough question, *ain't* it! *Yes*, sir, I k'n tell you what's tattooed on his breast. It's jest a small, thin, blue arrow; and if you don't look clost, you can't see it. *Now* what do you say—hey?"

Well, *I* never see anything like that old blister for clean out-and-out cheek.

The new old gentleman turns brisk towards Ab Turner and his pard, and his eye lights up like he judged he'd got the king *this* time, and says, "There—you've heard what he said! Was there any such mark on Peter Wilks's breast?"

Both of them says, "We didn't see no such mark."

"Good!" says the old gentleman. "Now, what you *did* see on his breast was a small dim p, and a w, and a dash between. Ain't that what you saw?"

Both of them spoke again, and says, "No, we *didn't*. We never seen any marks at all."

Well, everybody *was* in a state of mind now, and they sings out: "The whole *bilin'* of 'm 's frauds! Le's duck 'em! Le's ride 'em on a rail!" And everybody was whooping at once. But the lawyer he jumps up and yells, "Gentlemen—PLEASE! There's one way yet— let's go dig up the corpse and look."

That took them. "Hooray!" they all shouted. "And if we don't find them marks we'll lynch the whole gang!"

I *was* scared now, I tell you. But there warn't no getting away. They gripped us all, me and the four men, and marched us right along for the graveyard, a mile and a half down the river, and the whole town at our heels, for we made noise enough. It was now about nine in the evening. As we went by our house I wished I hadn't sent Mary Jane out of town; because now if I could tip her the wink she'd save me.

Well, we swarmed along down the river road; and to make it more scary the sky was darking up, and the lightning beginning to wink and flitter. This was the most awful trouble I ever was in; and I was kinder stunned; everything was going so different from what I had allowed for; stead of being fixed so I could have Mary Jane to save me when the close fit come, here was nothing in the world betwixt me and sudden death but just them tattoo marks. If they didn't find them—

I couldn't bear to think about it; and yet, somehow, I couldn't think about nothing else. It got darker and darker, and it was a beautiful time to give the crowd the slip; but that big husky had me by the wrist—Hines—and a body might as well try to give Goliar the slip.

When they got there they swarmed into the graveyard and washed over it like an overflow. And when they got to the grave they found they had about a hundred shovels, but nobody hadn't thought to fetch a lantern. But they sailed into digging anyway by the flicker of the lightning, and sent a man to the nearest house, a half a mile off, to borrow one.

So they dug and dug like everything; and it got awful dark, and the rain started, and the wind swished and swushed, and the lightning come brisker and brisker; but them people never took no notice of it. At last they got out the coffin and begun to unscrew the lid, and then such another crowding and shoving as there was, to scrouge in and get a sight; and in the dark, that way, it was awful. Hines he hurt my wrist dreadful pulling and tugging. Then all of a sudden the lightning let go a perfect sluice of white glare, and somebody sings out:

"By the living jingo, here's the bag of gold on his breast!"

Hines let out a whoop, like everybody else, and dropped my wrist to bust in and get a look, and the way I lit out and shinned for the road in the dark there ain't nobody can tell.

I had the road all to myself in the storm, and I fairly flew. When I struck the town I see there warn't nobody out, so I never hunted for no back streets, but humped in straight through the main one; and when I begun to get towards our house I aimed my eye at it. No light there; but at last, just as I was sailing by, *flash* comes the light in Mary Jane's window! My heart swelled up sudden, like to bust. She *was* the best girl I ever see, and had the most sand.

The minute I was above the town I begun to look for a boat to borrow, and the first time the lightning showed me one that wasn't chained I snatched it and shoved. It was a canoe and warn't fastened with nothing but a rope. The towhead was a rattling big distance off, but I didn't lose no time. When I struck the raft at last I sprung aboard and sung out:

"Set her loose, Jim! Glory be to goodness, we're shut of them!"

Jim was a-coming for me with both arms spread, he was so full of joy; but when I glimpsed him in the lightning my heart shot up in my mouth and I went overboard backwards; for I forgot he was old King Lear and a drownded A-rab all in one; and it most scared the livers and lights out of me. But Jim fished me out, and was going to hug me and bless me, and so on, he was so glad I was back and we was shut of the king and the duke, but I says:

"Not now; have it for breakfast! Cut loose!"

So in two seconds away we went a-sliding down the river, and it *did* seem so good to be free again and all by ourselves. I had to skip around and jump up and crack my heels a few times—but about the third crack I noticed a sound, and held my breath and waited; and sure enough, when the next flash busted out, here they come—a-laying to their oars and making their skiff hum! It was the king and the duke.

So I wilted right down onto the planks then, and give up; and it was all I could do to keep from crying.

CHAPTER XII

WHEN THEY GOT ABOARD the king shook me by the collar, and says, "Tryin' to give us the slip, was ye, you pup!"

I says, "No, your majesty, we warn't—*please* don't, your majesty!"

"Quick, then, and tell us what *was* your idea, or I'll shake the insides out o' you."

"Honest, I'll tell you everything just as it happened, your majesty. The man that had a-holt of me was very good to me, and kept saying he had a boy as big as me that died, and he was sorry to see a boy in such a fix; and when they was all took by surprise by finding the gold, he lets go of me and whispers, 'Heel it now, or they'll hang ye, sure!' and I lit out. It didn't seem no good for *me* to stay—so I never stopped running till I found the canoe; and when I got here I told Jim to hurry, or they'd hang me yet, and said I was afeard you and the duke wasn't alive now, and I was awful sorry, and so was Jim; you may ask Jim if I warn't."

So the king let go of me, and begun to cuss that town. But the duke says:

"You better a blame' sight give *yourself* a good cussing. You hain't done a thing from the start that had any sense in it, except coming out so cool and cheeky with that imaginary blue-arrow mark. That *was* bright; that trick took 'em to the graveyard, and the gold done us a still bigger kindness; for if the excited fools hadn't let go all holts and made that rush to get a look we'd 'a' slept in our cravats tonight—cravats warranted to *wear*, too."

They was still a minute—thinking; then the king says, kind of absentminded-like, "Mf! And we reckoned the *niggers* stole it!"

That made me squirm!

"Yes," says the duke, kinder slow and sarcastic, "*we* did."

After about a half a minute the king drawls out, "Leastways, *I* did."

The duke says, the same way, "On the contrary, *I* did."

The king kind of ruffles up and says, "Looky here, Bilgewater, what'r you referrin' to?"

The duke bristles up now, and says, "Oh, let *up* on this nonsense; do you take me for a blame' fool? Don't you reckon *I* know who hid that money in that coffin?"

"*Yes*, sir! I know you do, because you done it yourself!"

"It's a lie!"—and the duke went for him. The king sings out, "Take y'r hands off—leggo my throat!"

The duke says, "Well, you just own up, first, that you *did* hide that money there, intending to give me the slip one of these days, and come back and dig it up."

"Wait, jest a minute, Duke—answer me this one question, honest and fair; if you didn't put the money there, say it, and I'll b'lieve you, and take back everything I said."

"You old scoundrel, I didn't, and you know I didn't."

"Well, then, I b'lieve you. But as for me, I never done it either, Duke! I won't say I warn't *goin'* to do it, because I *was*; but you— I mean somebody—got in ahead o' me."

"It's a lie! You done it, and you got to *say* you done it, or—"

The king began to gurgle, and then he gasps out, "'Nough! *I own up!*"

I was very glad to hear him say that; it made me feel much more easier. So the duke took his hands off and says, "If you ever deny it again I'll drown you. And now dry up! I don't want to hear no more *out* of you!"

The king, still a-snuffling, sneaked into the wigwam and took to his bottle for comfort. Before long the duke tackled *his* bottle, too; and so in about a half an hour they was as thick as thieves again. They both got powerful mellow, and the tighter they got the lovinger they got, and went off a-snoring in each other's arms. Then Jim and I had a long gabble, and I told him everything.

WE DASN'T STOP AGAIN AT ANY TOWN for days and days; kept right along down the river. We was down South in the warm weather now, and we begun to come to trees with Spanish moss on them. So now the frauds reckoned they was out of danger, and they begun to work the villages again.

First they done a lecture on temperance; but they didn't make enough for them both to get drunk on. They tackled missionary-ing, and doctoring, and telling fortunes; but they couldn't seem to have no luck. So at last they got just about dead broke, and laid around the raft as she floated along, thinking and thinking, by the half a day at a time, and dreadful blue and desperate.

At last they took a change and begun to lay their heads together in the wigwam and talk low and confidential. Jim and me got uneasy; we judged they was studying up some kind of worse devil-try than ever, and was going to break into somebody's house or store, or was going into the counterfeit-money business, or some-thing. So then we was pretty scared, and made up an agreement that if we ever got the least chance we would give them the cold shake and clear out and leave them behind.

Well, early one morning we hid the raft in a good, safe place about two mile below a little shabby village named Pikesville, and the king he told us all to stay hid whilst he went up to town and smelt around to see if anybody had got any wind of the "Royal Nonesuch" there yet. (House to rob, you *mean*, says I to myself.) And he said if he warn't back by midday the duke and me would know it was all right, and we was to come along.

So we stayed where we was. The duke he fretted and sweated, and was in a mighty sour way. Something was a-brewing, sure. I was glad when midday come and no king; we could have a change, anyway—and maybe a chance for *the* chance. So me and the duke went up to the village, and hunted around for the king, and by and by we found him in a little low doggery, very tight, and a lot of loafers bullyragging him for sport. The duke he begun to abuse him for an old fool, and the king begun to sass back, and the minute they was fairly at it I lit out and spun down the river road like a deer, for I see our chance; and I made up my mind that it would be a long day before they ever see me and Jim again. I got there all out of breath but loaded up with joy, and sung out:

"Set her loose, Jim; we're all right now!"

But there warn't no answer, and nobody come out of the wigwam. Jim was gone! I run this way and that in the woods, whooping and screeching; but it warn't no use—old Jim was gone. Then I set down and cried; I couldn't help it. But I couldn't set still long. Pretty soon I went out on the road and I run across a boy walking, and asked him if he'd seen a strange nigger dressed so and so, and he says, "Yes."

"Whereabouts?" says I.

"Down to Phelps's place, two mile below here. He's a runaway nigger, and they've got him. Was you looking for him?"

"You bet I ain't! I run across him in the woods an hour or two ago, and he said if I hollered he'd cut my livers out—and told me to stay where I was. Been there ever since; afeard to come out."

"Well," he says, "they've got him. He run off f'm down South, som'ers. There's two hundred dollars' reward on him. I see the handbill. It tells all about him, to a dot, and tells the plantation he's frum, below New*rleans*."

"And *I* could 'a' had it if I'd been big enough! Who nailed him?"

"It was an old fellow—a stranger—and he sold out his chance in him for forty dollars, becuz he's got to go up the river and can't wait. Think o' that, now! You bet *I'd* wait. Say, gimme a chaw tobacker, won't ye?"

I didn't have none, so he left. I went to the raft, and set down to think. I thought till I wore my head sore, but I couldn't see no way out of the trouble. After all this long journey, and after all we'd done for them scoundrels, here it was all come to nothing, everything all busted up and ruined, because they could have the heart to serve Jim such a trick as that, and make him a slave again all his life, for forty dirty dollars.

Once I said to myself it would be a thousand times better for Jim to be a slave at home where his family was as long as he'd *got* to be a slave, and so I'd better write a letter to tell Miss Watson where he was. But I soon give up that notion for two things: she'd be mad and disgusted at his ungratefulness for leaving her, and so she'd sell him straight down the river again; and if she didn't, everybody naturally despises an ungrateful nigger, and they'd make Jim feel it all the time. And then think of *me!* It would get all around that Huck Finn helped a nigger to get his freedom; and if I was ever to see anybody from that town again I'd be ready to lick his boots for shame.

That's just the way: a person does a low-down thing, and thinks as long as he can hide, it ain't no disgrace. That was my fix exactly. The more I studied about this the more my conscience went to grinding me, and the more wicked and low-down I got to feeling.

At last it hit me all of a sudden that here was the plain hand of Providence slapping me in the face and letting me know my wickedness in stealing a poor old woman's nigger that hadn't ever done me no harm, and letting me know I was being watched all the time from up there in heaven. Then I most dropped in my tracks, I was so scared. I thought about the everlasting fire, and it made me shiver, and I about made up my mind to pray, and see if I couldn't try to quit being the kind of a boy I was and be better. So I kneeled down. But the words wouldn't come. Why wouldn't they? It warn't no use to try and hide it from Him. Nor from *me*, neither. I knowed very well why they wouldn't come. It was because my heart warn't right; it was because I was playing double. I was letting *on* to give up sin, but away inside of me I was holding on to the biggest one of all. I was trying to make my mouth *say* I would go and write to that nigger's owner and tell where he was; but deep down in me I knowed it was a lie, and He knowed it. You can't pray a lie—I found that out.

So I was full of trouble, full as I could be. At last I had an idea; and I says, I'll go and write the letter—and *then* see if I can pray. Why, it was astonishing, the way I felt as light as a feather right off. So I got a piece of paper and a pencil, and set down and wrote:

Miss Watson, your runaway nigger Jim is down here two mile below Pikesville, and Mr. Phelps has got him.

Huck Finn

I felt good and all washed clean of sin for the first time in my life, and I knowed I could pray now. But I didn't do it straight off, but laid the paper down and set there thinking—thinking how good it was all this happened so, and how near I come to being lost and going to hell. And went on thinking. And got to thinking over our trip down the river; and I see Jim before me all the time: in the day and in the nighttime, sometimes moonlight, sometimes storms, and we a-floating along, talking and singing and laughing. But somehow I couldn't seem to strike no places to harden me against him, but only the other kind. I'd see him standing my watch on top of his'n, so I could go on sleeping; and see him how glad he was when I come back out of the fog; and suchlike times; and how he would always call me honey, and do everything he could think of for me; and at last I struck the time I saved him by telling the men we had smallpox aboard, and he said I was the best friend old Jim ever had in the world, and the *only* one he's got now; and then I happened to look around and see that paper.

I took it up in my hand. It was a close place. I was a-trembling, because I'd got to decide, forever, betwixt two things, and I knowed it. I sort of held my breath, and then says to myself, All right, then, I'll *go* to hell—and tore it up.

It was awful thoughts and awful words, but they was said. And I let them stay said. I shoved the whole thing out of my mind, and thought I would take up wickedness again, which was in my line, being brung up to it, and the other warn't. And for a starter I would go to work and steal Jim out of slavery again.

Then I set to thinking over how to get at it, and at last fixed up a plan that suited me. As soon as it was fairly dark I crept out with my raft and went for a woody island that was down the river a piece, and hid the raft there, and then turned in. I slept the night through, and got up before it was light, and put on some clothes, and tied up the others in a bundle, and took the canoe and cleared for shore. I landed below where I judged was Phelps's place, and hid my bundle in the woods, and then filled up the canoe with rocks and sunk her where I could find her again, about a quarter of a mile below a little steam sawmill that was on the bank.

Then I struck up the road, and when I passed the mill I see a sign on it, PHELPS'S SAWMILL, and I see some farmhouses, two or three hundred yards further along. I didn't want to see nobody there just yet, so I just took a look and shoved along for town. Well, the very first man I see when I got there was the duke—sticking up a bill for the "Royal Nonesuch" three-night performance. They had the cheek, them frauds! I was right on him before I could shirk. He looked astonished, and says:

"Hel-*lo!* Where'd *you* come from?" Then he says, kind of eager, "Where's the raft—got her in a good place?"

I says, "Why, that's just what I was going to ask your grace."

Then he didn't look so joyful, and says, "What was your idea for asking *me?*"

"Well," I says, "when I see the king in that doggery yesterday I says to myself, We can't get him home for hours; so I went a-loafing around town to put in the time. A man up and offered me ten cents to help him pull a skiff over the river to fetch a sheep, and so I went along; but when we was dragging the sheep to the boat it got loose and run. We didn't have no dog, and so we had to chase him all over, and we never got him till dark; then we fetched him over, and I started for the raft. When I got there and see it was gone, I says to myself, They've got into trouble and had to leave; and they've took my nigger, and now I'm in a strange country, and ain't got no property no more, nor nothing; so I set down and cried. I slept in the woods all night. But what *did* become of the raft, then? And Jim—poor Jim!"

"Blamed if *I know*—that is, what's become of the raft. That old fool had made a trade and got forty dollars, and when we found him in the doggery the loafers had matched half-dollars with him and got every cent but what he'd spent on whiskey; and when I got him home late last night and found the raft gone, we said, 'That little rascal has stole our raft and shook us, and run off down the river.'"

"I wouldn't shake my *nigger*, would I—the only nigger I had in the world, and the only property?"

"We never thought of that. Fact is, I reckon we'd come to consider him *our* nigger; yes, we did consider him so—goodness knows we had trouble enough for him. And now that old fool the king has sold him, and never divided with me, and the money's gone."

"*Sold* him?" I says, and begun to cry. "Why, he was *my* nigger! Where is he? I want my nigger!"

"Well, you can't *get* your nigger, that's all—so dry up your blubbering. Looky here—" He stopped, and I never see the duke look so ugly out of his eyes before. "Blamed if I think I trust you. Do you think *you'd* venture to blow on us? Why, if you *was* to blow on us—"

I went on a-whimpering, and says, "I don't want to blow on nobody; and I ain't got no time to blow, nohow; I got to turn out and find my nigger."

He looked kinder bothered, and stood there thinking. At last he says, "I'll tell you something. We got to be here three days. If you'll promise you won't blow, and won't let the nigger blow, I'll tell you where to find him."

So I promised, and he says, "A farmer by the name of Silas Ph—" and then he stopped. You see, he started to tell me the truth; but when he stopped I reckoned he was changing his mind. And so he was. Soon he says, "The man that bought him is named Foster—Abram G. Foster—and he lives forty mile back in the country, on the road to Lafayette."

"All right," I says, "I can walk it in three days. And I'll start this very afternoon."

"No you won't, you'll start *now;* and don't you do any gabbling by the way. Just move right along, and then you won't get into trouble with *us*, d'ye hear?"

That was the order I wanted.

"So clear out," he says; "and maybe you can get Mr. Foster to believe that Jim *is* your nigger—some idiots don't require documents. Tell him anything you want to; but mind you don't work your jaw any *between* here and there."

So I left, and struck for the back country. After a mile I stopped; then I doubled back through the woods towards Phelps's. I reckoned I better start in on my plan straight off without fooling around, because I wanted to stop Jim's mouth till these fellows could get away. I'd seen all I wanted to of them, and wanted to get entirely shut of them.

WHEN I GOT TO PHELPS'S it was still and Sunday-like, and hot and sunshiny; the hands was gone to the fields; and there was them kind of faint dronings of flies in the air that makes it seem so lonesome and like everybody's dead and gone. It was one of these little one-horse cotton plantations, and they all look alike. A rail fence round a two-acre yard, with a stile; some sickly grass patches in the big yard, but mostly it was bare and smooth, like an old hat with the nap rubbed off; big loghouse for the white folks—hewed logs with the chinks stopped up with mud or mortar, and these mud stripes whitewashed; log kitchen, with a roofed passage joining it to the house; log smokehouse back of the kitchen; three little log nigger cabins t'other side of the smokehouse; outbuildings down a piece; hounds asleep round about in the sun; three shade trees away off in a corner; outside of the fence a garden and a watermelon patch; then the cotton fields begins, and after the fields the woods.

I clumb over the stile and started for the kitchen, not fixing up any particular plan, but just trusting to Providence to put the right words in my mouth when the time come.

When I got halfway, first one hound and then another got up and went for me, and of course I stopped and faced them. Such a powwow as they made! In a quarter of a minute I was a kind of hub of a wheel—spokes made out of dogs—circle of fifteen of them packed together around me a-barking and howling; and more a-coming; you could see them sailing over fences and around corners from everywheres.

A nigger woman come tearing out of the kitchen with a rolling pin in her hand, singing out, "Begone! *You* Tige! Spot! Begone!" And she fetched first one and then another of them a clip and sent them howling, and then the rest followed. Behind the woman comes a little nigger girl and two little nigger boys, and they hung on to their mother's gown, and peeped out, bashful. And here comes the white woman running from the house, about forty-five or fifty year old; and behind her comes her little white children, acting the same way as the little niggers. She was smiling all over so she could hardly stand—and says:

"It's *you* at last—*ain't* it?"

I out with a "Yes'm" before I thought.

She grabbed me and hugged me tight; and the tears come in her eyes; and she kept saying, "You don't look as much like your mother as I reckoned you would; but law sakes, I don't care, I'm *so* glad to see you! Children, it's your cousin Tom! Tell him howdy. And Lize, hurry up and get him a hot breakfast—or did you get breakfast on the boat?"

I said I had got it on the boat. So then she started for the house, leading me by the hand, and the children tagging after. When we got there she set me down in a chair, and says, "Now I can have a *good* look at you! We been expecting you a couple of days. What kep' you—boat get aground?"

"Yes'm—she—"

"Don't say yes'm—say Aunt Sally. Where'd she get aground?"

I didn't rightly know what to say, because I didn't know whether the boat would be coming up the river or down. I see I'd got to invent a bar or forget the name of one we got aground on—or—Now I struck an idea.

"It warn't the grounding. We blowed out a cylinder head."

"Good gracious! Anybody hurt?"

"No'm."

"Well, it's lucky; because sometimes people do get hurt. Two years ago your Uncle Silas was coming up from Newrleans on the old *Lally Rook*, and she blowed out a cylinder head and crippled a man. And I think he died afterwards. He was a Baptist. Your uncle's been up to the town every day to fetch you. And he's gone again, not more'n an hour ago. You must 'a' met him on the road, didn't you? Oldish man, with a—"

"No, I didn't see nobody, Aunt Sally. The boat landed just at daylight, and I left my baggage on the wharf boat and went looking around, to put in the time and not get here too soon, and so I come down the back way."

"How'd you get your breakfast so early on the boat?"

It was kinder thin ice, but I says, "The captain see me standing around, and told me I better have something to eat before I went ashore; so he took me in to the officers' lunch, and give me all I wanted."

I was getting so uneasy I couldn't listen good. I had my mind on the children; I wanted to get them to one side and pump them to find out who I was. But I couldn't get no show, and pretty soon Mrs. Phelps made the cold chills streak all down my back, because she says:

"But here we're a-running on this way, and you hain't told me a word about Sis, nor any of them. Now just tell me *everything*—how they are, and what they're doing, and every last thing you can think of."

Well, I see I was up a stump now—up it good. So I says to myself, Here's another place where I got to resk the truth. I opened my mouth to begin; but she grabbed me and hustled me in behind the bed, and says:

"Here he comes! Stick your head down; don't let on you're here. I'll play a joke on him. Children, don't say a word."

I see I was in a fix now. But there warn't nothing to do but just hold still, and try and be ready when the lightning struck.

I had just one little glimpse of the old gentleman when he come in; then the bed hid him. Mrs. Phelps she jumps for him, and says, "Has he come?"

"No," says her husband.

"Good-*ness* gracious!" she says. "What in the world *can* have become of him?"

"I can't imagine," says the old gentleman, "and I must say it makes me dreadful uneasy."

"Uneasy!" she says. "I'm ready to go distracted! He *must* 'a' come; and you've missed him along the road. I *couldn't* miss him along the road—*you* know that. I don't know what in the world to make of it, and I don't mind

135

acknowledging 't I'm right down scared. Sally, something's happened to the boat, sure!"

"Why, Silas! Look! Up the road! Ain't that somebody coming?"

He sprung to the window, and at that Mrs. Phelps stooped down quick at the foot of the bed and give me a pull, and out I come; and when he turned back from the window there she stood, a-beaming and a-smiling, and I standing meek and sweaty alongside. The old gentleman stared, and says:

"Why, who's that?"

"Who do you reckon 'tis?"

"I hain't no idea. Who *is* it?"

"It's *Tom Sawyer!*"

By jings, I most slumped through the floor! The old man grabbed me by the hand and shook; and the woman danced around and laughed and cried; and then how they both did fire off questions about Sid, and Aunt Polly, and the rest of the tribe! But if they was joyful, it warn't nothing to what I was; for it was like being born again, I was so glad to find out who I was.

Well, they froze to me for two hours; and at last I had told them more about the Sawyer family than ever happened to any six Sawyer families. Now I was feeling pretty comfortable all down one side and pretty uncomfortable all up the other; because by and by I hear a steamboat coughing along down the river; and then I says to myself, S'pose Tom Sawyer comes down on that boat? And s'pose he steps on in here and sings out my name before I can throw him a wink to keep quiet?

Well, I couldn't *have* it that way. I must go up the road and way-lay him. So I told the folks I reckoned I would go to the town and fetch my baggage. The old gentleman was for going along with me, but I said no, I could drive the horse, and I'd ruther he wouldn't take no trouble.

So I started for town in the wagon, and when I was halfway I see a wagon coming, and sure enough it was Tom Sawyer. I says, "Hold on!" and he stopped alongside, and his mouth opened up like a trunk, and stayed so; and he swallowed two or three times like a person that's got a dry throat, and then says:

"I hain't ever done you no harm. You know that. So, then, what you want to come back and ha'nt *me* for?"

I says, "I hain't come back—I hain't been *gone*."

When he heard my voice it righted him up some, but he warn't quite satisfied yet. He says, "Honest injun, you ain't a ghost?"

"Honest injun, I ain't," I says.

"Well—I—I— Looky here, warn't you ever murdered?"

"No. I warn't ever murdered—I played it on them. Come here and feel of me if you don't believe me."

So he done it; and it satisfied him; and he was that glad to see me again he didn't know what to do. And he wanted to know all about it right off, because it was a grand adventure, and mysterious. But I said, leave it alone till by and by; and I told his driver to wait, and we drove off a little piece, and I told him the kind of a fix I was in, and what did he reckon we better do? He thought and thought, and pretty soon he says:

"It's all right; I've got it. Take my trunk in your wagon, and let on it's yourn; and you turn back and fool along slow, so as to get to the house about the time you ought to; and I'll go towards town a piece, and take a fresh start, and get there a quarter or a half an hour after you; and you needn't let on to know me at first."

"All right; but wait a minute," I says. "There's one more thing—a thing that *nobody* don't know but me. And that is, there's a nigger here that I'm a-trying to steal, and his name is *Jim*—old Miss Watson's Jim."

He says, "What! Why, Jim is—" Then he stopped and went to studying.

I says, "*I* know what you'll say. You'll say it's dirty, low-down business; but what if it is? *I'm* low-down, and I'm a-going to steal him, and I want you to keep mum and not let on. Will you?"

His eye lit up, and he says, "I'll *help* you steal him!"

Well, I let go all holts then, like I was shot. It was the most astonishing speech I ever heard. I couldn't believe it. Tom Sawyer a *nigger-stealer!*

"Oh, shucks!" I says. "You're joking."

"I ain't joking, either."

"Well, then," I says, "joking or no joking, if you hear anything said about a runaway nigger, don't forget to remember that you and I don't know nothing about him."

Then he put his trunk in my wagon, and he drove off his way and I drove mine. I got home, and then in about half an hour Tom's wagon drove up to the front stile. Aunt Sally she see it through the window, and says:

"Why, there's somebody come! I do believe it's a stranger. Jimmy," (that's one of the children) "run and tell Lize to put on another plate for dinner."

Everybody made a rush for the front door, because, of course, a stranger don't come *every* year. Tom was starting for the house; the wagon was spinning up the road for the village, and we was all bunched in the front door. Tom had his store clothes on, and an audience—and that was always nuts for Tom Sawyer. In them circumstances it warn't no trouble to him to throw in an amount of style that was suitable. He warn't a boy to meeky along up that yard like a sheep; no, he come ca'm and important, like the ram. When he got a-front of us he lifts his hat ever so gracious and dainty, like it was the lid of a box that had butterflies asleep in it and he didn't want to disturb them, and says:

"Mr. Archibald Nichols, I presume?"

"No, my boy," said the old gentleman, "I'm sorry to say 't your driver has deceived you; Nichols's place is down a matter of three mile more. Come in, come in."

Tom he took a look back over his shoulder, and says, "Too late—he's out of sight."

"Yes, he's gone, my son, and you must come in and eat dinner with us; and then we'll hitch up and take you to Nichols's."

"Oh, I *can't* make so much trouble. I'll walk."

"But we won't *let* you walk—it wouldn't be Southern hospitality to do it. Come right in and make yourself at home."

So Tom he thanked them very hearty and handsome and come in; and he said he was from Hicksville, Ohio, and his name was William Thompson—and he made another bow.

Well, he run on, and on, making up stuff about Hicksville and everybody in it, and I getting nervous, and wondering how this was going to help me out of my scrape; and at last, still talking, he reached over and kissed Aunt Sally right on the mouth, and then settled back again in his chair and was going on talking; but she jumped up and wiped it off with her hand, and says:

"You owdacious puppy!"

He looked hurt, and says, "I'm surprised at you, m'am."

"You're s'rp— Why, what do you reckon *I* am? Say, what do you mean by kissing me?"

He looked kind of humble, and says, "I didn't mean nothing, ma'am. I—I—thought you'd like it. They—they—told me you would."

"*They* told you I would! Who's *they?*"

"Why, everybody. They all said so, m'am."

It was all she could do to hold in; her eyes snapped, and her fingers worked like she wanted to scratch him; and she says, "Who's 'everybody'? Out with their names!"

He got up and looked distressed, and fumbled his hat, and says, "They all said, kiss her and she'd like it. But I'm sorry, m'am, and I won't do it no more—till you ask me."

"Till I *ask* you! I lay you'll be the Methusalem-numskull of creation before ever *I* ask you!"

"Well," he says, "it does surprise me. But—" He stopped and looked around slow, and fetched up on me, and says, "Tom, didn't *you* think Aunt Sally 'd like me to kiss her, and open out her arms and say, 'Sid Sawyer—'"

"My land!" she says, jumping for him. "You impudent young rascal, to fool a body so—" and was going to hug him, but he fended her off, and says, "No, not till you've asked me first."

So she didn't lose no time, but asked him; and hugged him and kissed him over and over again, and then turned him over to the old man, and he took what was left. And after they got a little quiet again she says, "Why, dear me, I never see such a surprise. We warn't looking for *you* at all, but only Tom."

"It warn't *intended* for any of us to come but Tom," he says; "but I begged and begged, and at the last minute Aunt Polly let me come, too; so, coming down the river, me and Tom thought it would be a first-rate surprise for him to come here first, and for me to let on to be a stranger. But it was a mistake, Aunt Sally. This ain't no healthy place for a stranger."

"No—not impudent whelps, Sid. You ought to had your jaws boxed. But I'd be willing to stand a thousand such jokes to have you here."

We had dinner then, and there was things enough on that table for seven families. Uncle Silas he asked a pretty long blessing over it, but it was worth it.

There was considerable talk all the afternoon, and me and Tom was on the lookout all the time; but it warn't no use, they didn't happen to say nothing about any runaway nigger, and we was afraid to try to work up to it. But at supper one of the little boys says:

"Pa, mayn't Tom and Sid and me go to the show?"

"No," says the old man, "I reckon there ain't going to be any; and you couldn't go if there was, because the runaway nigger told Burton and me all about that scandalous show, and Burton said he would tell the people; so I reckon they've drove the owdacious loafers out of town before this time."

So there it was! Tom and me was to sleep in the same room; so, being tired, we bid good-night and went up to bed right after supper, and clumb out of the window and down the lightning rod, and shoved for the town; for I didn't believe anybody was going to give the king and the duke a hint, and so if I didn't hurry and give them one they'd get into trouble sure.

On the road Tom he told me all about how it was reckoned I was murdered, and how Pap disappeared, and what a stir there was when Jim run away; and I told Tom all about our "Royal Nonesuch" rapscallions, and as much of the raft voyage as I had time to; and as we struck into the town here comes a raging rush of people with torches, and an awful whooping and yelling and banging tin pans; and we jumped to one side to let them go by; and as they went by I see they had the king and the duke astraddle of a rail—that is, I knowed it was the king and the duke, though they was all over tar and feathers. Well, it made me sick to see it; and I was sorry for them poor pitiful rascals. Human beings *can* be awful cruel to one another.

We see we was too late. We asked some stragglers about it, and they said everybody went to the show looking very innocent; and laid low and kept dark till the poor old king was on the stage; then the house rose up and went for them.

So we poked along back home, and I warn't feeling so brash as I was before, but kind of ornery, and humble, and to blame, somehow—though *I* hadn't done nothing. But that's always the way; a person's conscience ain't got no sense, and just goes for him *anyway*. If I had a yeller dog that didn't know no more than a person's conscience does I would pison him. Tom he says the same.

By and by Tom says, "Looky here, Huck, what fools we are to not think of it before! I bet I know where Jim is."

"No! Where?"

"In that hut down by the ash hopper. Why, looky. When we was at dinner, didn't you see a nigger go in there with some vittles?"

"Yes."

"What did you think the vittles was for?"

"For a dog."

"So 'd I. Well, it wasn't for a dog."

"Why?"

"Because part of it was watermelon."

"So it was. I never thought about that. It shows how a body can see and don't see at the same time."

"Well, the nigger unlocked the padlock when he went in, and locked it again when he come out, and he fetched Uncle a key about the time we got up from the table. Watermelon shows man, lock shows prisoner; and it ain't likely there's two prisoners on such a little plantation, so Jim's the prisoner. All right—I'm glad we found it out detective fashion. Now you work your mind, and study out a plan to steal Jim, and I'll study out one, too; and we'll take the one we like the best."

What a head! If I had Tom Sawyer's head I wouldn't trade it off to be a duke, nor mate of a steamboat, nor clown in a circus. I went on thinking out a plan, but only just to be doing something; I knowed very well where the right plan was going to come from. Pretty soon Tom says, "Ready?"

"Yes," I says. "My plan is this. Tomorrow we fetch my raft from the island. Then the first dark night we steal the key out of the old man's britches after he goes to bed, and shove off down the river on the raft with Jim. Wouldn't that work?"

"*Work?* Why, cert'nly it would work, like rats a-fighting. But it's too blame' simple. What's the good of a plan that ain't no more trouble than that? It's as mild as goose milk."

I never said nothing, because I warn't expecting nothing different; but I knowed mighty well that whenever he got *his* plan ready it wouldn't have none of them objections to it.

And it didn't. He told me what it was, and I see in a minute it was worth fifteen of mine for style, and would make Jim just as free a man as mine would, and maybe get us all killed besides. So I was satisfied, and said we would waltz in on it. I needn't tell what it was here, because I knowed it wouldn't stay the way it was; he would be changing it around every which way as we went along. And that is what he done.

Well, one thing was dead sure, and that was that Tom Sawyer was in earnest, and was actually going to help steal that nigger out of slavery. That was the thing that was too many for me. Here was a boy that was respectable and well brung up; and had a character to lose. I *couldn't* understand it no way at all. It was outrageous, and I knowed I ought to just up and tell him so; and so be his true friend. And I *did* start to tell him; but he shut me up, and says:

"Don't you reckon I know what I'm about?"

"Yes."

"Didn't I *say* I was going to help steal the nigger?"

"Yes."

"*Well*, then."

That's what he said, so I let it go, and never bothered no more about it.

When we got home the house was all dark and still; so we went on down to the hut by the ash hopper for to examine it. We went through the yard so as to see what the hounds would do. They knowed us, and didn't make no noise. When we got to the cabin we took a look at the front and the two sides; and on one side I warn't acquainted with—which was the north side—we found a square window hole, up high, with just one board nailed across it. I says:

"Here's the ticket. This hole's big enough for Jim to get through if we wrench off the board."

Tom says, "It's too simple. I should *hope* we can find a way that's a little more complicated than *that*, Huck Finn."

"Well, then," I says, "how'll it do to saw him out?"

"That's more *like*," he says. "It's mysterious and troublesome. But I bet we can find a way that's twice as long. Let's keep looking around."

Betwixt the hut and the fence, on the back side, was a lean-to that joined the hut at the eaves, and was made out of plank. The door to it was at the south end, and was padlocked. Tom he went to the soap kettle and searched around, and fetched back the iron thing they lift the lid with; so he took it and prized out one of the staples. The chain fell down, and we opened the door and went in and struck a match, and see the shed was only built against the cabin and hadn't no connection with it; and there warn't no floor to the shed, nor nothing in it but some old rusty hoes and spades and picks. The match went out, and so did we, and shoved in the staple again, and the door was locked as good as ever. Tom was joyful. He says:

"Now we're all right. We'll *dig* him out. It'll take about a week!"

Then we started for the house, and I went in the back door— you only have to pull a buckskin latchstring, they don't fasten the doors—but that warn't romantical enough for Tom; no way would do him but he must climb up the lightning rod. He got up halfway about three times, and the last time most busted his brains out; but he allowed he would give her one more turn for luck, and this time he made the trip.

In the morning we was up at break of day, and down to the nigger cabins to make friends with the nigger that fed Jim—if it *was* Jim that was being fed. The niggers was just starting for the fields; and Jim's nigger was piling up a tin pan with bread and things; and whilst the others was leaving, the key come from the house.

This nigger had a good-natured, chuckleheaded face, and his wool was all tied up in little bunches to keep witches off. He said the witches was pestering him awful these nights, and he got so worked up, and got to running on so about his troubles, he forgot all about what he'd been a-going to do. So Tom says, "What's the vittles for? Going to feed the dogs?"

The nigger kind of smiled graduly and he says, "Yes, Mars Sid, *a* dog. Cur'us dog, too. Does you want to look at 'im?"

"Yes."

I hunched Tom, and whispers, "You going, right here in the daybreak? *That* warn't the plan."

"No, it warn't; but it's the plan *now*."

So, drat him, we went along. When we got in we couldn't hardly see, it was so dark; but Jim was there, sure enough, and could see us; and he sings out, "Why, *Huck!* En good *lan*'; ain' dat Misto Tom?"

I just knowed how it would be; and the other nigger busted in and says, "Why, de gracious sakes! Do he know you genlmen?"

We could see pretty well now. Tom he looked at the nigger, steady and kind of wondering, and says, "Does *who* know us?"

"Why, dis-yer runaway nigger."

"I don't reckon he does; but what put that into your head?"

"What *put* it dar? Didn' he jus' dis minute sing out like he knowed you?"

Tom says, in a puzzled-up kind of way, "Well, that's mighty curious." And turns to me and says, "Did *you* hear anybody sing out?"

And of course I says, "No; *I* ain't heard nobody say nothing."

Then he turns to Jim, and looks him over like he never see him before, and says, "Did *you* sing out?"

"No, sah," says Jim; "*I* hain't said nothing, sah."

"Did you ever see us before?"

"No, sah; not as *I* knows on."

So Tom turns to the nigger, who was looking wild and distressed, and says, kind of severe, "What do you reckon's the matter with you, anyway?"

"Oh, it's de dad-blame witches, sah, en I wisht I was dead! Dey do mos' kill me. Please don't tell nobody 'bout it, sah, or ole Mars Silas he'll scole me; he say dey *ain't* no witches—but I jis' wish to goodness he was heah now!"

Tom give him a dime, and said we wouldn't tell nobody; and told him to buy some more thread to tie up his hair with. And whilst the nigger stepped to the door to look at the dime, he whispers to Jim, "Don't let on to know us. And if you hear any digging going on nights, it's us; we're going to set you free."

Jim only had time to grab us by the hand and squeeze; then the nigger come back, and we said we'd come again sometime if the nigger wanted us to; and he said he would, more particular if it was dark, because the witches went for him mostly in the dark, and it was good to have folks around then.

CHAPTER XIII

IT WOULD BE MOST AN HOUR yet till breakfast, so we left and struck down into the woods; because Tom said we got to have *some* light to dig by, and a lantern makes too much; what we must have was a lot of them rotten chunks that's called fox fire, and just makes a kind of glow when you lay them in a dark place. We fetched an armful and hid it in the weeds; and set down to rest, and Tom says, kind of dissatisfied:

"Blame it, this whole thing is just as easy and awkward as it can be. And so it makes it rotten difficult to get up a difficult plan. There ain't no watchman to be drugged—now there *ought* to be a watchman. There ain't even a dog to give a sleeping mixture to. And there's Jim chained by one leg, with a ten-foot chain, to the leg of his bed; why, all you got to do is to lift up the bedstead and slip off the chain. Drat it, Huck, it's the stupidest arrangement

I ever see. You got to invent *all* the difficulties. Look at just that one thing of the lantern. When you come down to the cold facts, we simply got to *let on* that a lantern's resky. Why, we could work with a torchlight procession if we wanted to, *I* believe. Now, whilst I think of it, we got to hunt up something to make a saw out of the first chance we get."

"What do we want of a saw?"

"What do we *want* of a saw? Hain't we got to saw the leg of Jim's bed off, so as to get the chain loose?"

"Why, you just said a body could lift up the bedstead and slip the chain off."

"Well, if that ain't just like you, Huck Finn. You *can* get up the infant-schooliest ways of going at a thing. Why, hain't you ever read any books at all? Baron Trenck, nor Casanova, nor Benvenuto Chelleeny? Who ever heard of getting a prisoner loose in such an old-maidy way as that? No; the way all the best authorities does is to saw the bed leg in two, and leave it just so, and swallow the sawdust, so it can't be found. Then the night you're ready, fetch the leg a kick, down she goes; slip off your chain, and there you are. Nothing to do but hitch your rope ladder to the battlements and shin down it to the moat. It's gaudy, Huck. I wish there was a moat to this cabin. If we get time, the night of the escape, we'll dig one."

I says, "What do we want of a moat when we're going to snake him out from under the cabin?"

But he never heard me. He had forgot me. He had his chin in his hands, thinking. Pretty soon he says, "Anyway, he can have a rope ladder; we can tear up some sheets and make him a rope ladder easy enough. And we can send it to him in a pie; it's mostly done that way."

"Why, Tom Sawyer," I says, "Jim ain't got no use for a rope ladder."

"He *has* got use for it. He's *got* to have a rope ladder; they all do."

"What in the nation can he *do* with it?"

"*Do* with it? He can hide it in his bed, can't he? That's what they all do; and *he's* got to, too."

"Well," I says, "if it's in the regulations, and he's got to have it, all right; I don't wish to go back on no regulations; but there's one thing, Tom Sawyer—if we go to tearing up our sheets to make Jim a rope ladder, we're sure going to get into trouble with Aunt Sally. Now, the way I look at it, a hickry-bark ladder don't cost nothing, and don't waste nothing, and is just as good to load up a pie with—"

"Oh, shucks, Huck Finn, who ever heard of a state prisoner escaping by a hickry-bark ladder? Why, it's perfectly ridiculous."

"Well, all right, fix it your way; but if you'll take my advice, you'll let me borrow a sheet off the clothesline."

He said that would do. And that gave him another idea, and he says, "Borrow a shirt, too."

"What do we want of a shirt, Tom?"

"Want it for Jim to keep a journal on."

"Journal your granny—*Jim* can't write."

"S'pose he *can't* write—he can make marks on the shirt, can't he, if we make him a pen out of an old pewter spoon or a piece of an old iron barrel hoop?"

"Why, Tom, we can pull a feather out of a goose and make him a better one; and quicker, too."

"*Prisoners* don't have geese running around the donjon-keep to pull pens out of, you muggins. They wouldn't *use* a goose quill if they had it. It ain't regular."

"Well, then, what'll we make him the ink out of?"

"Many makes it out of iron rust and tears; but the best authorities uses their own blood. Jim can do that; and when he wants to send any little common message to let the world know where he's captivated, he can write it on the bottom of a tin plate with a fork and throw it out of the window. The Iron Mask always done that—"

He broke off there, because we heard the breakfast horn blowing. So we cleared out for the house.

Along during the morning I borrowed a sheet and a white shirt off of the clothesline; and I found an old sack and put them in it, and we went and got the fox fire, and put that in too. I called it borrowing, because that was what Pap always called it; but Tom said it warn't borrowing, it was stealing. But he said we was representing prisoners; and it ain't no crime in a prisoner to steal the thing he needs to get away with, Tom said; it's his right; and so long as we was representing a prisoner, we had a perfect right to steal anything we had the least use for to get ourselves out of prison with.

Well, as I was saying, we waited that morning till everybody was settled down to business, and nobody in sight around the yard; then Tom he carried the sack into the lean-to whilst I stood off to keep watch. By and by he come out, and we set down on the woodpile to talk. He says, "Everything's all right now except tools; and that's easy fixed."

"Tools for what?" I says.

"Why, to dig with. We ain't a-going to *gnaw* him out, are we?"

"Ain't them old picks and things in there good enough to dig with?" I says.

He turns on me, looking pitying, and says, "Huck Finn, did you *ever* hear of a prisoner having picks and shovels to dig himself out with? Why, they wouldn't furnish 'em to a king."

"Well, then," I says, "if we don't want the picks and shovels, what do we want?"

"A couple of case knives."

"To dig the foundations out from under that cabin with?"

"Yes."

"Confound it, it's foolish, Tom."

"It don't make no difference how foolish it is, it's the *right* way— and it's the regular way. They always dig out with a case knife— and not through dirt, mind you; generly through solid rock. And it takes them forever and ever. Why, one of them prisoners in the bottom dungeon of the Castle Deef in Marseilles dug himself out that way; he was at it *thirty-seven year*—and he come out in China. *That's* the kind. I wish the bottom of *this* fortress was solid rock."

"*Jim* don't know nobody in China."

"What's *that* got to do with it? You're always a-wandering off on a side issue. Why can't you stick to the main point?"

"All right—*I* don't care where he comes out, so he *comes* out;

148

and Jim don't either, I reckon. But there's one thing—Jim's too old to be dug out with a case knife. He won't last."

"Yes, he will *last*, too. You don't reckon it's going to take thirty-seven years to dig through a *dirt* foundation, do you?"

"How long will it take, Tom?"

"Well, we can't resk being as long as we ought to, because it mayn't take very long for Uncle Silas to hear from down there by New Orleans. Then his next move will be to advertise Jim, or something like that. So, things being so uncertain, what I recommend is this: that we really dig right in, quick; and after that, we can *let on*, to ourselves, that we was at it thirty-seven years. Then we can snatch him out the first time there's an alarm."

"Now, there's *sense* in that," I says. "Letting on don't cost nothing. It wouldn't strain me none to let on we was at it a hundred and fifty years. So I'll mosey along now, and smouch a couple of case knives."

"Smouch three," he says. "We want one to make a saw out of."

"Tom, if it ain't unregular to sejest it," I says, "there's an old saw blade sticking under the boarding behind the smokehouse."

He looked kind of weary, and says:

"It ain't no use to try to learn you nothing, Huck. Run along and smouch the knives—three of them." So I done it.

As SOON AS WE RECKONED everybody was asleep that night we went down the lightning rod, and shut ourselves up in the lean-to, and got out our pile of fox fire, and went to work. We cleared everything out of the way along the middle of the bottom log. Tom said we was right behind Jim's bed now, and we'd dig in under it, and when we got through there couldn't nobody in the cabin ever know there was any hole there, because Jim's counterpane hung down to the ground. So we dug and dug with the case knives till most midnight; and then we was dog-tired, and our hands was blistered, and yet you couldn't see we'd done anything hardly. At last I says:

"This ain't no thirty-seven-year job; this is a thirty-eight-year job, Tom Sawyer."

He never said nothing. But he sighed, and pretty soon he stopped digging. Then he says:

"It ain't no use, Huck, it ain't a-going to work. If we was prisoners it would, because then we'd have as many years as we wanted, and no hurry; and so our hands wouldn't get blistered, and we could keep it up year in and year out, and do it right. But *we* can't fool along; we got to rush; we ain't got no time to spare. If we was to put in another night this way we'd have to knock off for a week to let our hands get well—couldn't touch a case knife with them sooner."

"Well, then, what we going to do, Tom?"

"I'll tell you. It ain't right, and it ain't moral; but we got to dig him out with the picks, and *let on* it's case knives."

"*Now you're talking!*" I says. "Your head gets leveler and leveler all the time, Tom Sawyer. Picks is the thing, moral or no moral; and as for me, I don't care shucks for the morality of it, nohow. When I start in to steal a nigger, or a watermelon, what I want is the nigger, or what I want is the watermelon; and if a pick's the handiest thing, that's the thing I'm a-going to dig that nigger or that watermelon out with; and I don't give a dead rat what the authorities thinks about it nuther."

"Well," he says, "it might answer for *you* to dig Jim out with a pick, *without* any letting on, because you don't know no better; but it wouldn't do for me, because I do know better. Gimme a case knife."

He had his own by him, but I handed him mine. He flung it down, and says, "Gimme a *case knife*."

I didn't know just what to do—but then I thought. I got a pickaxe and give it to him, and he took it and went to work, and never said a word.

He was always just that particular. Full of principle.

So then I got a shovel, and then we picked and shoveled, turn about. We stuck to it about a half an hour, which was as long as we could stand up; but we had a good deal of a hole to show for it. When I got upstairs I looked out at the window and see Tom doing his level best with the lightning rod, but he couldn't come it, his hands was so sore. At last he says, "It ain't no use. What you reckon I better do? Can't you think of no way?"

"Yes," I says, "but I reckon it ain't regular. Come up the stairs, and let on it's a lightning rod."

So he done it.

NEXT DAY TOM STOLE a pewter spoon and a brass candlestick in the house, for to make some pens for Jim out of, and six tallow candles; and I hung around the nigger cabins and stole three tin plates for Jim to write messages on. Then Tom says, "Now, the thing is, how to get the things to Jim?"

"Take them in through the hole," I says, "when we get it done."

He just looked scornful, and said something about nobody ever heard of such an idiotic idea.

That night we went down the lightning rod a little after ten, and took one of the candles along, and listened under the window hole and heard Jim snoring. Then we whirled in with the pick and shovel, and in about two hours and a half the job was done. We crept in under Jim's bed, and took the candle and lit it, and then we woke Jim up gentle. He was so glad to see us he most cried; and he was for having us hunt up a cold chisel to cut the chain off his leg with right away, and clearing out. But Tom he showed him how unregular it would be, and told him all about our plans, and how we could alter them in a minute any time there was an alarm; and not to be the least afraid, because we would see he got away, *sure.* So Jim he said it was all right, and we set there and talked over old times awhile. Then Tom asked a lot of questions, and when Jim told him Uncle Silas come in every day to pray with him, and Aunt Sally come in to see if he was comfortable, Tom says:

"*Now* I know how to fix it. We'll send you some things by them."

He told Jim how we'd have to smuggle in the rope-ladder pie and other large things by Nat, the nigger that fed him, and he must be on the lookout, and not be surprised, and not let Nat see him open them; and we would put small things in Uncle's coat pockets and he must steal them out; and we would put things in

Aunt's apron pocket; and we told him what they would be and what they was for. And told him how to keep a journal on the shirt with his blood, and all that. Jim he couldn't see no sense in the most of it; but he said he would do it all just as Tom said.

Jim had plenty corncob pipes and tobacco; so we had a right down good sociable time; then we crawled out through the hole, and so home to bed.

In the morning we went out to the woodpile and chopped up the brass candlestick into handy sizes. Then we went to the nigger cabins, and while I got Nat's notice off, Tom shoved a piece of candlestick into the middle of a corn pone that was in Jim's pan, and we went along with Nat to see how it would work, and it just worked noble; when Jim bit into it it most mashed all his teeth out. Jim he never let on but what it was only just a piece of rock or something like that that gets into bread, you know; but after that he never bit into nothing but what he jabbed his fork into it three or four places first.

And whilst we was a-standing there in the dimmish light, here comes a couple of the hounds bulging in from under Jim's bed; and they kept on piling in till there was eleven of them. By jings, we forgot to fasten that lean-to door! The nigger Nat he just hollered "Witches" once, and he keeled over onto the floor amongst the dogs.

Tom jerked the door open and flung out a slab of Jim's meat, and the dogs went for it, and in two seconds he was out himself and back again and shut the door, and I knowed he'd fixed the other door too. Then he went to work on the nigger, coaxing him and asking him if he'd been imagining he saw something again. He raised up, and blinked his eyes around, and says:

"Mars Sid, you'll say I's a fool, but I see most a million dogs, er devils, er some'n. I did, mos' sholy! Mars Sid, I *felt* um—I *felt* um, sah! Dad fetch it, I jis' wisht dem witches 'd lemme 'lone!"

Tom says, "Well, I tell you what *I* think. What makes them come here just at this runaway nigger's breakfast-time? It's because they're hungry. You make them a witch pie; that's the thing for *you* to do."

"But my lan', Mars Sid, how's I gwyne to make 'em a witch pie? I doan' know how to make it."

"Well, then, I'll have to make it myself."

"Will you do it, honey—will you?"

"All right, seeing it's you, and you've been good to us. But you got to be mighty careful. When we come around, you turn your back; and then whatever we've put in the pan, don't you let on you see it at all. And don't you look when Jim unloads the pan—something might happen, I don't know what. And above all, don't you *handle* the witch things."

"*Hannel* 'm, Mars Sid? I wouldn' lay my finger on um, f'r ten hund'd thous'n billion dollars!"

So that was all fixed. Then we went away and went to the rubbage pile in the backyard and scratched around and found an old tin washpan to bake the pie in, and took it down cellar and stole it full of flour, and found a couple of shingle nails that Tom said would be handy for a prisoner to scrabble his name on the dungeon walls with, and dropped one of them in Aunt Sally's apron pocket which was hanging on a chair, and t'other we stuck in the band of Uncle Silas's hat, which was on the bureau, and then went to breakfast, and Tom dropped the pewter spoon in Uncle Silas's coat pocket, and Aunt Sally wasn't come yet, so we had to wait a little while.

And when she come she was hot and red and cross, and couldn't hardly wait for the blessing; and then she went to sluicing out coffee, and says:

"I've hunted high and I've hunted low, and it does beat all what *has* become of your other shirt."

My heart fell down amongst my lungs and livers and things, and a hard piece of corn crust started down my throat after it and got met on the road with a cough, and was shot across the table, and took one of the children in the eye and curled him up like a fishing worm, and let a cry out of him the size of a war whoop, and Tom he turned kinder blue around the gills, and it all amounted to a considerable state of things for about a quarter of a minute or as much as that, and I would 'a' sold out for half price if there was a bidder. But after that we was all right again—it was the sudden surprise of it that knocked us so kind of cold. Uncle Silas he says:

"It's most uncommon curious, I can't understand it. I know perfectly well I took it *off*, because—"

"Because you hain't got but one *on*. Just *listen!* I know you took it off. It was on the clo'sline yesterday—but it's gone now, and you'll just have to change to a red flann'l one till I can get time to make a new one. And the shirt ain't all that's gone, nuther. Ther's a spoon gone; and *that* ain't all. There was ten, and now ther's only nine. The calf got the shirt, I reckon, but the calf never took the spoon, *that's* certain."

"Why, what else is gone, Sally?"

"Ther's six *candles* gone—that's what. The rats could 'a' got the candles, and I reckon they did; I wonder they don't walk off with the whole place, the way you're always going to stop their holes and don't do it; but you can't lay the *spoon* on the rats, and that I *know.*"

"Well, Sally, I'm in fault, and I acknowledge it; but I won't let tomorrow go by without stopping up them holes."

"Oh, I wouldn't hurry; next year 'll do. Matilda Angelina *Phelps!*"

Whack comes her thimble, and the child snatches her claws out of the sugar bowl. Just then the nigger woman steps onto the passage, and says, "Missus, dey's a sheet gone."

"A *sheet* gone! Well, for the land's sake!"

"I'll stop up them holes today," says Uncle Silas.

"Oh, *do* shet up! S'pose the rats took the *sheet?* Where's it gone? I *never* see the beat of it in all my born days. A shirt gone, and a sheet, and a spoon, and six can—"

"Missus," comes a young yaller wench, "dey's a brass candlestick miss'n."

"Cler out from here, you hussy, er I'll take a skillet to ye!"

Well, she was just a-biling. She kept a-raging right along, running her insurrection all by herself, and everybody else mighty meek and quiet; and at last Uncle Silas, looking kind of foolish, fishes up that spoon out of his pocket. She stopped, with her mouth open; but not long, because she says:

"It's *just* as I expected. So you had it in your pocket all the time. How'd it get there?"

"I reely don't know, Sally," he says, kind of apologizing, "I was a-studying over my text in Acts Seventeen before breakfast, and I reckon I put it in there, not noticing, meaning to put my Testament in—"

"Oh, for the land's sake! Give a body a rest! Go 'long now, the whole kit and biling of ye; and don't come nigh me again till I've got back my peace of mind."

As we was passing through the setting room the old man he took up his hat, and the shingle nail fell out on the floor, and he just merely picked it up and laid it on the mantelshelf and never said nothing, and went out. Tom see him do it, and remembered about the spoon, and says:

"Well, it ain't no use to send things by *him* no more, he ain't reliable." Then he says, "But he done us a good turn with the spoon anyway, without knowing it, and so we'll go and do him one without *him* knowing it—stop up his rat holes."

There was a noble good lot of them down cellar, and it took us a whole hour, but we done the job tight and good. Then we heard steps on the stairs, and blowed out our light and hid; and here comes the old man with a candle in one hand, looking as absentminded as year before last. He went a-mooning around, first to one rat hole and then another, till he'd been to them all. Then he stood about five minutes, picking tallow drips off his candle and thinking. Then he turns off slow and dreamy towards the stairs, saying, "Well, for the life of me I can't remember when I done it. I could show her—but never mind—let it go." And so he went on a-mumbling upstairs, and then we left. He was a mighty nice old man.

Tom was a good deal bothered about what to do for a spoon, but he said we'd got to have it; so he took a think. When he had ciphered it out he told me how we was to do; then we went and waited around the spoon basket till we see Aunt Sally coming, and then Tom went to counting the spoons, and I slid one of them up my sleeve, and Tom says:

"Why, Aunt Sally, there ain't but nine spoons *yet*."

She says, "Go 'long, don't bother me. I know better, I counted 'm myself."

"Well, I've counted them twice, Aunty, and *I* can't make but nine."

She looked out of all patience, but of course she come to count—anybody would. "I declare ther' *ain't* but nine!" she says. "Why, what in the world—plague *take* the things, I'll count 'm again."

So I slipped back the one I had, and when she got done counting, she says, "Hang the troublesome rubbage, ther's *ten* now!" and she looked huffy and bothered both. But Tom says:

"Why, Aunty, *I* don't think there's ten."

"You numskull, didn't you see me *count* 'm?"

"I know, but—"

"Well, I'll count 'm again."

So I smouched one, and they come out nine, same as the other time. Well, she *was* in a tearing way—just a-trembling all over, she was so mad. But she counted and counted, and three times they come out right, and three times they come out wrong. Then she grabbed up the basket and slammed it across the house and knocked the cat galley-west; and she said cler out and let her have some peace, and if we come bothering around her again betwixt that and dinner she'd skin us. So we had the odd spoon, and dropped it in her apron pocket whilst she was a-giving us our sailing orders, and Jim got it all right, along with her shingle nail, before noon. We put the sheet back on the line that night, and stole one out of her closet; and kept on putting it back and stealing it again for a couple of days till she didn't know how many sheets she had anymore, either, and she didn't *care*, and warn't a-going to count them again not to save her life; she'd ruther die first. So we was all right now, as to the shirt and the sheet and the spoon and the candles, by the help of the calf and rats and the mixed-up counting; and as to the candlestick, it warn't no consequence, it would blow over by and by.

But that pie was a job; we had no end of trouble with that pie. We fixed it up away down in the woods, and cooked it there; and we got it done at last; but not all in one day; and we had to use up three washpans full of flour before we got through. We tore up the sheet all in little strings and twisted them together, and so we had a lovely rope that you could 'a' hung a person with. But it wouldn't go into the pie. Being made of a whole sheet, that way, there was rope enough for forty pies if we'd 'a' wanted them, and all we needed was just enough for the pie; so we throwed the rest away.

We didn't cook none of the pies in the washpan—afraid the solder would melt; but Uncle Silas he had a noble brass warming pan which he thought considerable of; it was hid away up garret with a lot of other old things that was valuable, and we snaked her out, private, and took her down to the woods. She failed on the first pies, because we didn't know how, but she come up smiling on the last one. We took and lined her with dough, and set her in the coals and loaded her up with rag rope, and put on a dough roof, and shut down the lid, and put hot embers on top, and stood off five foot, with the long handle, cool and comfortable, and in fifteen minutes she turned out a pie that was a satisfaction to look at.

Nat didn't look when we put the witch pie in Jim's pan; and we put the three tin plates in the bottom of the pan under the vittles; and so Jim got everything all right, and as soon as he was by himself he busted into the pie and hid the rope ladder inside of his straw tick, and scratched some marks on a tin plate and throwed it out of the window hole.

MAKING THEM PENS WAS a distressid tough job, and so was the saw; and Jim allowed the inscription was going to be the toughest of all. That's the one which the prisoner had to scribble on the wall. But he had to have it; Tom said he'd *got* to; there warn't no case of a state prisoner not scrabbling his inscription to leave behind. So whilst me and Jim filed away at the pens on a brick-bat apiece, Jim a-making his'n out of the brass and I making mine out of the spoon, Tom set to work to think out the inscription. He made up a lot, and wrote them out on a paper, and read them off, so:

"1. Here a captive heart busted.
   2. Here a poor prisoner, forsook by the world and friends, fretted his sorrowful life.
   3. Here a lonely heart broke, and a worn spirit went to its rest, after thirty-seven years of solitary captivity.
   4. Here, homeless and friendless, after thirty-seven years of bitter captivity, perished a noble stranger, natural son of Louis XIV."

Tom's voice trembled whilst he was reading them, and he most broke down. When he got done he couldn't no way make up his mind which one for Jim to scrabble onto the wall, they was all so good; but at last he allowed he would let him scrabble them all on. Jim said it would take him a year to scrabble such a lot of truck onto the logs with a nail, and he didn't know how to make letters, besides; but Tom said he would block them out for him. Then he says:

"Come to think, the logs ain't a-going to do; they don't have log walls in a dungeon: we got to dig the inscriptions into a rock. We'll fetch a rock."

Jim said the rock was worse than the logs; he said it would take him a pison long time to dig them into a rock. But Tom said he would let me help him do it. Then he took a look to see how me and Jim was getting along with the pens. It was most pesky tedious hard work and slow, and we didn't seem to make no headway, hardly; so Tom says:

"I know how to fix it. We got to have a rock for the inscriptions, and we can kill two birds with that same rock. There's a big grindstone down at the mill, and we'll smouch it, and carve the things on it, and file out the pens and the saw on it, too."

It warn't no slouch of an idea; and we allowed we'd tackle it. It warn't quite midnight yet, so we cleared out for the mill, leaving

Jim at work. We smouched the grindstone, and set out to roll her home, but it was a most nation tough job. Sometimes we couldn't keep her from falling over, and she come mighty near mashing us every time. We got her halfway; and then we was plumb played out, and most drownded with sweat. We see it warn't no use; we got to fetch Jim. So he raised up his bed and slid the chain off of the bed leg, and wrapt it round his neck, and we crawled out through our hole and down there, and Jim and me laid into that grindstone and walked her along like nothing, and got her through our hole.

Then Tom marked out them things on it with the nail, and set Jim to work on them, with the nail for a chisel and an iron bolt for a hammer. Tom told him to work till the rest of his candle quit on him, and then he could go to bed, and hide the grindstone under his straw tick and sleep on it. We helped him fix his chain back on the bed leg, and was ready for bed ourselves. But Tom thought of something, and says:

"You got any spiders in here, Jim?"

"No, sah, thanks to goodness I hain't, Mars Tom."

"All right, we'll get you some."

"Bless you, honey, I doan' *want* none. I's afeard un um. I jis' 's soon have rattlesnakes aroun'."

Tom thought a minute or two, and says, "It's a good idea. Yes, it's a prime good idea. Where could you keep it?"

"Keep what, Mars Tom?"

"Why, a rattlesnake."

"De goodness gracious alive, Mars Tom! Why, if dey was a rattlesnake to come in heah I'd bust right out thoo dat log wall, I would, wid my head."

"Why, Jim, you wouldn't be afraid of it after a little. You could tame it."

"*Tame* it!"

"Yes—easy enough. Every animal is grateful for kindness and petting, and they wouldn't *think* of hurting a person that pets them. Any book will tell you that. You try—just try for two or three days. Why, you can get him so that he'll love you; and sleep with you; and let you wrap him round your neck and put his head in your mouth."

"*Please*, Mars Tom—*doan*' talk so! I can't *stan*' it! I doan' *want* him to sleep wid me or shove his head in my mouf."

"Jim, blame it, can't you *try?* I only *want* you to try—you needn't keep it up if it don't work."

"But de trouble all *done* ef de snake bite me while I's a-tryin' him. Mars Tom, I's willin' to tackle mos' anything 'at ain't onreasonable, but ef you en Huck fetches a rattlesnake in heah for me to tame, I's gwyne to *leave*, dat's *shore*."

"Well, then, let it go, if you're so bullheaded about it. We can get you some garter snakes, and some rats, instead."

"Why, Mars Tom, I doan' want no rats either!"

"But, Jim, they all have 'em! Prisoners ain't ever without rats. They train them, and learn them tricks, and they get to be as sociable as flies. But you got to play music to them. You got anything to play music on?"

"I ain' got nuffn but a coase comb en a piece o' paper, en a juice harp; but I reck'n dey wouldn't take no stock in a juice harp."

"Yes, they would. *They* don't care what kind of music 'tis. A jew's harp's plenty good enough for a rat. All animals like music—in a prison they dote on it. Specially, painful music; and you can't get no other kind out of a jew's harp. Yes, you're fixed very well. You want to set on your bed nights before you go to sleep, and play your jew's harp; play 'The Last Link is Broken'; and when you've played about two minutes you'll see all the rats, and the snakes, and spiders and things begin to feel worried about you, and come. And they'll just fairly swarm over you, and have a noble good time."

"Yes, *dey* will, I reck'n, Mars Tom, but what kine er time is Jim havin'? Blest if I kin see de pint. But I'll do it ef I got to. I reck'n I better keep de animals satisfied, en not have no trouble in de house."

Tom waited to think it over, and see if there wasn't nothing else; and pretty soon he says, "Oh, there's one thing I forgot. Could you raise a flower here, do you reckon?"

"I doan' know; maybe I could, Mars Tom; but it's tolable dark in heah."

"Well, you try it, anyway. Some other prisoners has done it. You want to water it with your tears."

"She'll die on my han's, Mars Tom; kase I doan' skasely ever cry."

So Tom was stumped. But he studied it over, and then said Jim would have to worry along the best he could with an onion. He promised he would drop one, private, in Jim's coffeepot, in the morning. Jim said he would "jis' 's soon have tobacker in his coffee"; and found so much fault with it, and with the work and bother of jew's-harping the rats, and petting and flattering up the snakes and spiders, on top of all the other work he had to do on pens, and inscriptions, and journals, and things, which made it more trouble and worry to be a prisoner than anything he ever undertook, that Tom most lost all patience with him; and said he was loadened down with more chances than a prisoner ever had in the world to make a name for himself, and yet he didn't know enough to appreciate them, and they was just about wasted on him. So Jim he was sorry, and said he wouldn't behave so no more, and then me and Tom shoved for bed.

In the morning we went up to the village and bought a wire rat trap and fetched it down, and unstopped the best rat hole, and in about an hour we had fifteen of the bulliest kind of ones; and then we took it and put it in a safe place under Aunt Sally's bed. But while we was gone for spiders little Thomas Franklin Benjamin Phelps found it there, and opened the door of it to see if the rats would come out, and they did; and Aunt Sally she come in, and when we got back she was a-standing on top of the bed raising Cain, and the rats was doing what they could to keep off the dull times for her. So she took and dusted us both with the hickry, and we was as much as two hours catching another fifteen or sixteen, drat that meddlesome cub, and they warn't the likeliest, nuther, because the first haul was the pick of the flock. I never see a likelier lot of rats than what that first haul was.

We got a splendid stock of sorted spiders, and bugs, and frogs, and caterpillars, and one thing or another; and then we went for the snakes, and grabbed a couple of dozen garters and house snakes, and put them in a bag, and put it in our room, and by that time it was suppertime, and a rattling good day's work; and hungry? Oh, no, I reckon not! And there warn't a blessed snake up there when we went back—they worked out of that sack somehow, and left. But it didn't matter much, because they was still on the premises somewheres. So we judged we could get some of them again. No, there warn't no real scarcity of snakes about the house for a considerable spell. You'd see them dripping from the rafters and places every now and then; and they generly landed in your plate, or down the back of your neck, and most of the time where you didn't want them. Well, they was handsome and striped, and there warn't no harm in a million of them; but Aunt Sally couldn't stand them no way you could fix it; and every time one of them flopped down on her, it didn't make no difference what she was doing, she would just lay that work down and light out. I never see such a woman. And you could hear her whoop to Jericho. Why, after every last snake had been gone clear out of the house for a week Aunt Sally warn't over it yet; when she was setting thinking about something you could touch her on the back of her neck with a feather and she would jump right out of her stockings. It was very curious. But Tom said all women was just so. He said they was made that way for some reason or other.

We got a licking every time one of our snakes come in her way, and she allowed these lickings warn't nothing to what she would do if we ever loaded up the place again with them. I didn't mind the lickings; but I minded the trouble we had to lay in another lot. But we got them laid in, and all the other things; and you never see a cabin as blithesome as Jim's was when they'd all swarm out for music and go for him. Jim didn't like the spiders, and the spiders didn't like Jim; and so they'd lay for him. And he said that between the rats and the snakes and the grindstone there warn't no room in bed for him, skasely; and when there was, a body couldn't sleep, it was so lively, because *they* never all slept at one time, but took turn about, so when the snakes was asleep the rats was on deck, and when the rats turned in the snakes come on watch, so he always had one gang under him, in his way, and t'other gang having a circus over him, and if he got up to hunt a new place the spiders would take a chance at him as he crossed over. He said if he ever got out of this he wouldn't ever be a prisoner again, not for a salary.

Well, by the end of three weeks everything was in pretty good shape. The shirt was sent in early, in a pie, and every time a rat bit Jim he would get up and write a line in his journal whilst the ink was fresh; the pens was made, the inscriptions and so on was all carved on the grindstone; the bed leg was sawed in two, and we had et up the sawdust, and it give us a most amazing stomach ache. It was the most undigestible sawdust I ever see; and Tom said the same.

But, as I was saying, we'd got all the work done now, at last; and we was all pretty much fagged out, too, but mainly Jim. The old man had wrote a couple of times to the plantation below Orleans to come and get the runaway nigger, but hadn't got no answer; so he allowed he would advertise Jim in the St. Louis and New Orleans papers; and when he mentioned the St. Louis ones it give me the cold shivers. We hadn't no time to lose. So Tom said, now for the nonnamous letters.

"What's them?" I says.

"Warnings to the people that something is up. Sometimes it's done one way, sometimes another. But there's always somebody spying around that gives notice to the governor of the castle. When Louis Sixteen was going to light out of the Tooleries a servant girl done it. It's a very good way, and so is the nonnamous letters. We'll use them both. And it's usual for the prisoner's mother to change clothes with him, and she stays in, and he slides out in her clothes. We'll do that, too."

"But looky here, Tom, what do we want to *warn* anybody for that something's up? Let them find it out for themselves—it's their lookout."

"Yes, I know; but you can't depend on them. They're so confiding and mullet-headed, if we don't *give* them notice there won't be nobody or nothing to interfere with us, and so after all our hard work and trouble this escape 'll go off perfectly flat."

"Well, as for me, Tom, that's the way I'd like."

"Shucks!" he says, and looked disgusted. So I says:

"But I ain't going to complain. Any way that suits you suits me. What you going to do about the servant girl?"

"You'll be her. You slide in, in the middle of the night, and hook that yaller girl's frock."

"Why, Tom, that 'll make trouble next morning; because, of course, she prob'bly hain't got any but that one."

"I know; but you don't want it but fifteen minutes, to carry the nonnamous letter and shove it under the front door."

"All right, I'll do it; but I could carry it just as handy in my own togs."

"You wouldn't look like a servant girl *then*, would you?"

"All right, I'm the servant girl. Who's Jim's mother?"

"I'm his mother. I'll hook a gown from Aunt Sally."

"Well, then, you'll have to stay in the cabin when me and Jim leaves."

"Not much. I'll stuff Jim's clothes full of straw and lay it on his bed to represent his mother in disguise, and Jim 'll take the gown off of me and wear it, and we'll all evade together. When a prisoner of style escapes it's called an evasion. It's always called so when a king escapes, f'rinstance. And the same with a king's son."

So Tom he wrote the nonnamous letter, and I smouched the yaller wench's frock that night, and put it on, and shoved it under the front door, the way Tom told me to. It said:

Beware. Trouble is brewing. Keep a sharp lookout.
                                                Unknown Friend

Next night we stuck a picture, which Tom drawed in blood, of a skull and crossbones on the front door; and next night another one of a coffin on the back door. I never see a family in such a sweat. They couldn't 'a' been worse scared if the place had 'a' been full of ghosts laying for them. If a door banged, Aunt

Sally she jumped and said "Ouch!" If anything fell, she jumped and said "Ouch!" She was afraid to go to bed, but she dasn't set up. So the thing was working very well, Tom said; he said it showed it was done right.

So he said, now for the grand bulge! So the very next morning at dawn we got another letter ready, and was wondering what we better do with it, because we heard them say at supper they was going to have a nigger on watch at both doors all night. Tom he went down the lightning rod to spy around; and the nigger at the back door was asleep, and he stuck it in the back of his neck and come back. This letter said:

> Don't betray me, I wish to be your friend. There is a desprate gang of cutthroats from over in the Indian Territory going to steal your runaway nigger tonight, and they have been trying to scare you so as you will stay in the house and not bother them. I am one of the gang, but have got relligion and wish to betray the helish design. They will sneak down from northards, along the fence, at midnight, with a false key, and go in the nigger's cabin to get him. I am to be off a piece and blow a tin horn if I see any danger; but stead of that I will *ba* like a sheep soon as they get in; then whilst they are getting his chains loose, you slip there and lock them in, and can kill them at your leasure. Don't do anything but just the way I am telling you; if you do they will suspicion something and raise whoop-jamboreehoo. I do not wish any reward but to know I have done the right thing.
>
> Unknown Friend

CHAPTER XIV

WE WAS FEELING GOOD after breakfast, and took my canoe and went a-fishing, with a lunch, and took a look at the raft and found her all right, and got home to supper, and found them in such a sweat they didn't know which end they was standing on, and made us go right off to bed the minute we was done supper, and wouldn't tell us what the trouble was. As soon as we was half upstairs and her back was turned we slid for the cellar cupboard and loaded up a good lunch and took it up to our room and went to bed, and got up about half past eleven, and Tom put on Aunt Sally's dress that he stole and was going to start with the lunch, but says, "Where's the butter?"

"I laid out a hunk," I says, "on a piece of corn pone."

"Well, you *left* it laid out, then—it ain't here. Just you slide down cellar and fetch it. And then mosey down the lightning rod and come along. I'll go and stuff the straw into Jim's clothes to represent his mother in disguise, and be ready to *ba* like a sheep and shove soon as you get there."

So out he went, and down cellar went I. The hunk of butter, big as a person's fist, was where I had left it, so I took up the slab of corn pone with it on, and blowed out my light, and started upstairs very stealthy, and got up to the main floor all right, but here comes Aunt Sally with a candle, and I clapped the truck in my hat, and clapped my hat on my head, and the next second she see me; and she says, "You been down cellar?"

"Yes'm."

"What you been doing down there?"

"Noth'n."

"*Noth'n!*"

"No'm. I haint been doing a single thing, Aunt Sally, I hope to gracious if I have."

I reckoned she'd let me go now, and as a generl thing she would; but I s'pose there was so many strange things going on she was in a sweat; so she says, very decided, "You just march into that setting room and stay there till I come. You been up to something, and I lay I'll find out what it is before *I'm* done with you."

So she went away as I opened the door and walked into the setting room. My, but there was a crowd there! Fifteen farmers, and every one of them had a gun. I was most powerful sick, and slunk to a chair and set down. I did wish Aunt Sally would come, and get done with me, and lick me, and let me get away and tell Tom how we'd overdone this thing, so we could stop fooling around, and clear out with Jim before these rips got out of patience and come for us. Then at last she come and begun to ask me questions, but I *couldn't* answer them straight; because these men was in such a fidget now that some was wanting to start right *now* and lay for them desperadoes; and others was trying to get them to hold on and wait for the sheep signal; and here was Aunty pegging away at the questions, and me a-shaking all over I was that scared; and the place getting hotter and hotter, and the butter beginning to melt and run down my neck; and pretty soon, when one of them says, "*I'm* for going and getting in the cabin *first* and right *now*, and catching them when they come," I most dropped, and a streak of butter come a-trickling down my forehead, and Aunt Sally she see it, and turns white as a sheet, and says:

"For the land's sake, what *is* the matter with the child? He's got the brain fever fer shore, and they're oozing out!"

And everybody runs to see, and she snatches off my hat, and out comes the bread and what was left of the butter, and she grabbed me, and hugged me, and says:

"Oh, what a turn you did give me! And how glad and grateful I am it ain't no worse; for when I see that truck I thought we'd lost you, for I knowed by the color and all it was just like your brains would be if— Dear, dear, whydn't you *tell* me that was what you'd been down there for? Now cler out to bed, and don't lemme see no more of you till morning!"

I was upstairs in a second, and down the lightning rod in another one, and shinning through the dark for the lean-to. I told Tom as quick as I could we must jump for it—the house full of men, yonder, with guns!

His eyes just blazed; and he says:

"No! Is that so? *Ain't* it bully!"

"Hurry! *Hurry!*" I says. "Where's Jim?"

"Right at your elbow. He's dressed, and everything's ready. Now we'll slide out and give the sheep signal."

But then we heard the tramp of men coming to the door, and heard them begin to fumble with the padlock, and heard a man say, "I *told* you we'd be too soon; they haven't come—the door is locked. Here, I'll lock some of you into the cabin, and you lay for 'em in the dark and kill 'em when they come; and the rest scatter around a piece."

So in they come, but couldn't see us in the dark, and most trod on us whilst we was hustling to get under the bed. But we got under all right, and out through the hole, swift but soft—Jim first, me next, and Tom last, which was according to Tom's orders. Now we was in the lean-to, and heard trampings close outside. So we crept to the door, and Tom put his eye to the crack, but couldn't make out nothing, it was so dark; then we slid out anyway, not breathing, and slipped stealthy towards the fence in Injun file, and got to it all right, and me and Jim over it; but Tom's britches catched fast on a splinter on the top rail, and then he hear the steps coming, so he had to pull loose, which snapped the splinter and made a noise; and as he dropped in our tracks somebody sings out:

"Who's that? Answer, or I'll shoot!"

But we didn't answer; we just unfurled our heels and shoved. Then there was a rush, and a *bang, bang, bang!* and the bullets fairly whizzed around us! We heard them sing out:

"They've broke for the river! After 'em, boys, and turn loose the dogs!"

So here they come, full tilt. We could hear them because they wore boots and yelled. We was in the path to the mill; and when they got pretty close onto us we dodged into the bush and let them go by, and then dropped in behind them. They'd had all the dogs shut up, so they wouldn't scare off the robbers; but by this time somebody had let them loose, and here they come, making powwow enough for a million; but they was our dogs; so we stopped till they catched up; and when they see it warn't nobody but us, they just said howdy, and tore right ahead towards the shouting; and then we struck upstream again, through the bush to my canoe, and hopped in and pulled for dear life towards the middle of the river. Then we struck out, easy and comfortable, for the island where my raft was; and we could hear them yelling and barking at each other all up and down the bank, till we was so far away the sounds got dim and died out. And when we stepped onto the raft

I says, "*Now*, old Jim, you're a free man *again*, and I bet you won't ever be a slave no more."

"En a mighty good job it wuz, too, Huck. It 'uz planned beautiful, en *done* beautiful; dey ain't *nobody* kin git up a plan dat's mo' mixed up en splendid den what dat one wuz."

We was all glad as we could be, but Tom was the gladdest of all because he had a bullet in the calf of his leg.

When me and Jim heard that we didn't feel as brash as we did before. It was hurting him considerable, and bleeding; so we laid him in the wigwam and tore up a shirt for to bandage him, but he says:

"Gimme the rags; I can do it myself. Don't stop now, and the evasion booming along so handsome; man the sweeps, and set her loose! Boys, we done it elegant—'deed we did! Slick as nothing at all. Man the sweeps—man the sweeps!"

But me and Jim was consulting—and thinking. And after we'd thought a minute, I says, "Say it, Jim."

So he says, "Well, den, dis is de way it look to me, Huck. Ef it wuz *him* dat 'uz bein' sot free, en one er de boys wuz to git shot, would he say, 'Go on en save me, nemmine 'bout a doctor f'r to save dis one'? You *bet* he wouldn't! *Well*, den, is *Jim* gwyne to say it? No, sah—I doan' budge a step out'n dis place 'dout a *doctor;* not if it's forty year!"

I reckoned he'd say what he did say—so it was all right now, and I told Tom I was a-going for a doctor. He raised considerable row about it, but me and Jim stuck to it and wouldn't budge. So I left in the canoe, and Jim was to hide in the woods when he see the doctor coming till he was gone again.

THE DOCTOR WAS AN OLD MAN, a very nice, kind-looking old man. When I got him up I told him me and my brother was over on Spanish Island hunting yesterday, and camped on a piece of a raft we found, and about midnight he must 'a' kicked his gun in his dreams, for it went off and shot him in the leg, and we wanted him to fix it and not say nothing about it, because we wanted to come home this evening and surprise the folks.

"Who is your folks?" he says.

"The Phelpses, down yonder."

"Oh," he says. And after a minute he says, "How'd you say he got shot?"

"He had a dream," I says, "and it shot him."

"Singular dream," he says.

So he got his saddlebags, and we started. But when he see the canoe he didn't like the look of her—said she didn't look safe for two. I says, "You needn't be afeard, sir, she carried the three of us easy."

"What three?"

"Why, me and Sid, and—and—and *the guns*."

"Oh," he says.

But he put his foot on the gunnel and rocked her, and shook his head, and said he'd look around for a bigger one. But they was all chained; so he took my canoe, and said for me to wait till he come back, or maybe I better go home and get them ready for the surprise. I told him just how to find the raft, and then he started.

So then I crept into a lumber pile to get some sleep; and next time I waked up the sun was away up! I shot out and went for the doctor's house, but they told me he warn't back yet. Well, thinks I, that looks bad for Tom, and I'll dig out for the island right off. So away I shoved, and turned the corner, and nearly rammed my head into Uncle Silas's stomach! He says, "Why, *Tom!* Where you been all this time, you rascal?"

"*I* hain't been nowheres," I says, "only just hunting for the runaway nigger—me and Sid."

"Why, where ever did you go?" he says. "Your aunt's been mighty uneasy."

"She needn't," I says. "We was all right. We followed the men and the dogs, but they outrun us; and we thought we heard them on the water, so we got a canoe, but couldn't find nothing of them; so we cruised along till we got kind of tired; and tied up and went to sleep; then we paddled over here to hear the news, and Sid's at the post office to see what he can hear."

So we went to the post office to get "Sid"; but just as I suspicioned, he warn't there; so the old man he got a letter out of the office, and we waited awhile; then the old man said, come along, let Sid foot it home, when he got done fooling around.

When we got home Aunt Sally was that glad to see me she laughed and cried both. And the place was plum full of farmers and farmers' wives, to dinner; and such clack a body never heard. Old Mrs. Hotchkiss was the worst. She says:

"Well, Sister Phelps, I've ransacked that-air cabin over, an' I b'lieve the nigger was crazy. I says to Sister Damrell—didn't I, Sister Damrell?—s'I, he's crazy, s'I; everything shows it, s'I. Look at that-air grindstone, s'I; want to tell *me* any cretur 't's in his right mind 's a-goin' to scrabble all them crazy things onto a grindstone? Here sich 'n' sich a person busted his heart; 'n' here so 'n' so pegged along for thirty-seven year! He's plumb crazy, s'I; it's what I says in the fust place, it's what I says in the middle, 'n' it's what I says last 'n' all the time—the nigger's crazy—crazy 's Nebokoodneezer, s'I."

"An' look at that-air ladder made out'n rags, Sister Hotchkiss," says old Mrs. Damrell. "What in the name o' goodness *could* he ever want of—"

"The very words I was a-saying no longer ago th'n this minute to Sister Utterback. 'N' how in the nation'd they ever *git* that grindstone *in* there, *any*way? 'N' who dug that-air *hole?* 'N' who—"

"My very *words*, Brer Penrod! I was a-sayin'—pass that-air sasser o' m'lasses, won't ye?—I was a-sayin' to Sister Dunlap, how *did* they git that grindstone in there? Without *help*, mind you. Don't tell *me*, s'I; there *wuz* help, s'I; ther's ben a *dozen* a-helpin' that nigger; 'n' moreover, s'I—"

"A *dozen* says you! *Forty* couldn't 'a' done everything that's been done. Look at them case-knife saws and things, how tedious they've been made; look at that bed leg sawed off with 'm; look at that nigger made out'n straw on the bed! Why, dog my cats, they must 'a' ben a houseful o' niggers in there every night for four weeks to 'a' done all that work, Sister Phelps. Look at that shirt—every last inch of it kivered over with secret African writ'n done with blood!"

"People to *help* him, Brother Marples! Well, I reckon you'd *think* so if you'd 'a' been in this house for a while back. Why, they've stole everything they could lay their hands on. They stole that shirt right off o' the line! And as for that sheet they made the rag ladder out of, ther' ain't no telling how many times they *didn't* steal that; and flour, and candles, and candlesticks, and spoons, and the old warming pan; and me and Silas and my Sid and Tom on the constant watch day *and* night. Why, *sperits* couldn't 'a' done better. And I reckon they must 'a' *been* sperits—because, *you* know our dogs; ther' ain't no better; well, them dogs never even got on the *track* of 'm once! You explain *that* to me if you can—*any* of you!"

"Well, it does beat—"

"Laws alive, I never—"

"*House* thieves as well as—"

"Goodnessgracioussakes, I'd ben afeard to *live* in sich a—"

"'Fraid to *live!* Why, I was that scared I dasn't hardly go to bed; why, goodness sakes, if I warn't afraid they'd steal some o' the family! I says to myself, There's my two poor boys asleep, 'way upstairs in that lonesome room, and I declare I was that uneasy 't I crep' up there and locked 'em in! I *did*." And Aunt Sally stopped, looking kind of wondering, and then she turned around slow, and when her eye lit on me—I got up and took a walk.

Says I to myself, I can explain better how we come to not be in that room this morning if I go out to one side and study over it a little. So I done it. And when it was late in the day the people all went, and then I come in and told her the noise and shooting waked up me and "Sid," and the door was locked, and we wanted to see the fun, so we went down the lightning rod. And then I went on and told her all what I told Uncle Silas before; and then she said she'd forgive us; and so, as long as no harm hadn't come of it, she judged she better put in her time being grateful we was alive and well, stead of fretting over what was past and done. So then she kissed me, and dropped into a kind of a brown study; and pretty soon jumps up, and says:

"Why, lawsamercy, it's most night, and Sid not come yet! What *has* become of that boy?"

I see my chance; so I says, "I'll run right up to town and get him," I says.

"No you won't," she says. "You'll stay right wher' you are; *one's* enough to be lost at a time. If he ain't here to supper your uncle 'll go."

Well, he warn't there to supper; so right after supper Uncle went.

He come back about ten a bit uneasy; hadn't run across Tom's track. Aunt Sally was a good *deal* uneasy; but Uncle Silas he said there warn't no occasion to be—boys will be boys, he said, and you'll see this one turn up in the morning. But she said she'd set up awhile anyway, and keep a light burning so he could see it.

And then when I went up to bed she come up with me and tucked me in, and mothered me so good I felt mean; and she set down on the bed and talked with me a long time, and said what a splendid boy Sid was, and didn't seem to want to ever stop talking about him. And when she was going away she looked down in my eyes so steady and gentle, and says:

"The door ain't going to be locked, Tom, and there's the window and the rod; but you'll be good, *won't* you? And you won't go? For *my* sake."

Laws knows I *wanted* to go bad enough to see about Tom; but after that I wouldn't 'a' went, not for kingdoms. But Tom was on my mind, so I slept very restless. And twice I went down the rod in the night, and slipped around front, and see her setting there by the candle in the window with her eyes towards the road and the tears in them; and I wished I could do something for her, but I couldn't. And the third time I waked up at dawn, and slid down, and she was there yet, and her old gray head was resting on her hand, and she was asleep.

CHAPTER XV

THE OLD MAN WAS UP TO TOWN again before breakfast, but couldn't get no track of Tom; and both of them set at the table thinking, and not saying nothing, and their coffee getting cold. And by and by the old man says to Aunt Sally, "Did I give you the letter?"

"What letter?"

"The one I got yesterday out of the post office."

"No, you didn't give me no letter."

"Well, I must 'a' forgot it."

So he went off somewheres, and fetched the letter, and give it to her. She says, "Why, it's from St. Petersburg—it's from Sis."

I allowed another walk would do me good. But before she could break it open she dropped it and run—for she see something. And so did I. It was Tom Sawyer on a mattress; and that old doctor; and Jim, in *her* calico dress, with his hands tied behind him; and a lot of people. I hid the letter behind the first thing that come handy, and rushed. She flung herself at Tom, crying, and says, "Oh, he's dead, he's dead, I know he's dead!"

And Tom turned his head a little, and muttered something or other, which showed he warn't in his right mind; then she flung up her hands, and says, "He's alive, thank God! And that's enough!" and she snatched a kiss of him, and flew for the house to get the bed ready.

I followed the men to see what they was going to do with Jim; and the old doctor and Uncle Silas followed after Tom into the house. The men was very huffy, and some of them wanted to hang Jim for an example to all the other niggers around there. But the others said, don't do it; he ain't our nigger, and his owner would turn up and make us pay for him, sure. So that cooled them down a little.

They cussed Jim considerable, though, and give him a cuff or two side the head once in a while, but Jim never said nothing, and he never let on to know me, and they took him to the same cabin, and put his own clothes on him, and chained him again, and not to no bed leg this time, but to a big staple drove into the bottom log, and chained his hands, too, and both legs. Then the old doctor comes and takes a look, and says:

"Don't be no rougher on him than you're obleeged to, because he ain't a bad nigger. When I got to where I found the boy I see I couldn't cut the bullet out without some help, and he warn't in no condition for me to leave to go and get help; and he got worse and worse, and after a time he went out of his head, and wouldn't let me come a-nigh him any more; so I says, I got to have *help* somehow; and the minute I says it out crawls this nigger from somewheres and says he'll help, and he done it, too, and done it very well. Of course I judged he must be a runaway nigger, and there I *was!* So I had to stick plumb until daylight this morning; but I never see a nigger that was a better nuss or faithfuler, and yet he was risking his freedom to do it. I liked the nigger for that! I tell you, gentlemen, a nigger like that is worth a thousand dollars—and kind treatment, too. I had everything I needed, and the boy was doing as well there as he would 'a' done at home; but there I *was*, with both of 'm on my hands, and there I had to stick till dawn this morning; then some men in a skiff come by, and as luck would have it the nigger was setting by the pallet asleep; so I motioned them in quiet, and they grabbed him and tied him before he knowed what he was about. He ain't no bad nigger, gentlemen; that's what I think."

Somebody says, "Well, it sounds very good, Doctor, I'm obleeged to say"; and then the others softened up a little, too, and they all agreed that Jim had acted very well.

Then they come out and locked Jim up. I hoped they was going to say he could have the chains took off; but they didn't think of it, and I reckoned it warn't best for me to mix in, but I judged I'd get the doctor's yarn to Aunt Sally somehow as soon as I'd got through the breakers that was laying just ahead of me—explanations, I mean, of how I forgot to mention about Sid being shot. But I had plenty time. Aunt Sally she stuck to the sickroom, and every time I see Uncle Silas mooning around I dodged him.

Next morning I heard Tom was a deal better, and they said Aunt Sally was gone to get a nap. So I slips to the sickroom, and if I found him awake I reckoned we could put up a yarn for the family that would wash. But he was sleeping, and sleeping very peaceful, too; and pale. So I set down and laid for him to wake. In about half an hour Aunt Sally comes in, and there I was, up a stump again! She motioned me to be still, and set down by me, and begun to whisper, and said we could all be joyful now, because all the symptoms was first-rate, and he'd been sleeping like that for ever so long, and ten to one he'd wake up in his right mind. So we set there watching, and by and by he stirs a bit, and opens his eyes, and says:

"Hello! Why, I'm at *home!* How's that? Where's the raft?"

"It's all right," I says.

"And *Jim?*"

"The same," I says, but couldn't say it pretty brash. But he never noticed, but says, "Good! Splendid! *Now* we're all right and safe! Did you tell Aunty?"

I was going to say yes; but she chipped in and says, "About what, Sid?"

"Why, about the way the whole thing was done. About how we set the runaway nigger free—me and Tom."

"Good land! What *is* the child talking about! Dear, dear, out of his head again!"

"*No,* I ain't out of my HEAD; I know all what I'm talking about. We *did* set him free—me and Tom. We laid out to do it, and we *done* it. And we done it elegant, too." He'd got a start, and she just set and stared and stared, and let him clip along, and I see it warn't no use for *me* to put in. "Why, Aunty, it cost us a power of work— weeks of it—every night, whilst you was all asleep. And we had to steal candles, and the sheet, and the shirt, and your dress, and no end of things, and you can't think what work it was to make the saws, and pens, and inscriptions, and you can't think *half* the fun it was. And we had to make up the pictures of coffins and things, and get up and down the lightning rod, and dig the hole into the cabin—"

"Mercy sakes!"

"—and load up the cabin with rats and so on, for company for Jim; and then you kept Tom here so long with the butter in his hat that you come near spiling the whole business, because the men come before we was out of the cabin, and we had to rush, and they heard us and let drive at us, and I got my share, and then the dogs come, and we got our canoe, and made for the raft, and was all safe, and Jim was a free man, and we done it all by ourselves, and *wasn't* it bully, Aunty!"

"Well, I never heard the likes of it in all my born days! So it was *you*, you little rapscallions, that's been making all this trouble! To think—why, *you* just get well once, you young scamp, and I'll tan the Old Harry out o' both o' ye!"

But Tom, he *was* so proud and joyful, he just *couldn't* hold in, and his tongue just *went* it—she a-chipping in, and spitting fire all along, and both of them going it at once, like a cat convention; and she says, "*Well*, you get all the enjoyment you can out of it *now*, for mind I tell you if I catch you meddling with him again—"

"Meddling with *who?*" Tom says, dropping his smile.

"With *who?* Why, the runaway nigger, of course!"

Tom looks at me, and says, "Tom, didn't you tell me he was all right? Hasn't he got away?"

"*Him?*" says Aunt Sally. "The runaway nigger? 'Deed he hasn't. They've got him back, and he's in that cabin again, and loaded down with chains, till he's claimed or sold!"

Tom rose up in bed, with his eye hot, and sings out to me, "They hain't no *right* to shut him up! *Shove!* And don't you lose a minute. Turn him loose! He ain't no slave; he's as free as any cretur that walks this earth!"

"What *does* the child mean?"

"I mean every word I *say*, Aunt Sally. I've knowed him all his life, and so has Tom, there. Old Miss Watson died two months ago, and she was ashamed she ever was going to sell him down the river, and *said* so; and she set him free in her will."

"Then what on earth did *you* want to set him free for, seeing he was already free?"

"Well, that *is* a question, I must say; and *just* like women! Why, I wanted the *adventure* of it; and I'd 'a' waded neck-deep in blood to—goodness alive, AUNT POLLY!"

If she warn't standing right there, just inside the door, looking as sweet and contented as an angel half full of pie, I wish I may never!

Aunt Sally jumped for her, and most hugged the head off of her, and cried over her, and I found a good enough place for me under the bed, for it was getting pretty sultry for *us*, seemed to me. And

I peeped out, and in a little while Tom's Aunt Polly shook herself loose and stood looking across at Tom over her spectacles. And then she says:

"Yes, you *better* turn away—I would if I was you, Tom."

"Oh, deary me!" says Aunt Sally. "*Is* he changed so? Why, that ain't *Tom*, it's Sid; Tom's—why, where is Tom? He was here a minute ago."

"You mean where's Huck *Finn!* I reckon I hain't raised such a scamp as my Tom all these years not to know him when I *see* him. That *would* be a pretty howdy-do. Come out from under that bed, Huck Finn."

So I done it. But not feeling brash.

Aunt Sally she was one of the mixed-upest-looking persons I ever see—except one, and that was Uncle Silas, when he come in and they told it all to him. Tom's Aunt Polly, she told all about who I was, and what; and I had to up and tell how I was in such a tight place that when Mrs. Phelps took me for Tom Sawyer I had to stand it—there warn't no other way, and I knowed Tom wouldn't mind, because it would be nuts for him, being a mystery, and he'd make an adventure out of it. And so it turned out, and he let on to be Sid, and made things as soft as he could for me.

And his Aunt Polly she said Tom was right about old Miss Watson setting Jim free in her will; and so, sure enough, Tom Sawyer had gone and took all that trouble to set a free nigger free! And I couldn't ever understand before, until that minute, how he *could* help a body set a nigger free with his bringing-up.

Well, Aunt Polly she said that when Aunt Sally wrote to her that Tom and *Sid* had come all right, she says to herself:

"Look at that, now! I might have expected it, letting him go off that way without anybody to watch him. So now I got to go and trapse all the way down the river, eleven hundred mile, and find out what the creetur's up to *this* time, as long as I couldn't seem to get any answer out of you about it."

"Why, I never heard nothing from you," says Aunt Sally.

"Well, I wonder! Why, I wrote you twice to ask you what you could mean by Sid being here."

"Well, I never got 'em, Sis."

Aunt Polly she turns around slow and severe, and says:

"You, Tom!"

"Well—*what?*" he says, kind of pettish.

"Don't you what *me*—hand out them letters."

"What letters?"

"*Them* letters. I be bound, if I have to take a-holt of you—"

"They're in the trunk. There, now. I hain't touched them. But I knowed they'd make trouble, and I thought I'd—"

"Well, you *do* need skinning. And I wrote another one to tell you I was coming; and I s'pose he—"

"No, it come yesterday," Aunt Sally said. "I hain't read it yet, but *it's* all right, I've got that one."

I wanted to offer to bet two dollars she hadn't, but I reckoned maybe it was just as safe to not to. So I never said nothing.

THE FIRST TIME I CATCHED Tom private I asked him what was his idea, time of the evasion—what it was he'd planned to do if the evasion worked all right and he managed to set a nigger free that was already free before? And he said, what he had planned in his head from the start, if we got Jim out all safe, was for us to run him down the river on the raft, and have adventures plumb to the mouth of the river, and then tell him about his being free, and take him back up home on a steamboat, in style, and pay him for his lost time, and write ahead and get out all the niggers, and have them waltz him into town with a brass band, and then he would be a hero, and so would we. But I reckoned it was about as well the way it was.

We had Jim out of the chains in no time, and when Aunt Polly and Uncle Silas and Aunt Sally found out how good he helped the doctor nurse Tom, they made a heap of fuss over him. And we had him up to the sickroom, and had a high talk; and Tom give Jim forty dollars for being prisoner for us so patient, and Jim was pleased most to death, and busted out, and says:

"*Dah*, now, Huck, what I tell you up dah on Jackson Islan'? I *tole* you I got a hairy breas'; en I *tole* you I ben rich wunst, en gwineter be rich *ag'in;* en it's come true! Dah, now, doan' talk to *me*—signs is *signs*, mine I tell you!"

And then Tom he says, le's all three slide out of here one of these nights and get an outfit, and go for howling adventures amongst the Injuns, over in the territory, for a couple of weeks or two; and I says, all right, that suits me, but I ain't got no money for to buy the outfit, and I reckon I couldn't get none from home, because it's likely Pap's been back before now, and got it all away from Judge Thatcher.

"No, he hain't," Tom says. "It's all there yet—six thousand dollars and more; and your pap hain't ever been back since. Hadn't when I come away, anyhow."

Jim says, kind of solemn, "He ain't a-comin' back, Huck."

I says, "Why, Jim?"

"Nemmine why, Huck—but he ain't comin' back no mo'."

But I kept at him; so at last he says, "Doan' you 'member de house dat was float'n down de river, en dey wuz a man in dah, en I went in en didn' let you come in? Well, den, you kin git yo' money when you wants it, kase dat wuz him."

Tom's most well now, and got his bullet around his neck on a watch guard for a watch, and is always seeing what time it is, and so there ain't nothing more to write about, and I am rotten glad of it, because if I'd 'a' knowed what a trouble it was to make a book I wouldn't 'a' tackled it, and ain't a-going to no more. But I reckon I got to light out for the territory ahead of the rest, because Aunt Sally she's going to adopt me and sivilize me, and I can't stand it. I been there before.

Mark Twain
(1835–1910)

IN MARCH 1898, Samuel Clemens was notified in Vienna by his business manager, Henry Huddleston Rogers, that the last of his creditors had been paid. Few men of that time managed to recover from bankruptcy, but Clemens, better known to the world as Mark Twain, was no ordinary man. He had made a fortune and married another, then lost both through extravagant living and failed business ventures. It had taken him four years to repay his debts; he had undertaken a wildly successful around-the-world lecture tour and published two books. Yet within days of the news of his solvency Twain was again planning speculative ventures. He then amassed another fortune. When he died in 1910, his estate was valued at $600,000.

America's foremost humorist was born in 1835 and grew up on the Mississippi River in Hannibal, Missouri. His experiences in Hannibal—going to school, fishing, playing, fighting, swimming—were transformed into the lives of Tom Sawyer and Huck Finn in fictional St. Petersburg. Twain carried from his childhood a love of freedom, self-sufficiency, and imagination, which are important themes in *The Adventures of Huckleberry Finn* and *The Adventures of Tom Sawyer*.

Twain's father, John Marshall Clemens, an unsuccessful lawyer, died when his son was twelve years old, forcing the boy to go to work. A few years later he did his first writing, for his older brother Orion, in the Hannibal *Journal*. He left Hannibal in 1853 and worked as a printer around the country. In 1857, he became a cub pilot on the Mississippi River, realizing his boyhood's "permanent ambition," learning the river so well that "the face of the water, in time, became a wonderful book that . . . told its mind to me without reserve, delivering its most cherished secrets as clearly as if it had uttered them with a voice."

The Civil War put an end to the steamboat traffic and to Twain's career. After two weeks' military service for the Confederacy, he set out for Nevada with his brother Orion. It was in Nevada that he began using the name Mark Twain (meaning "two fathoms deep"). Soon he moved on to San Francisco, where he published "The Celebrated Jumping Frog of Calaveras County" in 1865. It was reprinted in newspapers all over the country.

In 1866, a newspaper sent him to Hawaii for five months. His reports were well received; one was published in *Harper's* magazine. When he returned to San Francisco in October, he began his lucrative lecture career, with ever-spreading fame. In December, he sailed for New York as a newspaper correspondent, and after a triumphant lecture at the Cooper Union, he sailed from New York to Europe and the Holy Land. The trip was pivotal for him: his letters formed the basis for the very successful book *The Innocents Abroad*, and aboard ship he met his future brother-in-law, Charles Langdon. Langdon showed Twain an ivory miniature of his sister Olivia. Twain resolved to marry her. Three years later, in Elmira, New York, he did.

In the following years, Twain's reputation grew steadily. He made an odd figure, with his trademark white suits and billowing hair, and he spoke with a deliberately quaint drawl. He loved to shock his conservative wife and friends and his audiences. He numbered among his closest friends William Dean Howells, the prominent editor, critic, and novelist, and also the disgraced and destitute former president, Ulysses S. Grant. Twain arranged for the publication of Grant's memoirs, which proved a financial success for both men. But despite all the trappings of his fame, Twain continually found himself considered merely funny. He was probably best known during his lifetime as a humorist and a speaker, rather than the great lyric writer and social critic we know him to be.

Twain's children—Langdon (who died in childhood), Susie, Clara, and Jean—were born over the decade from 1870 to 1880. By all accounts their home life was loving and very lively. The family traveled extensively in Europe, with the aim of reducing their expenses and making time for Twain to write. Unfortunately, the attempts to reduce expenses were never equal to the volume of spending.

In his later years, after bankruptcy and the loss of his wife and beloved daughter Susie, Twain's temperament became increasingly darker. "Pity is for the living, envy is for the dead," he wrote in 1899. Ten years later his gloom had deepened further. "I came in with Halley's comet in 1835. . . . It will be the greatest disappointment of my life if I don't go out with Halley's comet. The Almighty has said, no doubt: 'Now here are these two unaccountable freaks; they came in together, they must go out together.' " His daughter Clara married on October 6, 1909; his daughter Jean, who had been acting as his secretary, died on Christmas Eve that same year. Twain was desolate and alone. On a Thursday in April 1910, Halley's comet did appear. The next day Twain died.

Other Titles by Mark Twain

A Connecticut Yankee in King Arthur's Court. New York: Bantam, 1983.

Great Short Works of Mark Twain. New York: Harper & Row, 1967.

The Innocents Abroad. New York: New American Library, 1980.

Letters from the Earth. New York: Harper & Row, 1962.

Life on the Mississippi. New York: Penguin, 1985.

The Mysterious Stranger & Other Stories. New York: New American Library, 1962.

A Pen Warmed Up in Hell. New York: Harper & Row, 1979.

The Prince and the Pauper. New York: Bantam, 1983.

Pudd'nhead Wilson. New York: Penguin, 1969.

Tom Sawyer Abroad & Tom Sawyer, Detective. Berkeley: University of California Press, 1981.

The Unabridged Mark Twain. Philadelphia: Running Press, 1975.

The Unabridged Mark Twain, No. 2. Lawrence Teacher, editor. Philadelphia: Running Press, 1979.